REUNION

"Don't tempt me, Cheval," he said in a ragged voice.

Austin's breath fanned her lashes. "Why not? You tempt me."

"There's a difference. I'm capable of going through with anything I suggest. I'm not sure you are."

Was he challenging her? "I am," she said again, and as if it were a natural part of her everyday life to disrobe in front of this man, Cheval slipped out of the cotton robe and stood before him dressed only in the long-sleeved white nightgown. . . .

RAVES FOR GLORIA DALE SKINNER'S BOOKS

"[Skinner] provides the perfect Old South setting for this excellent sultry, sensuous story."

—*Rendezvous* on SULTRY NIGHTS

"A touching and sensuous story, as total strangers who are married begin to discover each other . . . and love."

—*Paperback Forum* on MIDNIGHT FIRE

"MIDNIGHT FIRE is a tender, sweetly poignant love story . . . a tale of healing and compassion, a gentle yet fiery romance."

—   in

"BEWITCHING is   d
betrayal that will   e
pages until the thri

D0802076

—Be   n

Other Zebra Titles
by
Gloria Dale Skinner

GEORGIA FEVER
TENDER TRUST
STARLIGHT
MIDNIGHT FIRE

BEWITCHING

GLORIA DALE SKINNER

ZEBRA BOOKS
KENSINGTON PUBLISHING CORP.

This book is dedicated
to children all over the world,
but especially to
my daughter Charla and my son Cameron.

After life's fitful fever, she sleeps well.
　　　—Betsy Bonaparte's Epitaph

Part One

The Journey

Prologue

Baltimore, 1804

Ordinarily, Austin wouldn't flinch when he looked down the barrel of a musket, but his mother sat beside him. He hadn't taken his eyes off the three highwaymen since they'd ridden out in front of him and stopped the carriage. His sword hung at his side, but that wouldn't be much defense against the long-barreled musket and two swordsmen. Niggling bumps of fear crawled up Austin's back, and his stomach filled with bubbles of apprehension.

"Please don't make trouble, Austin," Beatrice said, patting her son's arm nervously. "Give them your money, so they'll let us be on our way."

Austin studied the highwaymen as best he could with the late afternoon sun half-blinding him. The heavyset man with the gun had large round eyes, full cheeks and a grim twist to his misshapen lips. The closest man, who had a sword, wore a bushy beard. Thick, untamed hair fell to his shoulders. The robber farthest away wore a red coat, and a hardened scowl distorted his facial features.

All three men appeared muscular and fit beneath their worn clothing. It troubled Austin that they didn't try to hide their faces. That could mean the robbers didn't intend to let them live. He hoped he was wrong about that.

Dammit! He hadn't planned to travel so far from their home, but his mother had been enjoying the spring sunshine and fresh air so much he'd hated to bring the day to a close. He should have been more cautious, even though there had been no news of robbers in the area.

Wanting to prevent a fight, Austin carefully reached into his jacket pocket and pulled out his coin purse. "This is all I have." He extended the leather pouch to the one with the gun trained on him, hoping he'd lower the weapon, but the bearded man goaded his skittish horse closer to the carriage and took the money.

"We'll take yours, too," the heaviest man said looking straight at Beatrice.

"Oh, my goodness," she answered in a soft, flustered voice, fanning her face with her handkerchief. "I don't have any money with me. Why would I bring anything like that out on a Sunday ride?"

"We'll take your purse anyway." He pointed the gun barrel to the drawstring reticule lying in her lap.

Tight-lipped, Austin picked up the small bag and shoved it into the robber's hands. These men were serious, and he didn't want his mother hurt.

The bearded man stuffed the money pouch and

reticule down the front of his shirt. "A lady dressed as fancy as you is bound to have some valuables. Jewelry maybe? We'll take it."

Her eyes widened with fear and her hand went immediately to the braided cord attached to the collar of her fur-lined cloak. "B—but I don't."

A dark, angry feeling settled over Austin for the way these men were frightening his mother. Austin wasn't surprised his mother didn't do a good job of lying. She'd never had to.

"Take off your gloves and let me see your hands. Take the cape off, too. Be quick about it. We don't have all day." The man's horse snorted and shifted restlessly, sidestepping him closer to the carriage.

Clearly stunned they didn't take her word, Beatrice gasped and again clutched the braided cord that held her cloak on her shoulders.

Austin tensed. There was no way around it. A fight was coming. "Leave her alone," he said, stalling for time while he tried to figure out a way he could have a chance at beating all three men. He was afraid if he didn't come up with something neither he nor his mother would live. He should have let Jubal come with them. "She doesn't have anything of value on her. You have our money. Now let us pass. We don't want any trouble."

The robber lifted the musket a little higher and trained it on Austin's chest. "You say one more word and I'll put a hole in you the size of a cannonball." One corner of his mouth lifted in a snarl.

The man's cold eyes said he wouldn't hesitate to shoot and there wasn't much chance of his missing at this close range. Austin wished the sun lay at his back instead of right between his eyes.

"No, please. There's no need for that. Look, I'm taking off my gloves. See? I have no rings or bracelets." Beatrice held up her trembling hands.

"Take off your cloak. I want to see if you have a necklace round your neck or a brooch pinned to your dress."

"What?" Beatrice's eyes widened again. "I—I don't have anything pinned to my dress."

Austin cringed. His mother was lying again. He knew it. She knew it, and the robbers knew it. The locket pinned to her dress had been a gift from her husband on their wedding day. The small piece of gold was her most prized possession. She wouldn't give it up easily.

He had to make a quick decision. Did he risk losing his life and his mother's by trying to stop them now? Or did he allow things to continue on this course in hope they'd ride away without bloodshed?

The robber closest to them was as calm as any man Austin had seen holding a musket, but the horses the men rode were high-strung. That gave Austin an idea and, he hoped, an edge.

The man farthest away nudged his horse forward unexpectedly, startling all the horses. He rode up to the open carriage and backhanded Beatrice across the face. She gasped pitifully and fell backward against the cushioned interior of the carriage.

Rage flared within Austin. In one fluid movement, he rose from the seat. His hand closed over his sword hilt, sliding the blade from its fancy scabbard. He caught the nearest horse under the neck with the sharp edge. The horse screamed; the musket fired harmlessly into the air; men shouted; his mother whimpered. Swords screeched against scabbards.

The robbers prepared to fight.

The wounded horse reared and buckled, toppling the rider with the musket. Austin vaulted from the carriage and whacked the mare across the rump, hoping the frightened horse would run with the carriage and take his mother out of harm's way, but the animal merely bucked and snorted. Regaining his footing, Austin saw two of the men coming at him with drawn swords.

He pushed up the sleeves of his jacket and prepared for the onslaught. With a yell of excitement, the bushy-haired man charged. Austin hopped and skipped, thrusting forward with the sword, then backward and from side to side. Steel clinked against steel. The air rang with the clashing of metal. Sweat drenched him within seconds.

Austin strained to keep his gaze on the blades and the other two men at the same time. A split second of opportunity presented itself, and Austin slid his sword into the man's stomach and sliced up toward the rib cage. With his free hand, he shoved the robber backward as he withdrew the sword. The man collapsed in agony to the ground. Austin jumped back, quickly on guard again.

One of the men struck back and a blade whipped

across Austin's arm. He winced, hoisting his sword upward quickly to block a fatal blow. Sweat, mingled with tears of pain, rolled down his face and neck. Both men came at him at once with crashing, jabbing swords. He fought hard, quickly. He weakened. Keeping his thoughts on the man who'd struck his mother gave him strength to continue. While blocking one sword, Austin caught a slice across his midsection. Burning pain shot through him. His wounded arm ached from the loss of blood and the weight of the sword.

"Get the woman!" the bearded man yelled to his partner. "Kill her!"

Austin's blood pumped furiously. He trembled with fear for his mother. He wouldn't accept defeat. "Get out of here!" he yelled to Beatrice.

Beatrice frantically searched around her feet for the reins. Not finding them, she scrambled from the carriage and lifted her skirts to run. The robber easily caught her. His beefy arm grabbed her around the shoulders. He raised his sword to her neck.

Leaving his back unguarded, Austin let out an anguished yell and charged toward them. His heartbeat raced; his feet and legs did not move fast enough. Fear enveloped him. Panic filled him. He wasn't going to make it.

A shot rang out. The robber jerked. His sword stilled in mid-air. A red stain appeared on his shirt. He released Beatrice and dropped wide-eyed to the ground. The other man growled in rage and chased Austin with raised sword.

He was weakened by the fight, and it took all of Austin's strength to defend himself against the stronger man. He didn't have time to wonder who had saved his mother's life as the last robber's weapon clashed violently against his.

Within moments, a short, dark-haired man appeared at Austin's side and engaged the robber. Austin yielded his fight to the stranger and staggered to the side, lowering his sword.

Austin slumped to his knees, gasping for each breath. He bent double from the pain in his arm and midriff. His mother sank to her knees beside him, weeping. Thank God she was safe.

Yanking the front of his jacket around his chest, he pressed it tightly against his bleeding wound. The fresh face of Austin's helper dubbed him a young man—not yet twenty, Austin was sure—but he was an excellent swordsman. Austin's eyes blurred as he watched the skilled swordsman overpower the robber's blade and make short work of finishing him off.

In the distance behind them stood a magnificent mount with a silver and gold-threaded horse blanket and ornately decorated saddle. The stranger was elaborately dressed in a scarlet frock coat adorned with gold-colored braid and epaulets. Silver yarn fringed the dark-blue sash around his waist. Pheasant feathers trimmed his tricorn.

A burning pain skipped along Austin's stomach. He tugged his jacket tighter against the wound in his side as the stranger approached. Out of breath but grateful, Austin denied the weakness in his legs and forced himself to stand. Beatrice wrapped her arm around his waist to help him.

"I'm Austin Radcliffe. I'm indebted to you, sir."

The young man took off his hat and bowed politely. "Pleased to meet you. I'm Jerome Bonaparte, youngest brother to France's First Consul, Napoleon Bonaparte," he said in a heavily accented voice.

"Should you ever need a favor, I give my word to help you. You need only to ask and anything I have is yours."

The self-confident young man smiled and nodded in response. "I shall remember your vow, Mr. Radcliffe."

One

Baltimore: 1809

The first person he saw upon entering the smoky tavern was a golden-haired beauty. She glided across the room, carrying a tray loaded with tankards of ale to a table of rowdy men. Austin forgot about searching for the man he'd come to meet in favor of watching the young woman.

At a glance, he knew her to be more than a mere serving wench. She held her head too high, carried herself too well to belong in a taproom. She was tall for a woman, but small-boned. There was something distinctly alluring about her.

Why was such a polished woman serving drinks, he wondered? The firm set of her lips and cold expression in her eyes didn't detract from her lovely face. He smiled. She might be serving ale to a crowd of rowdy men, but she didn't like it.

The men at the table laughed loudly when she placed the tray of drinks in front of them. One of them cupped her buttocks with his palms at the same time another caressed her cheek. She swatted their hands, whirled from the table and stomped away.

She disappeared into another room, and Austin returned his attention to the reason he was on the wrong side of town. He didn't make a habit of meeting strange men in dock-side taverns, but this particular summons had brought back too many memories to ignore.

The Boar's Head Tavern was unfamiliar ground to him. It catered to the many sailors who walked the streets of Baltimore and its harbor looking for a place to spend their money and their time. Situated at the head of the busy Chesapeake Bay, Baltimore had miles of beautiful, functional waterfront, making the town one of the busiest seaports in the new world.

The serving wench walked back into the taproom with another tray and headed for a different table. Austin felt a rise in his manhood and chuckled to himself at the blatant reaction to this woman. He decided he needed to get away from his country estate more often and visit Miss Sophie's upstairs room in the Dock-Front Boardinghouse.

The taproom was larger than most of the ones he'd been inside in the last few years, but he quickly spotted a lone man sitting at a corner table away from the lamp light. Austin decided he must be the person he'd come to meet.

Throwing his waist-length cape over one shoulder, he strode into the room, bypassing one of the raucous groups the young woman had served. Low-burning lamps, cheroot and pipe smoke added to the room's hazy atmosphere. The scent of stale ale, food, and burned wood filled his nostrils.

He stopped in front of the man who didn't bother to look up at his approach and asked, "Auguste Le Camus?"

The stranger slowly lifted his head, showing a face with a large, hawk-like nose, small dark-brown eyes, bushy eyebrows, and thin lips. "I am he. You are Austin Radcliffe?"

The French accent didn't surprise Austin, but the lack of a smile or friendly greeting did. Brushing that aside, he nodded, then pulled out a chair and sat down at the small square table. If the man weren't cordial, there was no need to bother with pleasantries.

Getting right to the point, Austin asked, "Why did you ask me to meet you here? Why not just come to my office?"

"What I have to say is very important and for your ears only. No one must know we spoke." He kept his voice low. Both arms rested on the table, and he crouched over them, leaning toward Austin.

Austin agreed with what he said. He wasn't sure he wanted anyone in Baltimore to know he had had a liaison with Jerome Bonaparte's messenger. Even though he had great reason to appreciate Jerome, the rest of Maryland had reason to scorn him. Napoleon was at a zenith in France, but the Emperor and Jerome had made a laughingstock of one of Baltimore's finest citizens, Betsy Patterson.

After answering with a quick nod of his head, Austin stuck a finger down the shawl collar of his shirt, trying to loosen it. There could be only one reason this meeting had been arranged. Jerome had decided to call in the favor Austin had promised five years ago.

"Go on," Austin finally said.

"Do you remember the name Jerome Bonaparte?"

"Don't be absurd. I'm not likely to forget the man who saved my mother's life. You wouldn't be here if you didn't know about that incident. Besides that, there's not a person in Maryland who doesn't know who he is and what he did to Betsy Patterson."

Le Camus relaxed his shoulders in a lackadaisical manner. "Ah—yes, I assume your reference is to King Jerome's unfortunate relationship with Miss Patterson. It was at Napoleon's insistence, the Diocesan Court of Paris ruled Jerome and Betsy's marriage invalid in France. King Jerome begged Napoleon to accept his American wife. It was out of Jerome's hands what Napoleon did."

Austin didn't like the Frenchman's attitude or his tone. What kind of man allowed his brother to annul his marriage?

"That's not for us to argue. I'm here on a matter of extreme importance and the strictest confidence."

A commotion on the far side of the room caught Austin's attention. A sailor tried to force the young woman to sit on his knee. She struggled against his strength and managed to get away with only a quick slap to her bottom. The men howled as she hurried into the kitchen. Austin was tempted to go over and punch the man for harassing a woman who only tried to do her job.

It was time to find out what this man wanted from him, so he could concentrate on the serving wench. For some reason, he couldn't keep his eyes off her whenever she was in the room.

"Jerome is now King of Westphalia," Le Camus said. "Perhaps you've heard."

Pride shone in the messenger's eyes and rang in his voice. "I remember hearing Napoleon forced Jerome to marry a German princess for political reasons and rewarded Jerome by making him a king."

The hawk-nosed man leaned forward again. His dark gaze bored into Austin's face. "That's true. The question is, do you remember what Jerome did for you?"

Austin's eyes narrowed as he looked at the Frenchman. "I remember."

With acute awareness, Austin sensed the woman's presence before she spoke. A frisson stirred him. She had eased up to their table and stood behind his left shoulder, just out of his peripheral vision. Underneath the scent of dried ale on her dress and apron, he smelled the sweet nectar of clean skin and fresh-washed hair. His stomach quickened.

"A tankard of ale for you, sir?" the soft voice asked.

Austin ignored the man sitting across from him and turned to the woman. Eyes more rusty green than brown looked down at him. A fringe of golden-blonde hair framed her face and a small linen cap sat on top of her head, covering most of the chignon which rode low on the nape of her neck. Her eyebrows were a shade darker than her hair and slightly arched, emphasizing the roundness of her eyes. A smidgen of color stained high on her cheeks. His gaze fell to the full, sculpted shape of her lips. A tightening attacked his lower stomach. Beneath her bib apron and brown muslin dress, he saw the slight rise and fall of her chest.

She blinked a couple of times. "Ale for you, sir?" she asked again, her voice straining to be polite.

"No, port," he finally answered. "The best you have."

"I'll have another ale," Le Camus added before she turned away.

His reaction to her puzzled Austin. Everything about her had gained his attention. He hadn't looked a woman over so carefully in years. He danced with proper young ladies at parties, but he never seriously courted any of them. He enjoyed the naughty ladies at Miss Sophie's, but he seldom visited the same one twice in a row. What was it about this girl that made his gaze sweep the room to find her?

Le Camus continued to talk, but Austin wasn't listening. He strove to remember when he was last with a woman. By the way his lower body reacted to this young lady, it must have been months.

"Do you also remember vowing to return the good deed he bestowed upon you that day?"

That remark forced Austin to return his attention to the Frenchman. He had a strange feeling he wasn't going to like what this man had to say. He nodded once. "I remember. I'm merely waiting for you to say what Jerome wants from me. Naturally, I assumed that is why you asked me to meet you."

Le Camus sat back in his chair as the young woman placed their drinks on the table. Austin didn't look up at her this time. He didn't have to. He'd already memorized her face, her walk, her scent. The long sleeve on her dress rode above her wrist showing small, delicate bone structure. Her fingers and hands were smooth, not rough and reddened, her nails neatly trimmed. She hadn't been a tavern wench very long. When she walked away, her body movement stirred the air and left behind the gripping appeal of her fresh-washed hair. He closed his eyes and inhaled deeply. She was a bewitching little wench.

"Mr. Radcliffe?"

Austin's eyes popped open. He'd definitely been too long without a woman. This one was making him crazy. He leaned his chair back on its hind legs. It was time to get down to the business at hand. "What favor does Jerome ask of me?"

"He wants you to bring his son to France on one of your ships. He'll be waiting for you there."

"So, Betsy has agreed to go to him, even after his marriage to the German princess." Austin sipped his drink.

Le Camus waved his hand as if to dismiss Austin's statement. "No."

Austin's gaze never left Le Camus's face. "Betsy has agreed to let her son go to his father? Just the boy will be going?"

"Yes—but there's a little more to it than that. Not a big problem, though. She hasn't agreed. The boy will be taken."

"Damnation! You're going to kidnap the boy!" Austin's chair came down with a bang on the wood floor. His drink sloshed over the edge of the pewter goblet. The sweet liquid dribbled between his fingers.

Le Camus leaned over the table again. "Please, Mr. Radcliffe, must I remind you again not to bring attention to us?"

"Do you think I want to bring attention to us?" Austin pulled out his handkerchief and wiped his hand. "Jerome is a son-of-a-bitch to suggest such a thing as this, let alone to ask it of me." He snarled. "Does he think me a common criminal?"

"Need I remind you that it was you who made the unconditional vow that day? You said no desire of his would be too great a task. All Jerome had to do was ask. He's asking. He has no reason to doubt the child Miss Patterson bore in England is his. Because of Napoleon's great fortune, Jerome is now king of his own country and has the means to give the boy a life suitable to his station. It pains him not to have seen his son. Bo will be four years old in a matter of months."

It was Austin's time to lean over the table. "Kid-

napping is against the law, dammit! I didn't mean
I'd commit a crime for him when I made that
vow."

"Whose law? Is it breaking the law to take a
man's son to him? Does a mother have more right
to a son than his father? I think not. King Jerome
acknowledges the boy is his. How can it be against
the law to take a child to his father?" He spread
his hands in an unconcerned gesture.

"That's not against the law, I'm sure; but stealing him from his mother and taking him to France
is. He's an American."

"He is his father's son first. It is an act of kindness to this powerful man who wishes only the
best life for his son. Miss Patterson keeps the child
from Jerome only to hurt him for things that were
Napoleon's doing. The greater crime would be in
denying the boy his station in life as prince to the
throne of Westphalia and possibly to France."

Austin took a big swallow of the strong port. Le
Camus was right. Five years ago he hadn't put any
stipulations on the vow. How could he? Jerome
had not only saved his life but his mother's, too,
for surely the robbers would have killed them
both. He'd never forget how close that sword was
to his mother's throat before Jerome's shot rang
out. He didn't like going back on his word, but
what else could he do?

"Tell Jerome I'll do anything else he asks, but
I can't take a child from his mother."

"You'll have nothing to do with the actual kidnapping. I'll be responsible for getting the child

on board your ship. All you have to do is deliver him to France. The Patterson family knows me well. I've brought Miss Patterson letters from King Jerome. He's repeatedly asked for his son to be sent to him and even offered to make Miss Patterson the Princesses of Smalkalden so that she and the boy could be near him and have all the riches and titles they deserve."

A wry smile crossed Austin's face. He remembered well the newspaper's carrying Betsy's witty remarks concerning Jerome's ill-conceived offer. She told him Westphalia wasn't large enough for two queens and that she would rather be sheltered under the wing of an eagle than hang from the bill of a goose. In saying that, she refused Jerome's offer of a title and two hundred thousand francs a year in favor of Napoleon's offer of sixty thousand francs in exchange for staying in America.

Le Camus ignored Austin's irreverent smile and continued. "I doubt the kidnapping will be a great surprise, considering King Jerome's past efforts to obtain his son from Miss Patterson. The plan is already set in motion. You'll be on your ship and ready to sail as soon as the boy boards. I'll stay in Baltimore for the questions that are sure to come and when things settle down, as I'm sure they will, eventually go back to France. My brother Alexander is already there waiting for you."

Austin picked up his drink and drained the contents. The port stung his throat. He let out a loud breath and wiped his mouth with the back of his hand. "Damn! This is madness. I can't separate a child from his mother no matter the vow."

"Think back to that time five years ago. If Jerome had said, 'I will kill this man and save your mother if you'll bring my son to me,' would you have done it?"

He was trapped. "It didn't happen that way."

"It could have. Your mother is safe now, and it's convenient for you to forget how you felt that day after your life and your mother's had been saved. Do you wish that your mother had died and this vow hadn't been spoken?"

A heaviness settled in his chest. "Of course not. Your words are foolish."

"I agree. This is such a simple thing he asks of you to fulfill your vow."

Angered by the Frenchman's complacency, Austin reached over the table and grabbed the man by his cravat, roughly pulling him toward his face. "It's not simple. And I am a man of my word, but what you're asking me to do is a damnable thing." A table of men looked their way, and Austin let go of Le Camus.

The Frenchman remained cool as he straightened his cravat. He spread his hands in a helpless gesture again. "I will tell King Jerome you are not a man of your word. You Americans have no honor."

Austin gritted his teeth over those fighting words. How could Jerome question another man's honor after the way he had treated his American wife? He couldn't let the arrogant bastard think he was a man who went back on his word. "There is no honor in kidnapping a defenseless child."

"There is no honor in breaking your word to a man who not only saved your life, but also that of your mother."

"My integrity is not in question. Let the king ask for my life and I will travel to Westphalia and give it."

"His son's safe delivery to France is all that he seeks from you. You will be merely delivering a son to his father, who loves him so much."

Austin wasn't an idiot or a simpleton. It wasn't an easy decision to make. Was he bound by honor to do this terrible deed and take the kidnapped boy to France?

"Think about it. I have a room upstairs. I'll be here another day. But as I said, the plan is already in motion. If not you, someone else will take the boy to his father."

"Why ask me? Why not just hire someone to take the boy to him?"

"You are a respectable businessman. King Jerome would not trust his son's life to the hands of men who fight for money."

Le Camus rose from the table and left. Austin picked up the wine goblet and put it to his lips. It was empty. A foul taste coated his tongue and a bitter feeling stirred inside his stomach. He couldn't believe Jerome Bonaparte had the nerve to ask him to participate in the kidnapping of his son.

A man had to keep his word or he wasn't a man.

Honor demanded it. But, how could he do this horrible deed? Could he think about it as simply as Jerome and Le Camus did? He would merely be delivering a son to his father. How was that more wrong than a mother keeping a son from his father? When he looked at it like that, it made more sense. Besides there was always the chance she could get the child back through political channels. Austin knew he was rationalizing, but he had to come up with some damn good reasons before he could agree to Jerome's request.

Le Camus was right. He had a debt to pay. If it had been only *his* life, he'd gladly travel to France and give Jerome his sword and tell him to take it back. But, Jerome had saved his mother. And, to this day, his mother enjoyed a full, rich life. He owed Jerome, but could he justify the request?

No matter how he tried to rationalize it, he still didn't want to do it. Damn, he didn't want to do it.

Austin scanned the room for the serving girl. He needed another drink. He rubbed his eyes. He'd been so caught up in his conversation with Le Camus, he hadn't noticed the tavern had emptied.

Her feet hurt. Her head ached from lack of sleep. Cheval rubbed the back of her neck and down her shoulders as far as she could reach. She stretched first to the right, then left, trying to relieve the tension built from a week of working in the taproom from early morning until late at night. The tavern didn't close until midnight, and she had to be up at daybreak to help the cook with the morning meal for the guests staying at the inn.

Cheval couldn't wait for the tavern to close, so she could shed her clothes and splash water on her face and neck to rid herself of the stench of dried ale. She glanced around the taproom. The only man left had been at the table in the far corner for more than an hour.

She couldn't help but notice him. He'd watched her closely until he and his companion's conversation had become heated. Not many men were as tall or broad shouldered as he, nor as handsome. He wore his thick, dark-brown hair pulled back in a queue, though most men now boasted a shorter style. His clothing indicated a man of wealth. With that thought, Cheval huffed loudly and picked up the port bottle again. Maybe she could hurry him on his way so they could close. She'd found out the hard way that men of wealth could behave just as badly as the sea-worn sailors who sat at most of the tavern's tables.

Nearing his table, she asked herself why she put up with groping hands and lewd comments from the patrons. *Because I have nowhere else to go,* she answered herself. Thanks to the Duncans she had no choice, if she wanted a place to stay other than the street. It pained her greatly to think that, after a year of faithful service, the Duncans had not only ruined her reputation in Baltimore, but in the whole state of Maryland. Not one family had answered her letters inquiring about a new post

as a governess. No one had even responded to her
request for an interview. It seemed as if everything
had started to go wrong after her sister's death.

She had to find some other kind of work. She
hated all the pinches, fanny pats, and drinks
spilled on her. She didn't mind that she had to
work hard, but the behavior of the customers was
becoming increasingly difficult to endure.

"More port for you, sir?" she asked, stopping
beside the handsome stranger.

The patron lifted his face toward her. Cheval
looked down into a set of beautiful, greenish-gray
eyes. Her stomach fluttered. The man's forehead
was high and his cheekbones well defined. Dark-
brown eyebrows arched attractively, enhancing his
almond-shaped eyes. His nose was slightly pointed.
His full, chiseled lips parted as he said, "A bit
more, perhaps."

Why was she suddenly nervous? She had to hold
the wine jug with both hands to keep it steady while
she poured. Her breath shortened and her heartbeat increased. Fatigue, she assured herself. She
certainly didn't want to be attracted to a stranger
in the taproom.

"We'll be closing soon," she said, hoping to
hurry this disturbing man on his way. She moved
to turn away, but he caught her wrist and stayed
her.

Their eyes met. "How much to stay the night?"
he asked in a quiet voice.

She moistened her lips. "Our singles are occupied. A two-man bed is two dollars. If you want a room to yourself, it will be four."

He smiled. His thumb traced a slow pattern on the soft underside of her wrist. Her breathing became shallow. Why was he making her feel so light-headed?

"No. You misunderstood me. How much will it cost to share your room?"

Cheval shocked herself by taking a moment to consider his proposal. She must be going mad. Her aunt had taught her to be a woman of worth. How could it cross her mind, even for a fleeting moment, to consider his proposition? Was he that handsome? Had working at the tavern changed her? Maybe it was the spring air. Whatever the reason, she decided quickly that she couldn't continue to work at the tavern.

She moistened her lips and cleared her throat, wanting her voice to sound firm and stable. Her gaze didn't waver from his. She pulled her arm free. "I'm sorry, sir. I service the tables, not the rooms."

He laughed. "Name your price."

More strongly she said, "You'll have to go elsewhere for that."

He shook his head. "You're the one I want. Name your price," he said again.

Cheval had had too much for one night—enough to last her a lifetime. She'd been probed, pinched, poked, prodded, and propositioned. She was tired of it. She didn't care that this man was handsome, that she'd been drawn to his roguish good looks.

"I'm not for sale, sir, and I'm highly offended by your proposition." She turned and stomped away. His good-natured chuckle made her all the more furious. What gave men the right to behave so abominably toward women who had to work for a living?

She'd known she would have to fight off advances from drunken sailors when she had taken the job, but she hadn't expected it from the regular patrons and nicely dressed gentlemen.

When the Duncans had thrown her out of their house, they'd refused to pay her back salary. She'd only had enough money to stay at the boarding-house for two months while she'd tried to find another post. Her money ran out too quickly, and she wasn't able to obtain a job.

As a last resort, she'd agreed to work at the tavern to pay for her room and board. She'd asked to work in the kitchen where no one would see her, but the owner wouldn't agree. Mr. Muller said he needed the pretty ones serving the drinks. He and his wife did all the cooking and washing.

Weary, aching from her head to her toes, and upset, Cheval walked straight into the kitchen. She couldn't take any more. "Mr. Muller, I'd like to speak with you," she said in a tired voice.

The gray-haired man turned from banking the embers in the fireplace. Gray ash had settled on his clothes and the crown of his hair.

"Everyone gone?"

"No. There's one gentleman left. He's almost finished and will be gone soon." She took a deep breath and ran her hands down her stained apron, hating the feel of the soiled cloth. "I wanted to tell you I'm quitting."

"What?" He propped himself on one knee.

"I'm leaving. Most of the men who come in here think it's their right to touch me—proposition me. I can't take it any more."

He rose with a grunt and placating smile. "They mean no harm. It's all part of getting away from their wives for a time." He rubbed his flat nose with the back of his hand and left gray ash streaked across his face. "Don't give it a second thought. They won't hurt you."

Mr. Muller wasn't listening to her. "No, you don't understand. I'm quitting, leaving. I'm not working here any longer." Her voice was stronger this time, his lack of concern fueling her displeasure at her predicament.

"Don't get fastidious with me, girlie." He threw his shoulders back and raked the back of his hand under his nose again. "Why do you think I hired you? A comely wench like you brings many men into the tavern, just so they can look at you and slip a little feel of you every now and then. It won't hurt you. I've been tempted to feel of you a time or two myself."

Appalled by what the tavern-keeper said, Cheval gasped. He didn't mind that the men groped her. He wanted them to. Her anger was renewed.

Trying to keep a check on her temper, she said through clenched teeth, "I'll be leaving first thing in the morning."

She whirled toward the door; but just as quickly, he ran in front of her and blocked the doorway. His face glowed red with anger. His eyes twitched. "All right, I'll give you a dollar more a day. That should make a few pats on your backside worthwhile."

Her feet hurt. Her back ached. The strong odor of burned food and stale ale filled the room, making her sick to her stomach. Resolve strengthened her.

"Nothing is worth having leering men think they can touch me or say anything they want to me. I'd rather clean chamber pots in a boardinghouse. I'll be leaving first thing in the morning."

"No, girlie, you won't." His eyes narrowed. "If you're going to leave, it has to be now. I'm not giving you a bed for the night and have you walk out on me." He yanked her by the arm and pushed her forward out the kitchen door.

Pain shot up her arm. Cheval winced. A shove from the back sent her tumbling to the floor. Her legs tangled in her skirts. He reached down and grabbed her hair, yanking her cap off her head. She cried out in fear. His hand closed around her chignon, and he pulled her up by her hair. Intense pain spiraled through her. Cheval struck out at him. Her fist connected with the side of his face. The tavern-keeper's head snapped back. He grunted.

"Ungrateful bitch," he muttered and hit her with an open palm on the side of her head.

He swung her around and twisted her arm behind her back, shoving her forward again. He pushed her through the taproom, forcing her to run ahead of him.

Dazed from the stinging blow, Cheval found it difficult to focus. "My things," she called out when she realized what he was doing.

"As far as I'm concerned, you have no things here. Now get out!" He opened the front door and shoved her hard. She stumbled and fell into something that rocked, then crashed to the ground with her. The door slammed shut.

Cheval groaned and opened her eyes. Moonlight shone down, lighting the midnight darkness. She lay atop the stranger with greenish-gray eyes who'd propositioned her just minutes before.

He smiled up at her. "I guess this means you changed your mind about my offer."

Two

Cheval's eyes widened as she rolled off the man and scrambled to her feet. "I—I'm sorry. I didn't mean to knock you down." She brushed her hair out of her face. The coolness of the late night immediately chilled her, and she hugged her arms to herself.

Chuckling lightly, the man rose to his feet and dusted his clothes. "No harm. I've never had a woman fall so hard for me before. You know, you could have simply tapped me on the shoulder."

A large negro appeared out of nowhere and picked up the man's hat. Frightened he might hurt her, Cheval stepped away from him.

"Are you all right, Mr. Radcliffe?" he asked, helping brush dust from the gentleman's clothes.

"God, yes, Jubal, I'm fine. Don't fuss. I was standing on the porch, putting on my hat, and the next thing I know I'm lying on the ground with this lovely young woman on top of me. What happened?" His gaze darted to Cheval.

"I was watching from the carriage, sir. A man opened the taproom door and pushed her out on the porch, right into your back."

The whites of the negro's eyes shone brightly against his face and the black night. His voice wasn't frightening, and he didn't seem to be paying any attention to her. She relaxed a little.

The gentleman she'd knocked down looked over at her. Concern, showed in his features, warming her, though she still shivered from the coolness of the spring night and from the shock of the rough treatment by Mr. Muller.

"Is that true? Did you get thrown out?"

"Yes. I—I told him I was quitting in the morning. He wouldn't let me stay the rest of the night." Her voice grew fainter with each word.

What was wrong with her? She wanted to cry. She never cried. Many were the times she could have felt sorry for herself and given in to tears, but she was too strong for that. She had to be. It didn't matter that she was tired to the point of exhaustion. Her arm hurt as if it'd been ripped from its socket. She had the worst headache of her life. And being thrown out of the tavern and on top of the attractive man who'd propositioned her minutes ago was the worst thing that could have happened to her. She wished she could sit down and cry.

"Do you have a place to go?"

She swallowed hard and glanced toward the closed tavern door. She'd get no sympathy from Mr. Muller, but she couldn't tell this man that. He obviously hadn't given up on the idea of getting her into his bed for the night. "I'm sure I can find a place."

He looked at her doubtfully. "Do you have money?"

She decided to lie, just so he would go away and stop looking at her with those penetrating eyes and that soothing concerned expression. "Yes, but I'll have to get Mr. Muller to open up so I can get my things. Don't worry. I'll be all right." But, as she said the words, her stomach tightened. She knew that front door wasn't going to open for her tonight. What was she to do? She looked around the darkened street. If only her sister or brother-in-law were still alive, she wouldn't be so alone in the world. With their recent deaths she had no one.

The tavern was several blocks from the docks, but it wasn't a safe time for a woman to be out no matter the neighborhood. Two men stood huddled together on one corner, and the other three corners held clusters of men. She heard them talking, laughing. What would she do, if she couldn't find a boardinghouse to take her in without money in hand? And, how would she get past all those men without the protection of the tavernkeeper? Unbidden, a soft moan escaped her lips.

"Don't worry about tonight. You can come with me to my town house."

"No," she whispered, shaking her head. How many times did she have to turn this man down? Her ears rang. A pressing weight centered itself on her chest and tightened. For a moment she felt light-headed. She thought she might faint. "No—I can't go with you. I've told you I—I'm not like that." She slowly backed away from him until the back of her legs hit the porch.

"Calm down. Don't get upset." He held up his hands and approached cautiously. "I'm not asking you to be my doxy for the night. All right? I'm just offering help. No one's going to let you in this time of night without payment." He pointed to the tavern door behind her. "I don't think he will let you in at all."

Cheval's gaze darted around the street again. What was she to do? Dared she trust this man who'd propositioned her? She rubbed her forehead, trying to think clearly. He seemed sincere.

"I give my word you can trust me—Your name?"

She moistened her lips, then swallowed hard. "Cheval Worthington."

"I'm Austin Radcliffe, Cheval. You will be properly chaperoned at my town house." He turned around. "Tell her, Jubal."

The negro stepped forward. "He's telling the truth, Miss. His housekeeper Thollie won't let anybody mess with you, and I won't either."

Cheval had heard of Radcliffe Ship Builders and Sawmills and wondered if he were part of that family. His manservant seemed polished in his speech and his dress. She stared into the dark man's coal-black eyes. Did she dare trust either of them? She didn't know.

"I'll find a place to take me in," she managed to say on a breathy note, rubbing her arms to ward off the chill, the ache that had settled upon her.

"Do you really want to walk the streets, knocking on strangers's doors? You've found a place, Cheval. Come home with me."

Mr. Radcliffe spoke softly, his voice inspiring trust. He didn't act as if he intended to take advantage of her. Could she trust him? From down the street, she heard loud talking and laughing from the men lounging on the corners. Did she have a choice? She could spend the rest of the night on the street or be at the mercy of this man. Two men, smelling strongly of ale, shuffled by them. One of the men leered at her. She shivered again.

No. She was trapped. If she weren't so tired, maybe she could think of another way out. As it was, she'd be foolish not to take the offer of the properly dressed gentleman over the derelicts and wine bibbers on the street.

"All right," she whispered.

"Good," Austin said, taking his hat from the servant. "Jubal, get the carriage."

The negro trotted across the street. Cheval knew she could be making a big mistake; but feeling that tonight there was no other way, she resigned herself to putting her safety in this man's hands.

"Don't worry so, Cheval," he said, stepping closer to her. "You have no cause to be frightened of me. I know I was out of line earlier this evening, but I won't hurt you."

Moonlight shone down on his face and glowed in his eyes. She saw warmth, concern, and friendliness. She believed him. The carriage pulled up, and she allowed him to take her arm and help her inside. He climbed in, too, and closed the door, shutting out most of the light from the lanterns which hung on the outside wall of the carriage.

Her breathing became shallow again. Would she ever feel safe? Jubal snapped the whip and the horse took off, cantering down the street.

"You're cold."

"No, I'm fine," she lied, hovering in the corner, wishing it were light enough to see his face. Although he didn't touch her, she felt the warmth of his body. She tried to relax, but her whole body was stiff with fear of the unknown. What lay ahead of her?

"I don't think so. You're trembling." He took off his jacket and placed it over her chest and arms. "Here, take this and hold it up under your chin until you stop shaking."

He was right. She was cold. His coat buried her in warmth, soothing her almost immediately. She ached and hurt from her head to her feet. She was tired and so very sleepy. He helped her by tucking the collar of his coat under her chin.

"It's a long ride to my town house. Lay your head back and close your eyes, Cheval. Rest."

"Yes," she murmured, following his instructions. She'd close her eyes for a moment. She could think more clearly once she had a little rest.

Something touched her shoulder.

"Miss. Miss."

Someone shook her. Cheval's eyes popped open. She was staring into the dark-brown face of a woman with a curious expression on her face. Startled, Cheval got up quickly. The room spun and her eyes blurred. She grabbed her forehead and fell back against the pillows. Her head was throbbing.

"Are you all right, Miss? Do you need the doctor?"

What had happened? The last thing she remembered was crawling into the carriage with Mr. Radcliffe and getting warm. Cheval's gaze darted around the room. Hazy sunshine filtered through sheer curtains. Early morning or late afternoon? Cheval didn't know which. At a glance she saw an English dressing table with an oval mirror, a small chest, and a wardrobe—all fine furniture. A beautiful painting of a small girl running through a field of wildflowers hung on one wall. To her far right, the room had a spacious sitting area.

She quickly focused on the woman again. "Where am I?" Her voice sounded gravelly and thick.

The woman smiled pleasantly. "You in the home of Mr. Austin Radcliffe, Miss."

So he had brought her to his home. She remembered thinking last night that she'd heard his name before but knew nothing more than that he owned sawmills and ships. "And—and who are you?"

"I'm Thollie, Miss. I take care of this house for Mr. Radcliffe. He brought you in here early this morning. 'Bout three o'clock, I'd say. You've slept all day," she said good-naturedly, stepping back and looking down at Cheval. "I didn't have the heart to wake you."

Cheval couldn't believe she'd slept so long. She never slept late; but as she thought that, she remembered how exhausted she'd been from the long hours of work at the tavern. Mr. Muller had dealt her a stunning blow and her head was sore. Slowly this time, she raised her head. She wore only her sleeveless chemise. She prayed that Thollie was the one who'd undressed her during the night and not Mr. Radcliffe. The very thought of the handsome gentleman seeing her so scantily clad caused her cheeks to heat.

"My clothes?" she asked.

"Don't worry. I hung them when I undressed you last night."

Relief stole over Cheval. It appeared Mr. Radcliffe had lived up to his promise to be a gentleman.

"It's almost dinner time." The tall, buxom woman picked up a tray from the night table. "Here, I brought you some tea and biscuits to help you wake up. You need to be joining Mr. Radcliffe for dinner in less than an hour."

Dinner? She *had* slept the day away! Cheval was forced to sit up and take the tray. "Oh, I couldn't possibly join him for dinner, but thank him for asking me."

Thollie rested the heel of her hands on her hips, hiking the hem of her black dress. She tilted her head toward Cheval and pursed her lips. "He's expecting you, and we're not going to disappoint him. Now drink your tea. I'll help you dress and fix your hair."

"But you don't understand," Cheval hurried to say. "I don't have a proper dress for dinner." Thollie walked over to the wardrobe and pulled out one of Cheval's best dresses, a puce-colored sarcenet. "All my clothes are—" Cheval stopped in mid-sentence. Astonished, Cheval gasped. "How did you get my dress?"

Thollie's laugh was husky, friendly. "Mr. Radcliffe sent Jubal afta your things this morning." She laid the dress on the foot of the bed. "What Mr. Radcliffe sends Jubal afta, he comes back with. You remember that." She leaned against the cannonball post at the foot of the bed. "Now, you best start drinking that tea. We have to get you ready for dinner."

An hour later Cheval followed Thollie out the bedroom door, down the wide hallway to the stairs. Early evening twilight poured softly through the windows. She'd known last night that Austin Radcliffe was not only a man of education and wealth but also a man of means, and she appreciated all he'd done for her. She was embarrassed that she'd slept the day away. Instead, she should have been out finding a place to work and live. Since Mr. Radcliffe wanted her to join him for dinner, maybe he'd let her stay one more night, if she promised to leave first thing in the morning.

"That's the parlor in there," Thollie said, pointing to an arched entrance as they reached the bottom of the stairs. "Over on this side is the drawing room. Mr. Radcliffe's office is opposite the dining room down that way, and there's a small cook house out back. This house ain't as big as his country home, but he has more room than he needs, not having a wife and chilens. Go on into the drawing room. Mr. Radcliffe's waiting for you in there. I have to check on dinner." She waved for Cheval to go inside and kept walking down the hallway.

Cheval smiled. Thollie brimmed with information and didn't mind parting with it, making Cheval more comfortable in the house. She looked down at her dark-red dress, thankful she'd had it and two others made just before the Duncans had dismissed her. At least she looked presentable. The tunic style with the high waistline flared into a flowing skirt. A wide, buff-colored ribbon cuffed the long sleeves.

She rejected a moment of trepidation at the thought of facing Austin Radcliffe. Refusing to accept being tired as an excuse, she berated herself again for not getting up and out. She took a deep breath and walked over to the entrance into the drawing room.

Austin stood by a beautifully carved tambour desk at the far end of the room, reading a sheet of paper. A fluttering attacked her stomach. The same nervous jitter that had bothered her last night when she'd looked into his eyes. What was it about him that touched her so intimately, so intensely, so completely? He was handsome, kind, and generous. All those things appealed to her;

but she'd met handsome, kind, generous men before and not had her stomach flutter, her breath shorten, and her heart race. Why did she feel differently around this man?

He glanced up and caught her staring at him. Her cheeks and neck heated embarrassingly, but she didn't look away. His gaze swept slowly over her face, across her shoulders, down her breasts, and past her waist before lifting to meet her eyes again.

He folded the paper and laid it on the highly polished secretary. "Don't stand in the doorway staring. Come in and join me on the settee."

"Thank you," she murmured as she entered the room.

Austin walked over to stand in front of her. "You are a beautiful woman, Cheval. I'm pleased to have you in my home. Please sit down."

His words warmed her. She wondered why his voice was husky, why he used her first name, but only said, "Thank you, Mr. Radcliffe." She took a seat on the royal-blue-velvet-covered settee.

"The name is Austin, remember?"

He looked at her, waiting for her to respond. She nodded.

"Will you have a drink with me? A sherry, perhaps?"

The thought of any kind of spirits reminded her of the reeking odor of the tavern, and she wrinkled her nose. She looked up at him and caught his gaze as it lighted upon her face. "No, thank you," she answered politely. "I wouldn't care for anything."

He settled himself on the flower-printed wing chair opposite the settee. He held a short, fat glass in his hand. She noticed that his fingers were handsomely shaped and his nails neatly trimmed. A small smattering of hair graced his finger joints, making his hands look truly masculine.

"You look rested. How do you feel?"

"Much better than last night. I didn't realize how tired I was. I didn't mean to sleep all day."

"It was no matter. You obviously needed it."

She looked at her hands folded in her lap, then back up to his face. "Thank you for letting me stay last night, Mr. Radcliffe, and for sending Mr. Jubal to get my things. I'm so very grateful. I'm afraid Mr. Muller was unhappy with me last night and wouldn't let me get my clothes."

He smiled. The fluttering started again. She liked the way his eyes smiled with his lips. She liked that he made her feel at ease in his home. She liked the way he looked at her with genuine interest and not a leering gaze.

"His name is just Jubal. My housekeeper is Thollie, and I'd like for you to call me Austin."

Leaning forward, she protested. "Oh, I couldn't possibly be that forward, Mr. Radcliffe."

"Yes, you can. You have my permission. I'll call you Cheval and you'll call me Austin. I know we weren't properly introduced, but it's perfectly acceptable considering—how we met."

She wondered if she should bother arguing the

point with him. No, she decided. She wouldn't see him again after she left tomorrow. If she had only tonight in his company, then she didn't intend to annoy him. She'd relax, enjoy the evening, and call him Austin.

Accepting his invitation graciously, she said, "Thank you, Austin." She paused. He wasn't frightening or overbearing. He was kind, considerate, and friendly. She might as well ask him what was on her mind before she lost her nerve. "If you don't mind and it's not too much of an inconvenience, I'd like to ask that I be allowed to stay another night. I promise to be out first thing in the morning. By the time I awakened, I thought it too late in the day to start looking for lodging for the night." Lack of breath when she finished, made her realize how nervous she was that he might deny her request.

"It's not an inconvenience. I insist on your not only staying the night but staying until you find *appropriate* lodging."

She leaned forward. "Oh, I won't do that. I'm sure I'll find something tomorrow."

"But if you don't, I'll expect you back here before twilight bathes the sky."

"Thank you," she whispered again, knowing she'd already thanked him a number of times, but how could she not be grateful for all he'd done? Mr. Muller had left her to the mercies of the street.

"Tell me, Cheval, how did you come to be working in The Boar's Head? I had a feeling you didn't belong there when I first saw you."

Should she tell him she was horrified she had to work in that place? Old feelings rose to the surface and she asked in an accusing tone, "Still you propositioned me?"

A hint of a smile played on the corners of his lips. "Sometimes I'm a gentleman, and sometimes I'm just a man. I didn't want to pass up the chance, in case I was wrong about you."

She appreciated his saying that. It renewed some of the self-confidence she'd lost from all the pinches and lewd remarks she'd endured, but did she want to tell him about her past? She folded her arms across her chest, then quickly unfolded them and put her hands back in her lap before giving him her attention again. She couldn't lie to a man who'd been so good and generous to her.

Meeting his eyes she said, "I'm a governess. Unfortunately, I was dismissed not more than two months ago, and I haven't secured another post. When I ran out of money last week, I was forced to take whatever work I could find."

The studious expression on his face made her wonder if he were trying to figure out why she had been dismissed. Did she dare tell him she'd been falsely accused of trying to seduce her employer? Would he believe her, or the Duncans?

"You're a governess?" He set his drink aside and moved to the edge of his seat. "That means you know how to care for young children?"

That information had surprised him, but she wasn't quite sure whether it confused him or pleased him. He rubbed his chin thoughtfully as he studied her face. She wanted to know what he was thinking.

"Yes. I'm qualified to teach boys their lessons up to age ten; and of course, I can teach girls proper manners, needlework, and the basics of managing a household."

"You're a governess."

Austin repeated himself, but this time he made the comment a statement, not a question. She didn't understand his keen interest in her occupation. Was he deliberately overlooking her dismissal or had he not understood her?

Under his intense scrutiny she simply said, "Yes." She was afraid of not saying enough, and also of saying too much.

"Cheval, that gives me an idea. It just so happens I might be in need of someone to take care of a young child for a long journey."

Cheval's chest tightened at the thought. He needed a governess? Thollie had told her he wasn't married. "I don't understand. I wasn't aware you had a child."

"The boy's not mine. It's a bit complicated and nothing you need concern yourself about right now. Tell me, Cheval, do you have family obligations?"

Sorrow cloaked her at the thought of her sister's untimely death. Almost a year had passed since Loraine had swallowed the poison that ended her life. The pain hadn't lessened. "No family living," she answered softly before lifting her chin a little. "I wouldn't have resorted to working and living in a tavern if I'd had anyone to turn to for help."

Austin nodded, stood, and walked around behind the settee. "Tell me, are you opposed to taking a long sea voyage? Have you ever sailed on a ship?"

A brief shiver shook her, even though her curiosity was piqued. Loraine's husband, a seaman, had been lost at sea when his ship had sunk in a storm. She turned in her seat to follow him. No, she couldn't let that keep her from the possibility of a job. "I'm not opposed to a long journey; and although I've never been on board a ship, I see no reason why that should be a problem for me."

"Do you think you can handle—say thirty to forty days on a ship?"

"I don't see why not."

"Most of that time will be spent in a small cabin with a boy who's not yet four years."

"I can manage that, I'm sure."

"Sailing makes some people ill."

"I don't have a weak constitution."

"The food's bad and the facilities are limited. Will that bother you?"

He threw the questions at her so fast she had no time to think, only to respond with the first positive thought that came to her mind. His keen interest in her abilities surprised her. "I think so. I can't foresee any problems with the things you've mentioned. Why? Are you offering me the job?"

Austin shrugged his shoulders. "That's a good possibility. If you have no obligations, and if you're willing. I'll need someone to take care of him and see to his needs on the voyage."

Cheval's spirits lifted, soared. What luck! This

was her opportunity to win back her good name. If she did this for Austin, she was sure he'd give her a good recommendation for a permanent post. Just the Radcliffe name would be an excellent reference for her. And, getting away from Baltimore for a while would give the gossip the Duncans had spread about her time to die. With no family responsibilities, she was perfect for Austin's needs.

Excited, she moved to the edge of her seat. "I would very much like to do this for you. The money would pay my living expenses when we return until I could secure another post. I'm sure if the child's mother met me I could convince her I'm the best person for the job."

He hesitated. "Meeting the mother won't be necessary. I'm in charge of seeing that the child is cared for." A faraway expression clouded his eyes. "Yes, I think it would be better if there were a governess along to take care of the boy—if I decide to make the journey."

"It would mean a lot, if you'd allow me to do it," she said earnestly. "Not only would it help me, but it's a way I can repay you for taking me into your home."

Austin looked down into her eyes. "We might have to sail within a day or two."

Her heartbeat raced at the thought. "That's not a problem for me."

He studied her for a moment. "While final plans are being made, I'd like for you to stay here so you'll be available should I need you."

Cheval nodded. The thought of doing a good

job and reclaiming her good name filled her with joy, and a little voice reminded her that she wouldn't mind being on a ship with Austin for three or four weeks.

"Mr. Radcliffe, dinner's ready to be served," Thollie said from the doorway.

"Thank you, we'll be right in."

Austin smiled and extended his hand for Cheval. "You're hired."

Three

Austin rapped his knuckles three short times on the door of the upstairs room at the Boar's Head Tavern. He wanted to get this over with as soon as possible. The stench of dried ale and pipe tobacco lingered in the air of the windowless hallway. It was dark and damp, the only light afforded the narrow passageway came from the top of the stairs where it filtered up from below. Smooth, throaty laughter from a woman drifted past him from one of the other rooms. Already the tavern was receiving customers.

He was about to knock again when the door jerked open. A knowing smile crossed Le Camus's face, widening his hawk-like nose. "Why am I not surprised it's you?"

"Because you are a man of low principles and you recognize a dastardly deed."

"Perhaps King Jerome's request is all those things to you; but to me, it's simply a matter of you protecting your honor, which I assume you've decided to do or you wouldn't be here. Come in." Le Camus stepped aside and allowed Austin entrance into the small bedroom.

It bothered Austin that in theory the Frenchman was right. Austin was protecting his honor; but, he feared, in trying to protect it, he might end up losing it.

"You won't regret this, Radcliffe," Le Camus said, closing them inside the chilled room. "Jerome Napoleon—or Bo, as his mother so freely refers to him—deserves to be united with his father so that he may take his rightful place with this noble and imperial family of Bonapartes."

Austin grunted. Did the Frenchman think Americans weren't privy to the information about Napoleon's humble beginning and family heritage?

"The only thing I'm concerned with is fulfilling my vow to Jerome." And the only justification he could reason was that he was delivering the boy to his father. If the request had been for him to take the child anywhere else in the world, he would have refused.

"So all we need to do is make the final arrangements to take Bo from the Patterson house on South Street and delivering him to one of your ships."

"We'll use *Aloof*. She's the fastest. I've also hired a governess to take care of the boy."

"There's no need for that. I have a woman to look after the boy."

On this Austin would remain strong. "I want to use someone of my own choosing."

Le Camus held up his hand, a worried expression clouding his strong features. "Is she to be trusted?"

"Don't be stupid. I have too much to lose if word of this got out. I haven't been careless. She won't ask any questions. My captain will be the only one on board who'll know where we're going or what we're doing."

The Frenchman relaxed. "Very well. Let's get down to the details of where you are to land and whom you will meet. I have everything worked out."

Late afternoon sunshine glimmered off the brass shingle that read Bradley Thornhill, Attorney at Law. Austin stood in front of the side entrance to the large house on Wilderberry Street. A separate apartment connected to the home served as Bradley's office. Bradley was more than Austin's lawyer, he was his brother-in-law.

He was also a thorn in Austin's side most of the time. Bradley thought being William Radcliffe's lawyer and son-in-law gave him clout to question Austin on how he managed the ship building company since William died. Bradley was constantly stopping by Austin's office to question him or take issue with him about the business. Austin remained civil to him only because he was married to Winifred, his sister.

The shimmering brass shingle held Austin's attention and threw him deeper into thought. Was he crazy? A madman? Austin wondered as he stood in the waning light of day? Had he actually agreed to take this kidnapped little boy from his mother and sail him across the sea to a new land and a father he had never seen, all in the name of some intangible thing called honor? Would it make him less of a man for not keeping his word?

"Yes," he said with determination, jerking his thoughts back to the matter at hand. He had re-hashed the dilemma a number of times and always came up with the same answer. A man without honor was of no use to himself or anyone else. After Jerome Bonaparte had saved his mother's life, he would have done anything to repay Jerome. The deed the young soldier had done for him was no less commendable today than it had been five years before. Jerome deserved his reward. That Austin didn't like it was of no matter. It had to be done.

The plan was set. Le Camus was responsible for getting the child on board Austin's ship *Aloof,* which sat anchored offshore. He had Cheval, a trained governess, to care for the child. With no family, she was perfect for his needs. His stomach muscles tightened, forcing him to remember Cheval was not merely a governess but also a desirable woman. He'd be forced to keep those thoughts at the back of his mind. This was a mission, not a pleasure trip.

In Westphalia, Bo would be well cared for and lack nothing. Jerome was a king, the boy heir to the throne. No, he didn't like it, but he could justify it. A man deserved to have his son with him. He wouldn't think about the mother, Austin convinced himself. He couldn't. If he allowed himself to think about her anguish, he wouldn't go through with this, not even to save his honor.

Betsy Patterson's father was a wealthy man in his own right and would probably stop at nothing to get his grandson back. And, Austin had no doubt they'd know exactly where the boy would be. Everyone in the city knew Jerome had asked in numerous letters that his son be sent to him in Westphalia.

Austin knocked, then opened the door and walked into the law office.

A tall, lanky man with light-red hair and pale, freckly skin rose from his chair. A big smile stretched across his face. "Austin, come in and sit down. It's been awhile. Where have you been? What luck you've come by today. Stay for dinner. We have the most pleasant young woman dining with us this evening. You must meet her."

"Matchmaking again, Bradley?" Austin asked dryly. He shut the door and stepped farther into the darkly paneled room lit with oil lamps. The smell of beeswax, pipe tobacco, and burned oil hung heavily in the air.

"Certainly not." Bradley's face reddened. He pulled on the tail of his coat and threw his shoulders back as if affronted. "You've scolded me one time too many for that. I learned my lesson with Miss Peabody. If you're content to remain aloof—as you so aptly named your latest ship, then I shall respect your wishes."

Austin chuckled. He'd like to see the day Bradley respected his wishes without an argument. Maybe he'd been too hard on him for arranging the dinner party with the young and giggly Nora Peabody. When he'd been in his early twenties, he hadn't minded getting to know all the young women making their formal entrance into society, but they seemed to be getting younger each year. Austin had no use for a silly woman, no matter how beautiful.

His thoughts strayed to Cheval. A tightening stirred his lower body. She was beautiful, young—not yet twenty, he was sure—but definitely not silly.

"I had no idea you'd be stopping by today when Winifred told me she'd invited a new friend to dine with us." Bradley continued to defend his invitation.

"Of course you didn't," Austin said, dropping into the forest-green wing chair. He knew how to get Bradley off the taboo subject. "How is my dear sister?"

Bradley's countenance changed in the blink of an eye. His features softened, his shoulders relaxed. His mouth eased into a warm smile. "Beautiful. Your first nephew should arrive within two months."

Austin felt a tug at his heart. He hated that he wouldn't be here for the birth of his sister's fourth child. "Still so certain it's a boy this time?"

Bradley rolled his light-blue eyes upward. "After three girls—it has to be. Not even God would be so cruel as to give me *four* girls. Three lovely daughters running about the house crying after me is enough."

Both men laughed. Bradley walked around to

the front of his desk. Pushing the ink well aside, he leaned against the polished-oak, flat-top desk. Austin knew his brother-in-law was a soft touch for his family. Even though Bradley was a nuisance about the business, Winifred couldn't have picked a better husband for herself, or father for her children. The one thing he appreciated about Bradley was that he loved his family.

"Tell me, what made you stop by at the end of the work day, if not to join us for dinner?"

Austin sobered. "I'm here on business."

Bradley didn't hide his surprise well. And no wonder. Austin had never come to him on business. He folded his arms across his chest. "Your expression is serious. Do I need to be worried about you?"

"No," Austin lied. "I came to tell you that I'll be leaving Baltimore for a time."

Bradley squinted. "What? Leaving? What are you talking about?"

"I'll be sailing to Europe, and I'm not sure when I'll be back. I expect it to be a quick trip, but one never knows."

Shaking his head, Bradley said, "This isn't a good time to go to Europe, Austin. Surely I don't have to tell you there's a war going on."

"I'm aware of what's happening."

"I'm not sure you are, if you're willing to risk your life and one of your ships. Tell me, what is so important that you feel you must do this?"

"I can't."

"Nonsense. I've been in the family for six years. I can help you."

"Don't question me on this, Bradley. I have no answers for you. Just do as I ask."

"I have to advise you against this, Austin, no matter the reason. Europe is not safe. It's not like you to be foolhardy." He took a deep breath and stood straight.

"Your objection *and* observation are noted. Now, I don't want anyone to know where I've gone. If there are questions, you're to say I'm away on business, which I am, and leave it at that. I want you to keep an eye on mother. Take Winifred for a visit if you can. You know how lonely mama gets when I travel."

"You don't have to ask that of me but, my God, Austin, think about what you're saying. Napoleon's on the loose like a madman. This isn't the time to sail to Europe. You haven't thought this through, surely."

Austin remained calm. "No, you're wrong. I have thought it through. I realize there is some danger; but believe me, it's minimal." He pulled an envelope from his pocket. "However, should I not come back, open this. It will explain everything. Should I come back, I'll expect to reclaim this unopened."

Bradley reached for the envelope and laid it on the desk behind him without giving it a glance. "I need more information from you on this. Exactly where in Europe are you going, and when?

How long will you be gone? Whom should I contact for information should I not hear from you."

"We sail tomorrow night." Austin didn't intend to tell him his port of call or anything else.

His brother-in-law's eyes narrowed. He rubbed his chin with the backs of his fingers and started pacing in front of the desk. "Austin, something's wrong. I feel it. I don't like the sound of this. Tell me what is going on. I want to help you."

Austin rose from his chair and clapped his friend on the back, hoping to reassure him. "Don't worry about me. I know what I'm doing."

Jubal stopped the carriage at the front door of Austin's town house. He jumped out, splattering his shiny boots with muddy water. "The seas may be too choppy for you to row out to *Aloof* tonight," Austin said to his manservant as a chilling drizzle dampened the back of his neck, hitting that bare area between his coat collar and hat. Thollie had lit the lamp over the doorway, giving light to the pitch-black night.

"Yes, sir. You want me to wait or come back here?"

"Wait. I want to make sure that medicine bag is on board before we sail. I just hope the boy stays in good health and we don't need it. Now go. The rain has just started and with any luck the water won't be too rough yet."

Jubal headed for the carriage, and Austin opened the door and walked inside. Light from the dimly lit foyer immediately welcomed him with its comforting warmth and promise of safety. He took off his dripping hat and coat and hung them on the clothes tree behind the door. He wiped the dampness from his face and neck and sighed. Waiting was hell. He wished they sailed tonight.

He turned to go into the drawing room for a sip of brandy, but, with a rush of awareness, he stopped. Cheval stood in the doorway. The soft light framed her in its glow. The sight of her warmed him, taking the chill off the air. Their eyes met. His breath leaped. Austin knew he was in trouble. He desired her. He was falling victim to her quiet grace, her spirit, her charm. His gaze lingered on her face. Not only was she lovely, she was strong, resourceful, and intelligent.

Doubts tugged at his heart. Should he tell her that what he had asked of her could very well ruin her life? Was it fair to involve her, to involve anyone? Did he want to do that to her? No, of course not. If they were caught, she could possibly be in as much trouble as he. But, if they made it, he would be good to her and settle enough money on her that she'd never have to work again.

Finally he said, "You look lovely tonight, Cheval."

She waited a long time before she responded. "Thank you." She pulled a delicate handkerchief from the cuff of her sleeve and as softly as a warm wind, she stepped forward and handed it to him.

Without taking his gaze from hers, he took the small lace-edged square of cloth and gently touched it to each side of his neck, then to each cheek. He breathed deeply and inhaled the clean scent of Cheval on the handkerchief. He didn't want to give it back. He wanted to keep that part of her with him.

"The rain must have chilled you. I have hot tea in the parlor. Would you like a cup?"

Forgetting the brandy, touched by her consideration for him, he nodded and moved to her side, slipping the handkerchief into his jacket pocket.

Cheval poured tea while Austin took a seat on the settee. There was something—no, everything about this man she found appealing. All he had to do was look at her and her legs became watery. She felt like a young schoolgirl, blossoming with her first awareness of boys, rather than a woman who'd just turned twenty.

She had to be careful. The last thing she wanted was to develop any romantic feelings for her employer. She'd never forget what a shambles her last employer had made of her life. While Mr. Duncan was a handsome man, she'd never been attracted to him, no matter what he'd told his wife. Now that she *was* attracted to her employer, she had to be better than good, more than circumspect.

"Cream or sugar?" she asked.

Austin shook his head. "Neither. I'm surprised you're still up." He took the tea and sipped it.

"I slept so much yesterday I wasn't sleepy tonight. I hope you don't mind?"

"Actually, I'm glad. It gives me a chance to talk to you again." He paused, studying her. "I found out tonight that my journey is set. We sail tomorrow evening."

Excitement coursed through her. Her eyes lit with adventure. "That's wonderful. I'm ready to go whenever you give the word." The sooner she made this journey, the better. She could return and reestablish her good name and reputation as an excellent governess. She would take the best care of her charge and prove to the Duncans that she could rise above their perfidy.

His eyes turned serious. "Cheval, sit down. I want to talk to you."

She didn't like the sound of his voice. Her muscles tightened as she sat in a chair opposite him.

"This is not going to be an easy voyage. I'm beginning to wonder if it's fair of me to ask you to make this journey."

"What?" She poised forward in her seat, fear making her throat dry. "Have you found someone else to care for the child?"

"No, but I know you need to be here, trying to find a permanent post, and there is some danger in traveling to Europe at this time because of the war. I'm just not sure—"

"You have changed your mind about me." Her voice turned whispery. Even though he hadn't asked for references, he must have heard about the problem with the Duncans, and now he didn't want her. What was she to do? She needed this job. She *had* to have it.

She couldn't keep the hurt off her face, out of

her eyes, away from her voice. "You don't trust me?"

Austin rubbed the back of his neck. "That's not true. I—I don't know that I should involve you in this. It's a complicated matter, and I don't want you to get hurt. That's my only reason for having second thoughts."

Cheval clasped her hands together in her lap. She refused to let him deny her and go back on his word. "I need this position. Please let me go so I can prove myself."

"I know you're worried about a place to live while you look for new employment. You can stay here. Thollie would love it. Jubal will be going with me."

"No. You don't understand. I need this job. I'm not worried about sailing to Europe. I—I feel perfectly safe with you." She felt herself blush at admitting that to him but fear of losing out forced her to continue. "If you haven't found another to care for the child, why are you denying me this post?"

His eyes met hers. She felt as if he were trying to tell her something, trying to warn her of something. She wondered if she should simply tell him the whole story about the Duncans and beg him to give her a chance to prove she could take care of the child.

"There's a possibility one day you might regret accepting this position."

How could she regret what could very well restore her reputation? "No. I understand the dangers of sailing to Europe at this time. I'm prepared to accept them and do everything within my power to take care of that little boy."

Finally, he nodded reluctantly. "All right. Give Thollie a list of everything you might need for yourself and for the child. She'll purchase it for you and have it sent to the ship. You'll have all day tomorrow to get ready. We'll board late in the evening."

Cheval didn't realize how stiff she had been holding herself until she relaxed. Thank God, he was going to let her have the job. She'd prove to him she could take care of the child. And she'd stay as far away from Austin as possible. If he knew about the problem at the Duncan household, she'd see to it he'd had no reason to think she had anything on her mind other than caring for that child.

The ship rocked and creaked against the swift movement of the choppy water. It wasn't a great night to sail, but not impossible, Austin had assured her. Cheval wasn't sure she believed him. She was a ball of nerves as she sat in the dimly lit cabin, rocking back and forth, trying to comfort the dark-haired little boy whimpering in her arms. He'd cried for more than two hours.

Something wasn't right. The child's mother hadn't accompanied him, nor the father. Not even a nurse. Cheval had still been below preparing the cabin for them when she'd heard loud crying.

She'd met Austin coming down the stairs with the wailing and struggling child. As best he could, above the boy's screams for his mother, Austin told her that from here on she was in charge.

Above the roar of the wind and his crying she'd asked, "Where's his mother?"

"I really can't tell you much of anything about him," Austin had insisted. "Only that I'm delivering him to his father."

"Surely you can tell me the boy's name. If I know a little more about him, I'll be better equipped to take care of him."

"Bo. His mother calls him Bo. Take him below and give him some warm milk and a biscuit. We'll talk later."

It had been difficult to console Bo; but finally after two hours of rocking, singing, and soothing, he'd cried himself to sleep, asking for his Mama. It wrenched the very heart from her chest to see him so upset and unable to give him what he wanted. She ached to comfort him but knew nothing would take the place of his mother's arms.

She rocked him another hour, wanting to make sure he was sound asleep before she tried to lay him down. If he awakened, she was afraid he'd start crying again. Something wasn't right, she told herself again. She planned to find Austin and demand some answers.

Carefully she laid Bo on the small bed. He whimpered, but she patted his back until he slept soundly once more. She rubbed her neck and shoulders and tried to get the blood flowing in her arms again before tiptoeing from the room and down the gallery. As she neared the stairway, she heard muffled, angry voices coming from Austin's cabin. She walked closer and, noticing that the door wasn't completely shut, stopped. She started to knock and step inside, but angry words stopped her. Surprised by the harsh tone of Austin's voice, she listened.

"Dammit! Bradley, I can't believe you did this. I can't believe you're here."

"I told you. I wanted to try to persuade you once again to tell me what was going on. I had no idea you'd wait so late to board. I had a drink and fell asleep in your chair."

"Didn't you hear that child crying? Didn't that wake you?"

"I live in a house with three children. I'm used to crying."

Austin muttered another curse.

"Why is it so difficult to believe I wanted to try once again to talk you out of this foolish notion? Why can't you believe I wanted to help?"

"You can't help. For God's sake, Winifred's baby is due in less than three months. What were you thinking when you boarded?"

"I didn't plan on falling asleep. The brandy relaxed me."

"How much did you drink?"

"Well, I did wait a long time for you to retu— That's not important. I can assure you I didn't expect to have you rouse me a few hours later and tell me we're at sea, if that's what you mean. If you don't want my help, fine. Just turn the ship around and take me back to port."

Austin groaned lowly. "I can't."

"Of course you can. You own this ship."

"Look," Austin said in an irritated voice. "I don't like this any better than you do. You are the *last* person I would have wanted on this journey, but like it or not you are on your way to Europe."

"No! I won't hear of this foolishness. It may have been unwise of me to enjoy your brandy—"

"Unwise! That's a hell of an understatement."

Bradley chafed. "Well, now that I'm here you can't refuse to turn the ship around."

"I can't do it," Austin repeated, his voice losing some of its anger.

Bradley hissed his irritation. "Dammit, Austin, I insist you turn this ship around immediately."

Cheval heard swearing and the shuffling of feet. She gently pushed the door aside and in the yellow glow of lamp light she saw Austin pushing a red-haired man against the paneled cabin wall. Jubal stood to one side watching them.

"I can't take you back. That little boy you *didn't* hear crying down below has been kidnapped. By now the authorities are no doubt looking all over the city for him; and if I return, they will search the ship and throw all of us in jail!"

Bradley's face flamed red. "My God! Austin, you lie."

"No, I speak the truth. He's been kidnapped from his mother. I'm taking him to his father."

Cheval felt faint. Light-headed. The slow roll of

the ship unsettled her and she felt as if she were going to fall. She leaned against the wall, trying to get her breath. Her chest heaved. Her stomach churned. Surely, the nice man she was drawn to, the man who'd helped her hadn't done this horrible deed. Surely, she'd heard him incorrectly.

She squeezed her eyes shut. No, she hadn't. What must that little boy's mother be going through? Cheval opened her eyes, remembering her sister's cry of anguish, her lamenting when she'd awakened and found her son lost to her forever. Loraine had tried to overcome the loss of her son but her grief was too great. She never recovered.

In a moment of frantic passion Cheval knocked the cabin door open wide and rushed inside. Ignoring the other two men in the room, her eyes met Austin's.

"You bastard!" she said earnestly.

Four

Cheval walked farther into the dimly lit room. The ship creaked and swayed from the choppy seas. She steadied herself by grabbing hold of the back of a chair. A shocked expression rested on Austin's face, in his eyes, as he stared at her. The red-haired man Austin had shoved against the wall appeared stunned to see her, too. Only Jubal kept his feelings hidden behind a mask of indifference.

Her accusing gaze shot back to Austin, and he stepped away from the man he'd been struggling with. Cheval was bursting with outrage, with disappointment.

"I can't believe you! This child I've comforted and rocked to sleep has been kidnapped from his mother?" Her throat closed up on her as she said the words aloud, and her heart hammered in her chest. Again she felt that she might faint from the rage consuming her. "How could you?" she managed to force past her lips. "Have you no shame or mercy in your bones?" She didn't know if she were demanding an answer or making a damning statement.

"Who are you to barge in here like this?" the

red-haired man asked. He stepped in front of Austin, making it clear that even though he'd been fighting Austin just moments ago, he was now ready to take up for him against the person he considered an outsider.

"Her name is Cheval," Austin replied moving from behind Bradley. "I hired her to care for the boy on this journey. She's a governess."

The stranger squinted as if he had trouble seeing her in the hazy lamp light of the dark room. "You presume to speak to your employer in such a manner." He huffed and pulled on the tail of his coat. "This has nothing to do with you. Be off."

Astonished that the freckle-faced man made an attempt to put her in her place, Cheval stared mutely at him. In his skirmish with Austin, his hair had been ruffled and his cravat torn askew. While talking, he had maneuvered himself in front of her again so that he completely blocked her view of Austin.

Obviously, this man Austin had called Bradley hadn't yet realized they were on the same side. They both wanted the ship turned around immediately and headed back to Baltimore's harbor.

Determined not to be daunted by this man or Austin, she straightened her shoulders, trying to remain steady on her feet as she said, "I won't have you speak to me in such an unacceptable tone of voice. I'm not your servant to be ordered around. If Austin is involving me in a crime, it is very much my business what is said here."

"Austin, is it?" Bradley's color heightened. He turned around and faced his brother-in-law. "I can't believe you allow her to be so free with the use of your name or how she speaks to you."

Outrage gave Cheval courage she wouldn't otherwise have possessed. She stepped closer to the men. "I dare say you are in no position to argue with me or anyone else about my position on this ship. Stop this foolish nonsense about what is proper for me and what isn't." She felt as if every muscle in her body were on fire. She had to correct this terrible wrong. "We have a little boy who has been kidnapped and must be returned to his mother with all haste!"

Bradley lifted his chin and sniffed. "Quite true," he said as if the idea had been his own. He glared down at her as he brushed his straight hair away from his forehead with an open palm. "But I'll handle this."

"Stop this. Both of you," Austin interjected, pushing Bradley aside and stepping in front of him. His cold gray-green eyes scanned Cheval's face. "Who's with the boy?"

"No one, right now," she answered defensively. "He's sleeping peacefully. Don't worry, he won't awaken. I gave him a little laudanum. He was so distraught and crying for his mother I couldn't quieten him any other way."

Austin's eyes remained cold. "He shouldn't be left alone in any case. I want you—"

"Just a minute, Austin," Bradley chimed in, moving to stand beside him. "We need to clear this up so you can turn this ship around. Every minute we delay takes us farther from Baltimore. You can talk to this chit later." He rubbed his nose with his forefinger and sniffed again. "I have an idea I think will work. When we dock, I'll assume responsibility for the boy. I'll simply tell the authorities I found the youngster wandering around by himself. No one will ever know the truth of this night." His gaze darted from Cheval to Jubal, who still stood quietly in the corner of the small cabin and back to Austin. "It will be our secret."

Austin stared at Bradley with alarming steadiness in his eyes and his features but remained quiet.

Now that Cheval took the time to look at Austin, she could see he didn't look well. His lips were pale and a tightness showed around his mouth. He drew his dark eyebrows together in a frown as if he were in pain. Was he sick, or was he unhappy about what he was doing?

"No," Austin said.

"Have you lost your mind, Austin?" Bradley asked, holding up his hand. "You're not thinking this through."

Coming out of her reverie, Cheval took a step forward and said, "You have to turn around. Bo's mother is probably going out of her mind with worry. This is cruel. You can't do this to her."

"I'm sure she'll know exactly who has her son before she's told. She probably assumed his father might one day try to take him from her."

Cheval gasped and her neck stiffened. She wasn't

getting through to him the depth of a mother's love and what it would do to her to lose a child. "That's absurd. No mother would think that. I've never had a child, but my sister did. Believe me, I know what it will do to that poor woman to find her son gone. Please, you must take him back." Her voice shook. She felt on the brink of tears. "You must."

"I agree with *her*," Bradley commented, pointing at Cheval as if there were other women in the room.

Bradley emphasized the pronoun as if he couldn't remember her name. She could tell by his tone of voice he didn't like the fact that they were on the same side. But he didn't mind using it to his advantage.

"Austin, you must give word to turn the ship around. Not only for the boy and your social standing, but you know I have to get back to Winifred."

"I'm not unsympathetic to my sister's condition."

"What about Bo's mother? Think of what Bo's mother is going through," Cheval insisted, raising her voice louder to be heard above Bradley's pleadings.

Austin rubbed that small area between his eyebrows with his thumb and forefinger and winced. Cheval thought they were wearing him down until he said, "You're not listening to me. Even if I felt I could return him to Baltimore, there would be no way we could get him off this ship without someone seeing us. The docks will be covered with police. The mother will receive a note telling her that her son is safe and on his way to be with his father. Nothing can be reversed."

Her sister's pitiful face with tears streaming down her cheeks flashed before Cheval. She remembered what Loraine had gone through. The sleepless nights, the anguish, the crying, depression, and finally losing the will to live.

"You can't do this," Cheval insisted, suddenly grabbing Austin by his coat. She was wild with desperation. "Nothing could justify taking a child from his mother. Nothing! You must take him back! She can't live without him. I know it."

Austin took hold of her wrists and pulled her hands free, setting her away from him. "Neither of you are listening to me." Anger laced his voice. He looked from one to the other. "This is something I had to do. I can't explain it, and I don't expect you to understand. If—if I'd had any other recourse I would have taken it. The deed is done and in progress. I've given my word—such as it is."

He wasn't going to relent. Cheval understood that now. "You're a heartless man with no feelings in your bones," she whispered.

"You don't know me or what I'm feeling," he countered. "You have no right to judge me or my actions." His voice and features softened. "The two of you might as well save your breath." He turned toward Bradley. "There's only one way to get back to Baltimore. Swim. If you want to, be my guest. Otherwise, Jubal will show you a room." He turned to Cheval. "You have your room and your duties. The boy is in your hands, and I expect you to do a good job taking care—"

"All right! Damnation!" Bradley interrupted him. "Take this boy to God knows where if you must to fulfill your honor, but I demand you take me back to Baltimore first and at once. Then you're free to take off on this fool's errand for God's knows who and where."

Calmly, Austin said, "No."

"Hellfire! Austin, you're trying my soul."

A muscle worked in his neck but his tone remained even. "And you are trying mine. My patience is gone. If I have to say 'no' one more time, I'll have Jubal put you under lock. I pray you left word with Winifred what you were doing."

"We discussed this over dinner. She knew I was going to the ship to talk to you."

"Then I pray she knows your penchant for having a brandy after dinner and falling asleep."

Bradley's face fell, the angry redness of his complexion turned ashen, telling on him. "I—I had no idea you were under such constraints." A note of desperation entered his voice. He raised his hands in a helpless manner.

"Go with Jubal, Bradley. He'll see you settled into a cabin. We'll talk again later. I'll think of something."

"What is there short of returning?" With a defeated expression on his face, Bradley started to speak again, but closed his mouth and remained silent. He turned and walked out. Having never said a word, Jubal followed.

Austin turned away from Cheval and faced his desk. "You, too," he said. "Go back to your room."

For a moment, Cheval thought he was in pain again. She swallowed hard. How could this man she'd thought to be a gentleman do this? "Even though you know what you're doing to Bo's mother?"

Suddenly Austin whirled on her. "What about the father? Does he not have feelings for the young son he's never seen? Should the mother be the only one to know his love?"

"Will he never return to America again? Couldn't he visit if he wanted to see his son?"

"None of this concerns you. Just go and take care of the boy as you've been hired to do. You've been away from him too long as it is."

Sweat had broken out on his forehead. He was paler than before, she was sure. He didn't look well. Something told her she wouldn't get any farther with him than Bradley had. Not tonight anyway. And he was right. She needed to get back to Bo. He would be more frightened than ever if he awoke and no one was there to comfort him.

Without further words, Cheval turned and slowly made her way toward her cabin. Her heart ached. How could she make it up to that little boy for being torn from his mother's arms, snatched away from all he knew and loved?

Austin Radcliffe was a wealthy man from one of Baltimore's finest families. Surely he wasn't kidnapping the boy for money. But why?

Austin. How could this kind and gentle man who

took her off the streets and into his home and looked at her so lovingly just two nights ago possibly be involved in a kidnapping? Because he didn't understand a mother's love, she reasoned. Naturally, he wouldn't. He was a man, thinking like a man, helping another man. While she looked at this as an atrocity, he looked at it as taking a son to his father. It didn't surprise her that he assumed the boy would be better off with his father. Surely, most men would feel the same way, but that didn't make it right.

What could she do for Bo? With heavy feet, she walked back into the cabin where the boy lay. Lamp light bathed the room in a pale, yellow glow. He was so small. She touched his light-brown hair. It was fine, silky. She gently rubbed his forehead and caressed his reddened cheek with the tips of her fingers. He stirred briefly, but not enough to rouse him from sleep. Every little boy needed to be with his mother. Maybe when he was older, ready to learn to shoot, ride, and fight, he should be with his father. But not now. Not while he was still so young and innocent.

She had to do something, but what?

Cheval's thoughts turned closer to her heart, to Loraine. Her sister's child couldn't be returned. Two-year-old-Thomas had been lost forever to Loraine a year after her husband had been confirmed as missing at sea. Death couldn't be reversed, but Bo's situation could be reversed. Bo could be returned to his mother.

Cheval's breath caught in her throat. Her hand

stilled on Bo's soft cheek. Almost afraid to let her thoughts go further, she sat on the side of the bunk, covering her mouth with her hand. The lamp burned so low it gave only the faintest amount of light to the small room. The swaying of the ship seemed to have lessened, too, or maybe she was getting used to the continuous rocking motion. She squeezed her eyes shut. Dare she let her mind explore that intimidating avenue? Yes. Now that the idea had come to her, she had to explore it. She had to think about the possibility of returning Bo to his mother.

She opened her eyes and slipped her feet out of her soft-soled shoes, leaving her stockings on for warmth. She gently lay down on the bunk beside the youngster, not bothering to remove any of her clothes. She had too much to think about.

What could she do, she asked herself again? First, she had to find out who Bo's mother was. If the little boy couldn't tell her, maybe she could eventually get the information out of Austin.

She sat up in the bed so quickly Bo stirred and whimpered. She patted his shoulder and whispered softly to him, lulling him back to sleep.

That was it! If Austin could kidnap the boy from his mother, why couldn't she kidnap him from Austin? Cheval trembled with the shock, the fear of what she was thinking. Could she do it? Yes, she told herself immediately. She had to for Bo and his mother. But how? And when? She patted her lips with her fingers as she stared at the dark ceiling and contemplated.

Certainly not until they landed would she have a chance, but she'd start making plans now as to what to do when they reached land.

Bradley wanted to return quickly and see to his wife. She might be able to solicit his help and include him in her plan. No, she quickly dismissed that idea. She couldn't mention any plan to him. He'd made it clear he didn't approve of her or her friendly relationship with Austin. And he'd done it more than once, even though, like her, he wanted the boy, or more importantly the ship, returned to Baltimore.

All right, now that she'd decided she could do it and she'd have to do it alone, what would be the first thing she'd need? Money. Yes, she'd need that to buy passage back to Baltimore. What else would she need? A weapon in case anyone discovered her and tried to stop them. She trembled again, not knowing if it were her thoughts or the nip in the air making her cold. She pulled the blanket over her arms.

She would need money and a pistol, but where would she get them? From Austin, came the answer. More likely than not, he'd have a gun somewhere in his cabin—money, too. A sense of dread filled her. She would have to search his room. When the time came, near the end of the voyage, she'd have to know where to get both. Cheval forced down the emotions that prompted her to feel it was wrong to invade someone's privacy. Austin had already broken all the rules.

If Bo's father were a man of worth, he'd probably bring a nanny with him to care for the child. It occurred to her that she might not be allowed to disembark with Bo. If that happened, she would have to insist on going with them for a few days until the child got used to his new family.

Yes, surely his father would agree, not wanting Bo to be traumatized again so quickly. Once she talked them into letting her go with them, she'd have to be watchful and decide the best time to take the child and run. She'd keep the pistol with her and hope she wouldn't have to threaten anyone with it. She'd never shot a gun, and she hoped no one would give her reason to fire it.

Her plan needed some work, yes, but at least she had an idea and the determination to see it through. One thing she promised herself as she eased back down beside the little one sleeping peacefully beside her: When they dropped anchor, she would find a way to kidnap Bo and deliver him back to his mother. She wouldn't go back to Baltimore without him.

Austin rubbed his neck with one hand and held his stomach with the other. He winced. Damn! Since he was a youngster, no matter what he did, the first few days of sailing always made him ill. He never had a sick day in his life until he boarded a ship. From the first time he sailed when he was only ten years old, he had seasickness the first two or three days of the journey. He didn't know why.

He'd fought it for years, trying everything from

eating too much to not eating at all. He'd even had a doctor give him a mixture of herbs to put in his tea that was supposed to help. All that concoction had done was put him to sleep. He had still had the dreadful seasickness when he awakened.

Now that he had time to think about it, it bothered him that neither Bradley nor Cheval had shown any signs of the sickness. Maybe it was because they were too outraged, he thought irritably, hoping they were both hanging their heads over a bucket, heaving at this very moment.

The roiling continued as he walked over to his desk and sat down, propping his feet on top of it. He poured himself a cup of tea. It was barely warm, but he drank the black liquid anyway, hoping it would settle his churning insides.

He was upset and worried about Winifred. How could Bradley have been so stupid as to drink too much and fall asleep? Thank God Winifred knew where Bradley was going. He only hoped she wouldn't worry so about her husband that she couldn't figure out what had happened to him *Cheval*. The anger, the outrage he'd seen in her expression he could take, but the disappointment he'd seen in the depths of her eyes and heard in her troubled voice bothered him. But what was there to do about it now? The beautiful, bewitching young woman had haunted his dreams as no other woman had. He hated seeing the helplessness she felt in her eyes. She was desperate to take that little boy back to his mother. He hated seeing the loathing on her face for what he was doing.

But he had no choice, and he wouldn't defend himself to her or Bradley again. They would have to trust that if there had been any other course, he would have chosen it.

He liked that Cheval stood up for what was right. Many an employee would have been too frightened of losing his job to question him about any matter. Cheval was ready to do battle with him over the wrong she felt he was committing. There was no reason to worry about the safety of the child while in Cheval's care. What he had to worry about was the way he felt when he looked at her.

Austin sipped his lukewarm tea again and forced his thoughts away from Cheval. It was going to be a long voyage and there was no use torturing himself.

Bradley? What was he to do with him? How foolish of him to sit down and drink himself to sleep. It would be his own fault if he missed the arrival of his first son, but even worse for Winifred to go through the delivery alone.

Austin let his feet fall to the floor. Damn, he had to lie down. His stomach was churning. And damn Bradley's soul for the worry and anguish he would cause Winifred when she discovered him gone.

Betsy Patterson's father's ship the *Erin* had made it to Lisbon in a record twenty-one days. If the weather held, maybe they could match that record. Then, with good weather, a fast ship, and a load of luck, he could have Bradley home inside the two months. If not in time for the baby, then shortly afterward, surely.

After blowing out the lamp, he lay down on his bunk, placing an arm over his eyes to block out the hint of light that shone through the small porthole.

He didn't like fighting with Cheval or Bradley. He moaned aloud. He was too sick to worry himself with it any longer tonight. They didn't understand why he was doing it, and he couldn't tell them. The less they knew about what was going on, the better off they would be.

The one he could count on not to judge him was Jubal. He trusted the large man with his life. Since that fateful day five years ago when Jerome made his heroic appearance in his life, Austin always took Jubal with him. He'd vowed never to be caught unaware again.

With his stomach settling down, Austin's thoughts drifted back to Cheval. He felt a stirring of his manhood. It wasn't just her beauty that stimulated him, though she had plenty of that. She was intelligent, capable, and soft-hearted.

He smiled. He hadn't heard her giggle once, an annoying habit of most of the young women who caught his eye at Baltimore's endless parties. While he must have enjoyed giggles and batting of eyelashes when he was younger, he found now that he was nearing thirty it irritated him.

Austin rolled over onto his side and buried his face in his pillow. Damn, he wished he'd taken time to visit Miss Sophie's upstairs room before he'd boarded *Aloof.*

It was going to be a long trip to Lisbon with that beautiful woman on board his ship and his needing a woman in his bed.

Five

A soft whimpering awakened Cheval. She wiped her dry eyes as she lay in the small bunk. At first she was dazed, not sure where she was. She blinked several times. A faint sway reminded her she was on Austin's ship. Her arms shot out beside her. Bo wasn't there. Fear raced in her heart. She rose up in the bed. By the dim daylight afforded by the small porthole in the cabin, she looked down at the end of the bed and saw Bo sitting at her feet, staring at her. She took a labored breath and relaxed.

Confusion showed in his round, expressive eyes. His nose was red from where he'd rubbed it, and his bottom lip trembled slightly. His little face said it all. Bo didn't know why he'd been taken from his mother, his home. Her heart went out to him and his mother. But no matter how much she wanted to, she couldn't change anything today. Right now, her job was to take care of Bo and make him feel as safe and happy as possible.

She smiled. "Good morning. How do you feel today?"

He just looked at her and rubbed his nose again,

sniffling. His brown hair was sticking out on one side where he'd slept on it, and his white shirt had wrinkled from his tossing and turning in the bed.

He didn't respond to her question. Looking at him, she wondered how well he could understand her and if he could put a sentence together. Some three-year-olds were still learning the art of speech communication while others spoke with ease. Bo should talk very well since he was almost four years. Last night, in his distraught condition, all he'd been able to do was call for his Mama.

"Is your nose stuffy?" she asked when he continued to rub it with the back of his chubby hand. "Do you think some fresh air would help you to breathe better?"

"I want Mama," he replied, his bottom lip quivering, his wide eyes nervously searching the room.

Taking him to his mother was the one thing she couldn't do for him—not yet. Her heart constricted again, but she pushed that soft feeling aside. What Bo needed was for her to accept their position and make the best of it—until she could do something about it.

She threw back the covers and immediately felt the chill in the air. Her best bet was to keep Bo busy to take his mind off his mother. Thinking about her would only make him miserable and make him cry. Cheval had great sorrow for the woman and what she was going through. For now, the only thing Cheval could do for her was to love Bo and care for him as if he were her own—until she could return him. And she wouldn't rest until she did.

She hoped to talk with Austin again, too. As much as she hated to admit it, she new this damning incident hadn't faded her attraction to him. He'd said he was doing this because of honor. What kind of honor demanded that a child be stolen from his mother and taken across the seas? She needed to understand.

Cheval swung her feet to the side of the bed and stood up, brushing the wrinkles from her skirt. Either the ship was sailing along smoothly or she was getting used to the rocking. She didn't feel as if she were swaying back and forth anymore. The creaking and cracking sounds seemed to have all but disappeared, too.

From the one porthole she saw that it was a sunny day. That one little window didn't afford enough light to chase away the dreariness of the small, dark cabin. The first thing she would do after breakfast was ask Austin if there were a larger room they could have—one with at least two portholes. If not, she'd probably have to keep a lamp burning all day. A bright room was a cheerful room, and she wanted Bo to be as happy as possible.

She patted her stomach and looked down at Bo. "Mmm, I'm hungry. How about you? Ready for something to eat?"

He watched her with curious eyes but made no response to her question.

Dropping to her knees, she searched the small

bed for pins that had fallen out of her hair during the night. She didn't usually sleep with her hair up or her clothes on, but last night had not been ordinary.

"Mama."

Cheval glanced up at Bo. It looked as if he might start crying at any moment. There was a quiver in his rounded cheeks. She had to get his mind off his mother before he would get better. She quickly picked up the pins and walked, on her knees, down to the foot of the bed.

Looking at him lovingly she said, "I can't take you to your mama right now. But I will take very good care of you until I can. Don't be frightened of me or anyone. I won't let anyone hurt you. All right?" She reached her hand out to Bo.

"Mama's gone bye-bye."

She took a deep breath. In a way he understood what was going on. He wasn't with his mother. The most important thing was that he feel safe.

"Yes. Now, take my hand. We'll go over to the basin and wash our faces. Then we'll go to the galley and find something to eat. Would you like that? Wouldn't you like something to drink?"

He continued to look at her with those big, watery eyes and slowly lifted his arms toward her. She smiled and closed his hand in hers. He didn't try to pull away from her. Bo jumped off the bed as she rose from the floor. She brushed his straight brown hair away from his face. In height, he came up to the top of her hip. He wasn't very tall for being almost four years old.

As she looked at Bo, Cheval found herself wondering who his father might be and why he felt the need to kidnap his son. She also couldn't help but wonder why his mother and father lived thousands of miles apart in different countries. Why didn't the father simply visit his son? Why did he have to steal him from his mother? She couldn't help but feel there was something very important about this little boy.

"When I talk to you, do you understand everything I'm saying to you?" she asked, trying a different approach to make him feel comfortable with her and to get him to talk.

He remained quiet, looking at her, running his tongue over his lips as if his mouth might be dry.

"Well, no matter." She smiled again as they padded over to a corner where a small chest with a pitcher and wash basin stood. "We'll get along just fine anyway. How old are you?" she asked, knowing most young boys were proud of their age and how tall they were.

Bo held up three fingers.

She placed a mock look of surprise on her face and praised, "My goodness. You're a big boy to only be three years old. I think you're old enough to help me pour water from the pitcher, don't you?"

He nodded.

Cheval pretended the pitcher was heavy, and Bo reached up with his little hands and helped her hold it. After they set it down, she wet the end of the towel and squeezed out the chilled water. She wiped the cloth over his eyes, down his rounded cheeks, and across his pink lips. He remained passive, letting her wash him. With the pads of her fingers, she touched his cheek. Soft, smooth skin caressed her. Her heart went out to the sweet child. How could she not love the little boy who, today, was acting like a grown-up little man?

She rinsed the towel in the cold water again and cleaned her own face and neck, wishing she could sink down into a tub of warm water and wash away all her nagging fears.

Last night the only thing she'd thought about was the trauma Bo and his mother would endure by their separation, but this morning she could see this was going to affect her, too. When Mr. and Mrs. Duncan had ruined her reputation with their lies, she had hoped in time to overcome their viciousness. She almost laughed, remembering how she looked upon this job as the one to redeem her reputation and help her secure a post with a good family somewhere in Maryland.

How would this affect her job prospects? Surely Bo's mother would thank her, of that there was no doubt, but would she want to recommend a woman who'd been hired by kidnappers? Would anyone believe Cheval had no prior knowledge of the kidnapping? And if she succeeded in returning Bo, could she turn Austin over to the authorities?

Cheval closed her eyes for a second and chased that thought away. There were too many other things to consider right now. The only important thing to consider was returning Bo to his mother because *it* was the right thing to do. Anything and everything else, including her livelihood, could be decided later.

But as she thought that, she remembered how the night before they boarded the ship Austin had tried to talk her out of accepting the assignment. She was the one who had insisted he keep his word and allow her to take the job. But had she known its true nature, would she have accepted it?

Cheval looked down into Bo's trusting expression. Some of the fear had left his eyes. If she hadn't seen him, maybe she could have declined involvement; but now she was glad she had been given the opportunity to care for him, because she intended to make a difference. She vowed to take him back to his mother; another governess might not have wanted to accept that responsibility.

A knock sounded on the door and a moment later it opened. Austin walked inside. "Good morning," he said.

Cheval slowly laid the towel in the basin and looked at him. Her heartbeat increased. Her breath grew short. His presence almost filled the small room. He was alarmingly handsome, his white shirt gleaming against his dark breeches and black surcoat. How could she be attracted to a man who would steal a child? It was a violation of herself, of all she held to be just and right. Denial rose up within her but quickly faded as she looked at him.

How could she condone his strength of conviction when it was so wrong? Why did she like the way his gaze swept across her face with appreciation? Why did she tense with anticipation whenever she saw him? Why did she want him to smile at her, to tease with her, find favor with her, and embrace her?

What was wrong with her? Thank God she'd found out what kind of man Austin was before her feelings for him went any further. It was best she know now that he was a hard, unscrupulous man who felt no remorse about stealing a child from his mother.

Bo wrapped his arms around her legs and hid his face in the wrinkled folds of her skirt. She slipped her hand down to his shoulder and held him to her, offering security. She didn't want him to be afraid.

"Good morning," she finally answered.

Austin's gaze fell to Bo. "How is he?"

Her anger at what he'd done had gone, she realized, and in its place only a need to make right his wrong. "He's not crying right now, but of course he misses his—" She didn't finish her sentence, catching herself before saying the word 'mother.' "Family," she finished.

"I'm glad you've quieted him. He could be heard all over the ship last night."

Taking offense she lifted her chin and said, "I'm sorry if he disturbed you."

Austin's eyes narrowed. "He didn't disturb anyone. I only meant I was concerned about how upset he was. Has there been any sign of seasickness from either you or the boy?"

Cheval grabbed hold of her long hair and wound it on top of her head. "None," she answered, inserting the pins into the bun of hair. "We've both taken to the seas quite well so far. I hope that won't change after we've eaten."

He nodded.

Knowing further argument was futile, she let her hands drop to her side and stepped forward. She had to ask him one last time. "Is there any chance that this morning you've changed your mind and we're heading back to Baltimore?"

His composure remained firm. "No."

Her hand squeezed Bo's shoulder tighter and she pressed him toward her leg. "Then, I feel I must ask you one more time to please return him to his family."

"I can't do that."

Cheval swallowed and knew he meant what he said. She wouldn't ask again. He had made his decision just as she had made hers last night. If Austin could kidnap Bo, so could she. Now all she had to figure out was how. In the meantime, she would stay quiet, bide her time, and make her plans.

"All right. Might I ask if there is by chance a larger cabin we might occupy. This one is very small for all the time we will have to spend in it."

"There are no large staterooms on this ship. *Aloof* was built for speed not home comforts. However, there is another cabin that's empty. It's right beside mine. It's the same size as this one, though."

"Do you mind if I take a look at it? If it's not in use, maybe we can make a play room and school room out of it. It will at least give us a change and reason to move about the ship."

"Take it for whatever you need."

She nodded. "Thank you. I hope you have plenty of candles and oil for the lamps. It's so dark in this part of the ship, I'm afraid he'll become more unhappy and sickly if we don't keep the light in here."

"We've enough. Just keep him healthy."

While he was being so agreeable she continued. "I'll need to take him on deck each morning and afternoon for exercise. He'll need plenty of sunshine to counter the dampness and chill. Should that be a problem?"

"Not at all."

His manner changed. She thought she saw a smile lift the corners of his lips. Why he was playing with her, teasing her, smiling at her! She'd done or said something that humored him. But what? She thought she was being rather demanding. But she had to admit that she liked him in this mood. This attitude was one of the things that made him so attractive to her—and that wasn't good for her.

She cleared her wayward thoughts. She couldn't let Austin distract her from her mission. "He's a smart boy. After he gets used to me, I will start teaching him his letters, colors, and numbers.

Things like that. He's still a little young, and we're limited with what we can do on this ship as far as playtime. The busier I keep him, the less he will cry for his mo—family."

"There you are, Austin," Bradley said, sauntering into the cabin, smirking. "Why doesn't it surprise me that I find you in here." He looked down at Bo and sniffed. "So this is the little devil who caused you to take leave of your good senses. Fetching."

Cheval cringed. She refused to suffer this man again. No reason she should have to. "Excuse me," she said, taking Bo's hand. "We were just on our way to the galley for a bite to eat." She smiled sweetly, turning her face first to Austin, then to Bradley. "You two stay and chat as long as you want. It will be awhile before we return." She whisked past them with Bo at her side.

Bradley opened his mouth to speak, but Austin held up his hand. "Don't say anything. I got very little sleep last night, and I'm in no mood to hear your harping. You got yourself into this, Bradley; now you're going to have to take it like a man."

Austin's stomach wasn't feeling much better. The black tea was helping, but hadn't cleared up his problem. What made it worse was knowing that Cheval, Bradley, and Bo seemed to be in fine form and having no stomach problems whatsoever. *He was the cursed one!*

"But what about my law practice? I have clients who need me. And what will Winifred do? Austin, surely you can't put your sister through this? She knows I was going to your ship, but what will she think when I don't return? She and your mother will assume I've been attacked and left for dead."

"I'm sure your brother will step in and handle your clients. And obviously, I have more faith in my sister and mother than you do. When your body doesn't show up and they check and see *Aloof* is gone, I'm sure they'll assume you did exactly what you did."

He sniffed loudly. "I was tired and fell asleep."

"After you drank a half-bottle of brandy."

"That was not my fault. You—"

"Yes, I know. It was my fault because I didn't arrive when you thought I should." Austin rubbed his forehead. "No more whining, Bradley. Damnation, I have enough to contend with right now without you."

Bradley's face flamed. "Ah—Ugh—I wouldn't have had to follow you if you'd been truthful with me in the first place. I knew something was up and I was right. Austin, I don't think you understand how serious kidnapping is."

"You're wrong. I do understand. I know I'll be thrown in jail if the authorities find out my involvement."

"And yet you're willing to risk it. Why? And for whom?"

"The less you know, the better off you'll be."

Exasperated, Bradley said, "I want to help."

Austin was too sick for this. Maybe the fresh air on deck would make him feel better. "I'll put you on a ship back to Baltimore as soon as we reach our destination. That's the best I can do for you."

"Can you at least tell me our destination?"

"No. Now excuse me. I have other things to attend to."

Jubal sat at the rectangular, wooden table in the dining hall, which was located on the opposite end of the ship from the sleeping quarters. He stood up when Cheval and Bo entered and picked up his empty plate. A large, ruddy-cheeked man with a bushy, graying beard who sat beside Jubal rose, too.

"Morning, Miss Worthington," Jubal said.

"Good day to you, Miss," the other man chimed in behind Jubal, splaying his fingers on his rotund middle.

"Good morning," she greeted both men with a smile. "Have either of you met Bo?" She patted Bo's shoulder reassuringly while keeping her gaze on the two men. "I'm sure your captain has told you we have a special guest on board with us."

The robust man looked from Cheval to Jubal and cleared his throat. "I—I'm the captain, Miss. You must be talking about Mr. Radcliffe."

"Oh, I assumed Mr. Radcliffe was the captain." Her questioning gaze darted to Jubal. "Austin was certainly acting as if he were in charge last night."

"Oh, no, Miss. Well—I mean he is, in that he owns *Aloof,* sure enough, but he's not a captain. He knows a lot about the ships his men build, but he doesn't care anything about being captain of one. Doesn't have the stomach for it."

"I see. Well, I'm pleased to meet you, Captain—"

"Hammersfield, Miss."

She smiled again. "It's nice to know that someone can put Mr. Radcliffe in his place. Tell me, captain, where and what time should we come for our meals each day?"

"I can have Jackson prepare a tray for you and the boy and take it to your cabin, if you'd like."

"No. That won't work." She tapped her finger on her chin. "The cabin is too small as it is, and we'll have to spend enough time there anyway. I need to get Bo out of that room as much as possible. He will get sick if I try to keep him shut in that small room all day and all night, too."

Both men nodded but said nothing. Cheval continued, "A growing boy needs to have properly prepared foods served at the same time each day. Will there be a problem with that?"

"No, Miss."

"And he must get as much exercise as possible. Going up and down those stairs and playing on deck will be good for him."

Captain Hammersfield nodded, brushing his beard with an open palm.

"Mr. Radcliffe is going to let us take the room next to his office as a teaching and play room. What I'd like is a checkerboard and some game pieces. Captain, do you think your cook might be able to come up with some corn cob or pieces of wood that I could use."

"I think we can take care of that for you."

"I can make a board for you." Jubal spoke up for the first time.

"Oh, I would appreciate that, Jubal. Thank you," she said and made a mental note to remember to keep an eye on Jubal. Cheval turned back to the captain. "Staying active is important to Bo's well-being. I'm pleased we'll have freedom to roam about the ship. He's a well-behaved—"

"Limited freedom, I'm afraid," Austin countered from the doorway, interrupting her sentence.

Cheval turned to see him lounging in the doorway. His coloring didn't look much better than it had last night. It was her guess that the sea was not treating him well. "What do you mean? Captain Hammersfield has—"

"Captain Hammersfield handles the men and the sailing of the ship. When I'm on board I make decisions concerning any passengers."

"Especially if they are unwilling passengers, I presume." Her hand tightened around Bo's, but he didn't make a sound. She looked down at him. He had his fingers in his mouth, twisting them around. He was looking at Austin.

"Yes."

"I take it you overheard of my conversation with Captain Hammersfield. What rules do you have for us?"

"You are free to roam about the ship; however, you'll not be allowed to talk to any of the crew other than the captain, Jubal, or me. Oh, and of course, Bradley. Should you choose to talk to him.

The other men are here to work and will not have time for conversation with you. Feel free to take your meals wherever you feel inclined."

"Thank you," she mumbled with no real appreciation in her voice. "Do you mind if I speak to the cook this once to learn what foods are available on the ship and discuss how I'd like Bo's food prepared?"

A hint of a smile lifted one corner of his mouth. "Be my guest."

She started to make an angry retort about being a hostage not *guest* but changed her mind before she spoke. Instead, she simply whisked by him for the second time that morning.

Austin was irritated at Cheval's attitude toward him. He started to follow her and tell her the truth. That he was doing this because Jerome Bonaparte had saved his mother's life, but Austin couldn't do that. The less she knew, the better off she'd be when they returned to Baltimore. Hammersfield was the only one who knew they were sailing to France, but not even the captain knew why.

A smile tugged at the edges of Austin's mouth even though he felt like hell. He liked the way Cheval handled Hammersfield. She took her job of caring for Bo seriously and that was what he'd hired her for. He couldn't help but be pleased when he overheard her tell the captain just what the boy needed and how she expected them to be treated. He liked that about her. He liked the way she assumed her responsibilities and took charge.

"How are we doing?" Austin asked Hammersfield from the doorway.

"Making good time, sir. I don't think we'll beat the *Erin's* record, but we'll be close."

"Good. This is one journey I want over as quickly as possible. Tell the men to stay away from Cheval and Bo. Jubal, keep a keen eye on Bradley. He's desperate to return to Baltimore. Hammersfield, make sure none of the men leave their weapons around for him to get his hands on. He might try something foolhardy."

"I'll have a talk with them all."

"Jubal, it's also your job to look after Cheval and Bo. Make sure they come to no harm, and if they need anything, let me know. And don't forget to make her that board you promised."

"Yes, sir."

Austin turned back to the captain. "Give Robert a little freedom from his chores to help Cheval with the boy."

"I'll take care of it. You're looking a bit better today. How are you feeling?" the captain asked.

"Like hell, as usual. Dammit, after all these years why does it take me so long to get my sea legs?"

"You know how it is. Some people never do," Hammersfield said, his beard moving back and forth as he talked. "You're just one of those people who takes awhile for your body to adjust to the rocking motion of the ship. Has nothing to do with a man's constitution otherwise."

"I'm going on deck to clear my head. Let me know if you need anything."

Six

"I was very proud of the way you crawled into bed last night and went to sleep by yourself," Cheval said to Bo on the third morning of their journey. She knelt in front of him, helping him dress for the day. "Most boys your age aren't as big-acting as you are," she praised him.

"Mama says a prince isn't supposed to cry."

Cheval stiffened. Her hands went still. *A prince?* Was Bo's father a king? Surely not. His mother probably thought of Bo as a prince. But just as quickly she remembered they were on their way to Europe where there were many kings. She thought back to that first night when Austin had spoken to her about this journey. Had he mentioned a country? No. She was certain he'd only mentioned Europe. What was their destination?

She'd hope to question Austin about Bo's parents, but he'd managed to avoid being alone with her the past two days. She hadn't wanted to question Bo about his mother or father for fear of upsetting him and making him cry.

Since he had mentioned his mother, maybe he was ready to talk about her. Now that he had gotten used to Cheval he was more talkative. She had to try.

Bo held up his arms and Cheval slipped his white shirt over his head. "Did your mother tell you you were a prince?" she asked softly, watching Bo's face as she buttoned his shirt.

He nodded, placing his hands on her shoulders to steady himself as he stepped into his breeches. "Mama says Papa is a king. He's an im—portant man like I'm going to be someday."

Cheval wasn't sure she wanted to believe him, but the glistening pride she saw in Bo's eyes convinced her he thought his father was a king.

"Have you ever seen your papa?" she questioned.

He shook his head as she buttoned his breeches. "He doesn't live with us. He lives far away. Across the water."

She trembled with expectancy. "Do you know his name?"

"His name is the same as mine," he said and sat down on the bed so she could help him with his shoes.

Maybe his mother used the word prince as a pet name, she thought. She didn't know any kings by the name of Bo, but then she remembered Austin saying that Bo was a pet name, too.

"Do you know your complete name?"

Bo laughed for the first time, a lighthearted giggle that made her feel good. It pleased her greatly to see him adjusting to this new life that had been forced upon him. "Of course I know my name. Mama says I'm a smart boy."

She smiled and buckled the first shoe onto his foot. "You are a smart young man." When he remained quiet for a moment she was forced to ask, "What is your full name?"

"Jerome Napoleon Bonaparte," he stated loudly.

Cheval gasped so loud she coughed to try to cover her surprise. It couldn't be. He had to be wrong! His face beamed proudly with his announcement. He told the truth. Her breath quickened as she asked, "Is your mother's name Elizabeth?"

Bo shook his head and Cheval was about to relax her shoulders when Bo continued by saying, "Her name is Betsy."

With trembling fingers, Cheval buckled his other shoe. Yes, of course. Betsy was a pet name for Elizabeth, just as Bo was obviously a nickname for Bonaparte. Cheval moaned inwardly. She didn't want to believe this.

Austin? Why was he involved in this? How could he have taken this little boy away from that poor woman after all she'd been through? Everyone in Baltimore knew her sad story.

Cheval looked into Bo's bright eyes and remembered. The dashing young Jerome Bonaparte, Napoleon's youngest brother, had come to America for a visit. He and the beautiful Betsy Patterson met, fell in love, and married a few months later. Napoleon called Jerome home to France, and he took his pregnant bride with him. Napoleon refused to let the ship carrying Betsy and Jerome dock in France. The young couple was forced to sail on to Lisbon where a few days later, Jerome left Betsy and traveled on to Milan to meet with Napoleon, wanting to persuade his brother to accept his marriage.

Jerome never returned to claim his wife. Betsy was forced to sail to England, where her son was born, and later she returned to Baltimore. A year later Napoleon bribed a priest into annulling Betsy's marriage to Jerome so Jerome could remarry for Napoleon's political gain. For bowing to his wishes, Napoleon honored Jerome by making him a king of his own country and handpicking his new wife.

Cheval groaned as she looked into Bo's innocent little face. No wonder Jerome wanted his firstborn son. Bo was in line for the throne of Westphalia. But how could Austin have done this to Betsy? After what that wretched Jerome had put her through, how could Austin justify stealing her child? Had this something to do with Austin selling his ships to Napoleon? Was he in some way indebted to Jerome? What could it be? She refused to let herself believe Austin, who'd been so kind to her, had done this horrible deed for profit, but what else could it be?

She rose and took Bo's hand, leading him over to the wash basin. This was more complicated than she'd realized, but she wouldn't let that stop her. It made her more determined to see her plan through. She would kidnap Bo from Austin and take him back to his mother where he belonged. And she would never forgive Austin if Betsy Patterson did something as drastic as killing herself as her sister had. Like Loraine, Betsy had lost her husband and her son.

Until she could do something about this terrible wrong, she had to pray that Betsy was stronger than her sister had been.

After a meal of bread, butter, cooked figs, and tea, Cheval asked Robert, a fifteen-year-old cabin boy who'd been a great help to her to watch Bo while he played on deck. She'd been anxious all through the meal, wanting to talk with Austin about her newfound information. She'd already decided she couldn't make him change his mind, but she could let him know what a despicable man she knew him to be.

Finding Austin in his cabin, she knocked on the open door. He looked up from his desk. As their eyes met, she knew he immediately saw that she was upset.

"Come in," he said and rose from his chair.

No longer able to hold it all inside her, Cheval said, "I can't believe you'd stoop so low as to take that poor woman's son. After all Jerome put her through, how could you do it? Did Napoleon promise you a kingdom, too, if you betrayed her?"

She shook, and that made her angry. She'd wanted to calmly tell him what a loathsome man she thought him to be, but she was too emotional to remain unaffected.

Remaining calm, Austin said, "I take it Bo's decided to talk. I was hoping he wouldn't be old enough to tell you very much."

"All I needed to know was his real name. The

rest of the story has been in the papers for years. We're taking Bo to his father in Westphalia, aren't we?''

Austin walked over to the door, shut it, then leaned against it, his hand behind him. His eyes darkened as he looked at her. She didn't like the way his eyes searched her face. He looked at her as if he were measuring her. She didn't want to be aware of every little detail about him, like the soft rise and fall of his chest.

"Actually, we're sailing to France. Someone will meet us there and take the boy on to his father. Have you mentioned this to anyone?''

"What? Who Bo really is? Of course not. I came straight to you."

"Good. Cheval, I know I don't have to tell you that the less anyone on board knows about this, the better off they will be. I suggest you tell Bo not to say anything about his real name to anyone else."

Cheval's skin prickled. "Why doesn't that surprise me? I assume the reason you don't want anyone to know is so they won't be able to tell on you when you return to Baltimore. You plan to pick up with your life as if you've done nothing wrong."

"Naturally I'd like for it to be that way. My crew knows nothing about this journey. It wouldn't matter if they did. They're loyal. Bradley knows how judicious it would be for him to remain quiet about this. So—''

Cheval stiffened. It irritated her that he remained

so collected. "So that only leaves me for you to worry about."

He shook his head and moved away from the door and closer to her. "I'm not worried about you either, Cheval. If the authorities find out Bo was on this ship, they will blame anyone on board, including you."

A knot of fear grew inside her, but she fought its overwhelming force. She walked closer to him, her legs weak with frustration and looked directly into his eyes. "I promise not to tell anyone of your involvement in this, if you'll turn the ship around right now and take us back."

"I'm committed to this journey."

"Have you thought about what this will do to Bo's mother?" How could she make him understand what that woman must be going through? Maybe if she told him about her sister he'd find compassion in his heart and do the right thing.

Forcing the tears to remain in her eyes she said, "I'm worried about Betsy's sanity. I—my sister's story is so like hers. Loraine's husband was lost at sea, and year a later her son took a fever and died. She wouldn't eat. She wouldn't sleep. She wouldn't talk. I—I tried to comfort her, but she wouldn't be consoled. She took her life a few weeks after her son's death."

"I'm sorry, Cheval. I know that couldn't have been easy for you."

His eyes soften with such compassion for her that for a moment she wanted to forgive him everything and rush into his arms and let him comfort her.

Don't weaken.

He wants your understanding.

She shouldn't have told him. She didn't want his sympathy; she wanted his cooperation.

In an act of desperation, she took hold of his shirt front and pulled him closer to her. Her heart pounded. "Austin, please, no amount of money, no promise from that devil Napoleon is worth what you're putting that woman through."

Austin grabbed her wrists and gently shoved her up against the desk, pressing his body against hers to hold her there. His eyes bored down on her. "Cheval, you know nothing about this. You know nothing about me."

"Then tell me so I'll know. I want to understand. I don't want to believe you're capable of this madness, but what am I to think when Bo is proof of your crime?"

"Cheval. Leave it alone. This cannot be changed."

"You feel no remorse for what you're doing," she countered.

His hands tightened around her wrists, and he lowered his face to hers. She felt him tremble. "How would you know what I'm feeling? I'm not doing this for any kind of profit, and I'm not any happier about it than you are."

She felt his breath, his warmth, his sincerity. Looking into his eyes and seeing the integrity and the weariness written in his face, she softened. "Then you must be doing this because you believe

Bo should be with his father, the king, rather than his mother."

"I believe this should have been settled between the mother and the father before it came down to this action. My reasons for doing this are my own; and as much as I'd like you to understand, I can't share them with you."

His voice was like a soothing balm, quieting her. He was asking for her trust. She wanted to give it. She wanted to think only about the way he held her now and looked at her, the way he made her feel inside, but no. How could she when she didn't trust him?

She stirred and Austin released her without hesitating. She walked to the door and opened it, but suddenly looked back at Austin. "You don't have to worry about me, either. I'll never tell anyone you were involved in this."

Cheval walked out into the companionway and pulled the door behind her. She was shaking. Austin left her no choice. She had to find a way to take Bo away from him.

Austin muttered a curse as soon as the door shut behind her. Had she believed him when he told her he didn't like this any more than she did? He ran his hands through his hair and returned to his desk. He wondered if she knew how close he'd come to kissing her. Did she know how desirable she was to him? He didn't think so. She was too busy hating him to see the signs.

Had she ever noticed how his eyes followed her whenever they were in the same room. Did she feel the tremble in his body when he'd leaned against her just now? She was working her way into his heart, and he didn't know what he was going to do about it. He couldn't seem to stop it. He liked the way she moved, the way she walked, the way she held her head. He couldn't stop watching her.

When he'd thought her a tavern wench, he'd understood his attraction to her. Every man in the tavern that night had wanted her. That was why she had gotten so much attention. But now that he knew she wasn't just a whore to take a tumble with, his feelings should have changed.

Austin sighed. They hadn't. He still wanted her.

Seven

It was subtle, but Cheval had noticed the change in the wind as she sat on deck mending the hem of one of her dresses and watching Jubal teach Bo how to tie knots in roping. She appreciated his help and understanding; and although Bo had been frightened of Jubal at first, he soon learned to think of Jubal as his best friend.

When they'd first come on deck half an hour ago, there had been no clouds in the sky. A bright sun had hung midway down the western sky, and the day had been relatively calm. Now, the air had turned decidedly warmer, but it was much stronger, whipping at loose strands of her hair and blowing her sewing thread in all directions. The sun lay hidden behind light-gray clouds and the horizon looked dark and puffy.

Bo no longer cried for his mother as he had the first few days of his journey. He'd turned into a rambunctious, inquisitive little boy who wanted to know about everything from how the sails worked to why the moon and stars hung in the sky.

The worst time for him seemed to be at night, when it was time for him to go to sleep. Even that

was getting better. She didn't mind his fitful behavior. Every little boy wanted his mother at nighttime to tuck him into bed. Now it worried her that
he might be already forgetting about his mother.
A couple of times he'd called her Mama instead
of Miss Cheval, but she'd quickly reminded him
that she wasn't his mother and he would be seeing
his mother soon.

Because she kept the little boy busy, the days
seemed to fly by for them. She found she was usually so tired in the evenings from running after
Bo that she slept like a baby herself each night.
She'd come to welcome the slow roll of the ship
to help lull her to sleep in the evenings.

From the corner of her eye, Cheval saw Austin
come out of the main deck cabin and approach
the captain, who stood at the helm, not far away.
She tensed. She had to watch him carefully, as she
had the past few days. This could be the opportunity she'd been waiting for to slip into his cabin
and search it.

On the pretext of looking through the sewing
materials in her lap, she watched the two men talk,
point, look at the sky, and talk again. She wondered if a storm were brewing. A slight chill of
fear touched her, but she quickly dismissed it.
Surely not. Austin and the captain didn't appear
alarmed. The wind carried their voices toward
her, but she couldn't make out what they were
saying.

She noticed that Austin's mode of dress was
more relaxed than it had been in Baltimore. On

board he didn't bother with a cravat and stickpin, preferring to leave his shirt open at the neck. On warm days, like this one, he left his waistcoat off, too. She liked seeing him dressed so casually. Without his jacket and waistcoat she could see how his broad shoulders complemented his narrow hips and powerful-looking legs. His hair was always held in a queue with a black ribbon at the back of his neck.

The ship was so small it was impossible not to see Austin several times a day as she and Bo explored the ship and played on deck in the fresh air. Her plan to escape with Bo was never far from her thoughts. She was constantly watching for an opportunity to search Austin's cabin for the money she'd need for passage back to Baltimore. She found it wasn't easy to get Austin, Jubal, the captain, and Bradley all together at one time. When she looked for Austin's money bag and a weapon, she'd like to have every one of them accounted for in one place.

Throughout the first week on board, she'd watched Austin with Jubal, Bradley, and the captain and his men. He was always calm, easygoing, just as he was with Bo and with her. There was nothing about him to suggest he was the kind of man who could participate in the kidnapping of a child.

Robert, the young cabin boy, barely in his teens, had been assigned to help take care of Bradley, but the young man couldn't seem to do anything right for the finicky lawyer. She couldn't help but smile at times when Bradley complained to Austin.

Cheval noticed that Austin seemed to have unlimited patience with the young man when teaching him to tie knots or work the sails, but every time she saw Bradley he was always in an agitated state because of something Robert hadn't done or hadn't done right.

Her admiration for Austin had grown, even though she tried to make no further judgments about him. His involvement in the kidnapping should have clinched her unfavorable feelings for him. But no matter how hard she tried to ignore the owner of the ship if he were around, she found herself watching him, admiring him, just as she was doing right now.

Cheval laid her mending in her lap and looked at Jubal and Bo. Their heads were bent together, both intent on the task at hand. The large negro had been a great help to her in caring for Bo, hardly leaving their sides.

One of the men who was working the sails walked over and joined Austin and the captain. They pointed toward the southern sky again. A prickle of excitement touched her. There would never be a perfect time to search Austin's cabin. She took a deep breath to steady her nerves. Now was as good a time as any.

Bo and Jubal were busy and so was Austin. Bradley was the only one not accounted for, and he was probably in his room either sleeping as he was prone to do, or on the other side of the ship in the dining hall sipping tea with some of the crew.

She rubbed her hands together, fighting for the courage she needed to get up off her seat and go invade Austin's privacy. She moistened her lips and looked out at the beautiful, dark-blue water. She didn't want to do this, but what else could she do? If she escaped with Bo and had no money, they'd be no better off. She had to know she could get her hands on some money when they neared their destination.

"Jubal, I need a few minutes to myself," she said, using the phrase she used when she needed to take care of her bodily functions. "Would you mind watching Bo for me?"

"No, Miss. We'll be right here working on this when you get back."

She smiled and lay her stitching aside, trying to act perfectly normal when inside she'd already started to tremble. She didn't look at Austin or the other men as she went through the doorway which led to the steps that took her to the cabins below.

Her stomach jumped. She denied her feelings of fear and forced her legs to move quickly. At the bottom of the steps, she waited for a minute to see if Austin or anyone followed her. She listened and heard nothing. Quickly, she turned and hurried down the companionway, past her own room. If she were gone a long time, Austin or Jubal might get suspicious and come looking for her.

Austin's office was dark. Like all the staterooms she'd been in, it had only one porthole. She went straight to Austin's desk, hoping to find both the items she need there so she could get out quick. The desk was the typical early-Georgian style with a shallow drawer in the middle and three matching drawers running down each side.

Opening the center drawer first, Cheval saw it contained only pen, ink, and paper. The second drawer she pulled on was locked. She hesitated only a moment to glance at the door before passing it and going on to the next. That drawer contained various records about the ship and its crew members.

She listened for sounds other than the creaking of the ship as she continued to search for a money pouch or pistol. The last drawer on that side held several bottles of liquor and glasses. Hardly daring to breathe, Cheval glanced at the doorway again and moved to the other side of the desk to search the three drawers. They contained nothing but papers, maps, and charts of varying sizes. She'd come up empty-handed for the two things she had to have to aid her escape with Bo.

She looked at the locked drawer again. Should she simply assume Austin kept the money and his pistol under lock, which, she agreed, would be the logical and safe thing to do, or should she take a chance on trying to open the lock with a kitchen knife? The only problem with that was the possibility of breaking the lock and giving Austin reason to be more cautious. Reluctantly, she decided that, even though she didn't know for sure, the best thing to do for now was to wait.

Cheval started to leave, but something made her stop and scan the room. Now that her immediate search was over, something inside her made her want to linger and look around Austin's cabin. Her heartbeat settled into an easy rhythm, and she started to breathe easier.

The ship-owner's cabin was larger than the others she'd seen on the ship. His bunk sat fastened to the far wall as in all the cabins she'd seen. Two leather wing chairs sat to the side with a small game table between them. In the corner behind the chairs stood a tall chest which she assumed held Austin's clothes. A shaving plate and mirror and pitcher and basin sat on top of it. She walked over to the chest and opened it. Austin's coats hung neatly in a row, and his breeches and stockings were folded at the bottom. She closed the door, then picked up his shaving plate. She breathed in deeply and inhaled the clean smell of soap. Austin's scent.

Bookshelves lined the wall behind the desk. Slowly she let her fingertips glide along the spines of the books on the middle shelf as her gaze scanned the room again. It surprised her that she didn't feel odd about searching through Austin's things. There was the fear of getting caught, but for some strange reason she felt comfortable in his room.

Her eyes caught sight of a horn-shaped instrument on Austin's desk. The brass had a beautiful shine to it. She picked it up and looked through the small end and to her delight found it was a spyglass.

"What are you doing?"

Her heart jumped in her chest. Cheval almost dropped the spyglass at the sound of Bradley's irritated voice breaking through her thoughts. Calming herself, she lowered the instrument and said, "You nearly scared the life out of me. Why did you speak to me in such an angry tone?"

"Who do you think you are to question me?" He sauntered into the room, fully dressed in his jacket, waistcoat, and cravat with his pearl stickpin. "I asked you, what are you doing in Austin's cabin, looking through his things?"

She had to think quick. Her eyebrows rose and her lips rounded as she pretended shock. "Looking through his things? I—I merely came in here hoping to find a book to read and saw this beautiful piece of brass and thought to examine it," she lied, but not without a twinge of guilt.

His keen gaze bore down sharply on her. "Did you hope to find a book inside the spyglass? Or should you have been looking on the bookshelf behind you?"

Cheval could have kicked herself for not leaving the minute she finished searching the desk. But no, she had to look, touch, and smell Austin's possessions. How would she ever explain this to Austin? Bradley wouldn't miss the opportunity to tell him. She gritted her teeth to keep her anger in check.

She replaced the brass tube. She couldn't hurry out of the office as she wanted to; that would indicate guilt, but she couldn't let Bradley intimidate her either. He'd never leave her alone if she allowed him to cower her.

Faking a confidence she didn't feel, she turned to the bookshelf and casually picked up a book. Thumbing through it she said, "It's a very nice piece. I was simply looking at it."

"You have only one mission on this ship, and that is to look after that child."

Bradley was so pompous and rigid Cheval wanted to bend him. She put the book away and took another to inspect. She had to remain calm and not let Bradley fluster her.

"I know my place, Mr. Thornhill. There's no reason for you to be so irate. I know you're unhappy Austin wouldn't take you back to Baltimore, but—"

"You presume too much, Miss Worthington."

Cheval put the second book away, deciding to look at one more, then politely excuse herself from this horrible man and Austin's office. She'd have to justify her actions to Austin, but not Bradley.

She took a large book off the shelf and opened it. Stunned, she quickly closed it again. Her heartbeat increased. Turning her back to Bradley so he couldn't see the surprise on her face, she carefully put the book back on the shelf. Her heartbeat increased. *Thank God!* She'd found a pistol. How clever of Austin to have hidden it in a hollow book. Forgetting about Bradley, she read the spine of the book so she'd be able to find it again. *The Study of Ancient Insects.* That should be easy enough to remember.

Masking her face with indifference she turned back to Bradley. "I'm sorry what did you say?"

"I think you were in here looking for something else." Bradley walked so close to her she was forced to lean back against the bookshelf to get away from him.

"What?" It was impossible not to flinch, he was so close. "I don't know what you're talking about. What could I possibly be looking for?" She tried to keep the tremor of guilt out of her voice but wasn't sure she had.

"Anything that might help you get what you want. I know how badly you want to return that child to his mother. Maybe it would help you if you knew whom the child belonged to and why Austin is taking him to his father."

Cheval's stomach quaked and her chest felt tight. "You're accusing me of having the same thoughts as you. I know how badly you want to return to your wife," she countered, hoping to cast doubt on him. "Were you just passing by this cabin or were you bent on doing what you accuse me of?"

"You little bitch." He grabbed hold of her upper arms. "I'll—"

"Bradley! Cheval. What's going on in here?" Austin burst into his cabin, a scowl darkening his face.

Bradley spun away from Cheval, but didn't let Austin's arrival shake him. "I'm glad you're here, Austin," he said, pulling on the tail of his coat. "I was walking by your cabin and saw her," he pointed at Cheval, "standing here by your desk."

Cringing inside, filled with fear, Cheval remained quiet, rubbing her arms where Bradley had grabbed her. She couldn't have spoken if she'd wanted to. She felt that her heart had jumped into her throat.

Austin's eyes narrowed and his gaze raked across Cheval's face before concentrating on Bradley again. "What was she doing?"

"Well." He pulled on the tail of his jacket again. "I don't know what she was doing before I came in, but she was—looking at your spyglass when I saw her."

Cheval kept her eyes on Austin while berating herself. If she'd left as soon as she'd checked the drawers, Bradley wouldn't have found her. Why had she felt the need, the desire, to inspect Austin's things? They didn't matter to her plan. She'd been careless. Now she'd gotten caught, and it would be harder for her to get back in his room to continue her search for some money.

"Is that what you were doing, Cheval?"

"Yes. I was looking at your spyglass," she answered, happy it wasn't a lie. She had a feeling Austin would be able to see right through her if she were not telling the truth. Austin remained composed, but she was keenly aware of his scrutiny.

"She said she came in for a book," Bradley

added. "But she wasn't looking on the bookshelf. She was at your desk. I think she was trying to find out more information about that little boy."

Austin didn't take his gaze off her. "Would you like a book to read?"

She nodded. Again, she told the truth and passed his test.

Passing by an irritated Bradley, Austin walked over to the bookshelf and stood beside Cheval. Her heart beat so fast she thought she might get light-headed. His nearness made her tremble inside, but she managed not to flinch. He reached on the shelf and took down two books and handed them to her. "I think you'll enjoy these."

Holding her gaze steady on his she said, "Thank you. I have to get back to Bo, if you'll excuse me."

He looked down into her eyes. "Cheval, the next time you'd like to see anything in my room, would you just ask me?"

"Of course," she said, already moving away from him. "Good day, Mr. Thornhill."

Austin walked over to his desk and sat down, thinking about what he'd just witnessed. He didn't believe Cheval had lied to him about wanting a book to read, but was that the only reason she had come into his office? Bradley's suggestion was a good guess, but Cheval already knew who Bo was. That Bradley and Cheval disliked each other there was no doubt. But they did have a strong desire in common. They both wanted to go back to Baltimore.

He looked up at his brother-in-law. "I can see

I'll have no privacy with you and Cheval on board, Bradley. I find it intriguing that both of you had to pass your rooms to get to mine. I don't suppose the two of you are planning anything, are you?" he needled Bradley.

"Planning anything? With her? Absolutely not!" Bradley's words were hissed.

He had a feeling Bradley was in his office to do exactly what he accused Cheval of. Still Austin decided it would be a good idea to keep better watch on both of them.

Austin smiled. "So you're planning something on your own."

"What?" Bradley's face reddened. "Ah—no, of course not. I'm resigned to my fate. I passed by your cabin only because I was stretching my legs. There's not enough walking space on the ship as it is." Bradley turned to go but stopped. "What *she* was doing in here, I haven't a clue. I'll leave it to you to find out." Bradley turned and stalked away.

Austin rubbed his chin as he sat down at his desk. He checked the drawer on his right where he kept his pistol and cash box. Locked. He looked at it closely. It didn't appear the lock had been tampered with. He rose and looked at the fake book where he kept an extra gun. It appeared undisturbed, too.

He could make a pretty good guess as to what Bradley wanted. He'd love to get his hands on a gun and force them to sail back to Baltimore, but what was Cheval looking for?

He remembered how his body had quickened when he'd walked up beside her. She'd been apprehensive. He'd felt it in her.

She obviously wanted to find out something about him or the kidnapping. But why? Would it change her mind about the act itself? No. And it wouldn't change her mind about him either.

It didn't matter how attracted he was to Cheval or she to him. She'd never forgive him for his role in this abduction, making any relationship between the two of them impossible.

Eight

The late afternoon dragged by. Bo became irritable when a strong wind and light rain drove them inside. The high waves formed deep troughs, making the ship dip and roll. At times the waves beat against the ship, rocking it so Cheval almost lost her footing. The drizzling rain made the temperature drop, so Bo and Cheval wore their cloaks to stay warm.

Robert and Jubal had checked on them shortly after dark, but she hadn't seen Austin since she'd left him in his cabin mid-afternoon. Apparently he'd accepted her excuse for being caught in his room. She'd really expected him to seek her out and question her again about it when Bradley wasn't around to offer his opinion. Now that she'd found the pistol, all she had to do was find enough money to book passage back to Baltimore. And she had a feeling she would find that locked in the top drawer of Austin's desk. All she had to do was find the right time and a way to get it out.

Bo had fussed and whimpered so during the early part of the night that Cheval took him in her arms and rocked him as she had the first night he was on board the ship. She knew if he ever quieted long enough, he'd fall asleep. It took an hour of rocking and softly singing to him before he gave up the fight and slept.

For more than an hour Cheval walked the floor, pacing back and forth in front of the bed, hoping the wind and rain wouldn't turn into a bad storm. Before he had retired for the evening, Jubal had told her that a storm lay south of them but the captain didn't expect it to reach them. She wasn't so sure he was right. The light rain and blowing wind could easily turn into a bad storm.

She remembered every horrible story she'd heard about being lost at sea. She'd heard about too many Baltimore residents who had lost loved ones to the sea, her sister's husband among them.

Cheval wished Austin had come down to their cabin to check on them. It was crazy, she knew, but she wanted him to tell her that everything was going to be all right. She chided herself for coming to depend on him for anything. Even though she found herself attracted to him, she had to remember he was a man without principles or noble character. That he'd shown her a kindness that night she was thrown out of the tavern mattered little when she thought of Bo's mother.

Finally, giving up hope that Austin would come and check on them, she struggled into her nightgown and lay down beside Bo, praying the rain would be over and the sun out when she awakened.

Later that night, Cheval awoke to the ship's creaking and swaying, almost rolling her from the mattress. She lay on the bed beside Bo for a moment longer, but as she awakened fully, remembered that it had been raining when she'd gone to bed. The ship was rocking and pitching harder than at any other time all the days they'd been out to sea. The room brightened suddenly, and she glanced toward the porthole.

Lightning.

The rain shower *had* turned into a storm.

Cheval tensed. She looked at the lamp, set in its holder, hoping the flash of light had been from the flickering flame and not lightning. A quick glance told her she hadn't been wrong. The low flame of the lamp couldn't have caused the bright flash. It had been lightning.

She rose from the bed and immediately had to grab hold of a chair to steady herself. Rain beat against the porthole. The ship tossed and pitched.

Her fear mounted.

When she had agreed to accept this job, she hadn't thought about the possibility of a storm at sea. Now she had to. And, she had to remain calm. It was her responsibility to take care of Bo. It didn't matter that she was frightened, she told herself.

Determined to find out if they were in any real danger of sinking, she grabbed her robe and scrambled into it while trying to keep her balance.

The air in the cabin had gotten much cooler. She rubbed her arms to ward off the damp chill. The room brightened again. In the brief flash of light she saw rain slashing against the porthole. Seconds later, thunder rumbled outside. There was no mistaking it now. No wonder the ship pitched from side to side. They were in the middle of a fierce storm.

Austin would know what was going on. She had to find him.

Her stomach muscles tightened; her anxiety increased. She laid a hand to her chest trying to calm herself. Cheval wasn't afraid of storms, but she was afraid of being on the water in a storm. After belting her robe with a sash, she tied the ribbons that held it together at the neckline. She struggled to keep her balance as she stepped into her slippers.

With cold, trembling fingers she turned up the flame on the lamp and picked it up. Carefully, she walked to the bed to check on Bo. He was sleeping soundly.

She had no idea of the time, but knew she couldn't go back to sleep until she found out if the ship was in any danger of sinking in the storm. Bo slept peacefully. She pulled the blanket up over his slender shoulders and lightly sifted her fingers through his fine hair. A picture of her sister and nephew flashed across Cheval's mind and tugged at her heart. She couldn't let anything happen to Bo. She had to return him to the safety of his mother before the woman did something foolish.

She held up the lamp and steadying herself against the rocking, headed for the door. Her hands and feet were cold as she made her way down the darkened, narrow hallway to Austin's cabin, the

lamp light flickering as she went. She held on to
the wall to steady herself as she walked the four
doors down until she came upon Austin's door.
Leaning a hip against the wall to keep from falling,
she knocked lightly. There was no answer. Thunder
rumbled outside and she quickly knocked again,
louder the second time.

Fearing he may not have heard her or that he
might not be inside, she reached and opened the
door.

"Austin," she called, stepping inside the room.

She saw him bolt upright in bed, his bare skin
gleaming in the lamp light, a mat of dark, curly
hair covering his chest. He blinked rapidly.

"Cheval? What's wrong? Is it Bo?" He reached
and grabbed his breeches at the end of the bunk,
then threw the covers aside. By the time she realized he was nude and slipping into his breeches,
he had them pulled up and was walking toward
her, steadying himself with outstretched arms. His
hair, loose from its queue, fell to the top of his
shoulders.

"What's wrong?" he asked again, blinking against
the offending light from her lamp.

Her eyes widened. She was speechless for a moment. She wasn't in the habit of seeing men without
their shirts on and with their breeches unbuttoned.
Austin's open breeches showed much more of his
flat belly than what was intended for a woman to
see.

It was crazy, she knew, but she wished she had
the time to just look him over and examine his

body. She would have liked to reach out and touch his skin, run her hand over it, feel the hardness of the muscles that showed beneath his golden-colored skin. She'd wondered what Austin looked like beneath all those clothes he always wore, and she liked what she saw. Maybe it was the danger she felt from the storm and the comfort she sought that caused her sensual reaction to Austin.

"And why are you walking around holding that lamp with the ship pitching like a buoy. Let me have it before you're thrown against the wall and catch yourself on fire."

He took the light from her and hung it on a bracket on the wall. He was not happy she'd awakened him.

She had no reason for why, but she felt safer just being near him. "It's raining."

"Raining?" He looked back toward his porthole in time to see lightning streak across the darkened sky and shimmer off the pelting rain. "Is that all? You came in here and woke me in the middle of the night to tell me it was raining."

"Oh, ah—I," she stammered, flustered that he seemed to be angry with her. "I think we're in the midst of a storm. Haven't you heard it? Didn't it awaken you?" She was babbling like an idiot and trembling from fear and from the chill in the air. "I just want to know that we're going to be all right." Her voice shook and that bothered her.

Why had she come here looking for anything from this man? Hadn't he already shown himself to be a man who didn't care about a woman's feelings? But as soon as she thought that, Austin's features softened and he gently took hold of her arms.

His eyes searched her face. "Hey, you're really upset, aren't you?"

"Yes," she said, trying to collect herself, hating to admit that weakness.

"Everything is going to be all right. You nearly scared the life out of me, coming in here like this. Are you sure the boy is all right? I thought for sure something had happened to Bo."

Suddenly the ship pitched and threw Austin into Cheval, knocking her against the wall. Austin stretched his arm out behind her to keep her from hitting the wall hard as his body was thrown against hers.

"Damn!" he mumbled, regaining his footing, holding himself against her.

Austin's gaze swept down her face, and hers swept up his. Their faces were so close she felt his breath. Their chests were so close she felt his heartbeat. Their bodies were so close she felt the spring of desire in his lower body.

He bent his head toward her, and for a moment, she thought he was going to kiss her. She held her breath and remained motionless, looking into his beautiful, grayish-green eyes.

Lightning flashed.

Thunder rumbled.

The ship rocked again.

Austin moved away from her.

Cheval cleared her throat and moistened her

lips. She felt bereft. She'd wanted him to kiss her. Her breathing became laborious. How could she be concerned by the fact that she'd wanted him to kiss her when the ship was rocking violently?

"Bo's all right," she said too quickly. "He's sleeping like a babe. I guess I'm the one who's fretful tonight."

His eyes didn't leave her face as he gave her a reassuring smile. "I'm sorry I didn't realize earlier you were so frightened." His voice was gentle. "You didn't tell me you were afraid of storms when we spoke about your making this journey."

"Storms don't worry me when I'm on land. It's the storm on water that bothers me. I've heard about ships that are lost at sea and m—my sister's husband sailed on one that never returned. I'm not frightened, really," she lied. "Just a little concerned and wanting to know that everything is going to be all right and that we're not in danger of sinking."

Austin cupped her cheek and said, "We're not going to sink. I'll finish dressing and go on deck and talk to the captain, see what I can find out. Will that make you feel better?"

She smiled and nodded.

"All right. But to put your mind at ease right now, I'll tell you that if we were in any real danger, Hammersfield would have already awakened me. So try not to worry until I get back." He lifted her chin with the tips of his fingers. "Give me a smile."

How could she be worried when he spoke so

softly, when he stood so near, when he promised her they would be safe? She couldn't. How could she not trust him when he looked at her with his beautiful eyes? She felt calmer already.

"Go back to your room and wait for me there. I'll have a look around on deck and come back and let you know what I find out. All right?"

She nodded. "Thank you," she whispered. Shaking from the effects of his touch, she held onto the wall and hurried back to her room. She trembled, but not from fear. She'd actually wanted Austin to kiss her! How could she be attracted to a man she knew to be so cruel as to kidnap a child? But, she reminded herself, he'd said he had good reason. No, now she was trying to make excuses for him because he hadn't thought her silly for being frightened, because she liked him, because she was attracted to him, because she had wanted him to kiss her.

"No," she whispered to herself. She couldn't think that way. No reason was good enough for what he'd done.

Just because his first concern tonight was for Bo when he saw her in the doorway doesn't mean anything, she told herself. Of course he worried about the child. He wouldn't get whatever he'd been promised by the Bonapartes if Bo wasn't delivered safely.

But why would a family like the Radcliffes need blood money?

She shivered as she set the lamp back in its safety lock. She'd feel better once daylight brightened the sky and the sun chased the storm clouds away.

Austin climbed the small stairway to the deck. He pulled up the collar of his raincoat and settled a wide-brimmed, oil-cloth hat over his head before opening the door that led outside. The cold, pounding rain hit him immediately. A vicious wind blew rain in his face, almost blinding him. Waves crashed against the side of the ship, tossing it from side to side.

There was no brightness in the sky. Only darkness. A light shone through the night from the helm. The captain and two of his men stood at the wheel. Austin ducked his head against the raging elements and grabbed the line the captain had rigged so no one would go overboard as they moved about the deck.

The ship tossed and pitched on the rough seas, making him almost lose his footing a couple of times on the slippery, rain-slick deck.

"You didn't have to come out. We have everything under control," the captain yelled above the roar of the crashing waves and driving wind and rain as Austin drew near him.

"What do you think we're in for?" Austin asked, the wind whipping his words away.

"There's always a chance we could be in for a bad one, but I don't think so," the captain said, water dripping from his hair and beard. "If it doesn't get any worse than this, we'll be all right.

Bishop awakened me 'bout an hour ago when the wind kicked up and the swells started surging. He said it has been lightning most of the night. The clouds we saw late this afternoon have caught up with us."

"Maybe it's too early in the year for a severe storm," Austin said, hoping that were true.

"Unusual that's for sure, but freakish things have been known to happen."

Lightning flashed and Austin saw the rain pelting the deck in what looked like solid sheets of water. Thunder crashed overhead and reverberated in his ears. "Are we off course?"

"A bit. I can't tell you anything for certain until the storm passes. If it calms in the next hour or two, we'll be all right. Let's just pray this weather doesn't follow us the rest of the way to Europe."

Hammersfield was his best captain. He'd never lost a ship or a man at sea. And Austin didn't want this voyage to be his first. Austin clapped Hammersfield on the back. "Do what you can."

"The wind's not giving us much trouble and won't as long as it holds its current direction," Hammersfield said. "The seas appear to be about twelve to fifteen feet. If they don't get any higher than that, we should be all right. Go on back to bed. I'll call you if we need you. You can't do anything right now."

Austin nodded. "I'm going to check on our passengers. I'll be back later."

"It's best if they can sleep through the worst part of this."

That was not likely to happen with Cheval already awake, Austin thought, but said nothing to Hammersfield as he turned and followed the line back to the doorway leading into the hull.

At the bottom of the steps Austin took off his hat and coat and hung them on a peg. He wiped the water from his face with his open hand. Rain had dripped down his collar and wet his shirt, but his boots and coat had kept his feet and legs dry. The ends of his hair were also wet. The hull was cold and the damp shirt clinging to his back chilled him immediately.

Remembering how frightened Cheval had appeared, he decided to change after he talked to her. He wanted to ease her mind. He wanted to let her know that she'd be all right. She and Bo were safe from harm.

Her door was ajar, so he stopped in the doorway and looked inside. She stood by the small chest in the far corner, combing her hair. No, she was doing more than combing her hair. The slow, fluid movement of her slender arm as she stroked the silky hair with the brush tightened his whole body.

Lamp light shone on her golden-blonde hair, making it appear more the color of gold than honey. The long tresses fell down her back in shimmering strands so thick and lush he ached to grab them in his hands and crush them beneath his fingers. Her hair looked like a solid sheet of flowing gold with a hint of silver making it glimmer and shine with each gentle motion of her wrist.

Austin wanted to brush her hair.

Each stroke of her hand hardened his manhood, twisted his insides with desire so potent he thought he might grab her and ravish her. He grew so hard with wanting, he was afraid he couldn't move. He wanted to throw her down on the bed and cover himself with the blanket of silk that was her hair. He wanted to bury his face in its loveliness and breathe deeply, inhale it. He wanted to walk up behind her, reach his arms around her waist and press her backside against his male firmness. He wanted to hold her to his chest and fondle her breasts while he kissed the back of her neck, her shoulders. He wanted to breathe in her scent, take in her essence. He wanted to make her his.

Without even being aware he was there, she tempted him. His desire for her deepened, intensified. He wanted to crush her in his embrace.

"Austin? What's wrong?" she asked when she turned and saw him standing in the doorway.

His gaze flew to her troubled face. His hands dropped to hang and clasp in front of his breeches. The passion and the hunger she raised in him startled him. Had Cheval bewitched him? What was wrong with him? He'd never been as hot for a woman as he was for this one. He'd never wanted to comb a woman's hair before, either. Dammit, he'd never cared one way or the other about a woman's hair until tonight. What was happening to him?

He shook his head, wondering if it were the storm or Cheval who had him swaying on his feet. He should have taken the time to visit miss Sophie's upstairs room before sailing; but even as he thought it, he knew that right now, Cheval was the only woman he wanted. Dammit, he couldn't have Cheval bewitching him like this. He wanted her plain and simple, but he couldn't have her. End of story.

Just touch her, his mind told him.

But his thoughts weren't through with her. It didn't matter that he liked having her on board his ship. It didn't matter that he wanted to spend more time with her. She wasn't a trollop to be used for a time, then tossed aside. She might be a woman of meager means, but she was a lady.

"How bad is the storm?" Cheval asked when he remained silent.

Feeling his body relax a little, Austin raised a hand and wiped at water dripping down the side of his face as he walked farther into the dimly lit room. He had to stand legs apart to keep his balance.

"Nothing to worry about right now. No promises, but Captain Hammersfield thinks we'll run out of this in another hour or so." He deliberately embellished the captain's words.

"Thank God we're not in any danger of sinking."

A smile lifted the edges of his mouth. He stared into her face, not wanting to take his eyes off her.

"You wouldn't want to be on deck right now, but there's a good chance the sun will shine by midday."

"That's good news. I'll put in more time on Bo's lessons in the morning so we'll have extra play time when the weather clears."

Cheval walked over to Austin. She picked up the skirt of her robe and wiped the water that ran down his cheek.

Austin's breath quickened.

Just touch her.

He was reminded of the time she had given him her handkerchief and how he'd reluctantly passed it on to Thollie to wash and iron before giving it back to Cheval. He'd wanted to keep it. And now he wanted to keep her here in front of him. He felt the heat from her body, and it warmed him like a fire.

Looking down into her eyes, he raised his arm and closed his hand around her wrist. Her beautiful lips parted just enough to invite him to kiss her. But, did she know what she was doing? Did she know that every movement she made, every word she said invited him to take her into his arms and love her? He heard a soft moan but didn't know if it came from Cheval or himself.

Lightning flashed brightly and a clap of thunder shook the ship. Cheval squeezed her eyes shut and muffled a scream behind her hand. Austin's arms flew around her, bringing her up close to his hard chest.

"Cheval, it's all right," he whispered against her ear. "You're safe. We're going to be all right. *Aloof* is the best ship that's made. Thunder won't hurt it."

Damn, she felt good in his arms. He held her close and threaded his fingers through her golden curls, savoring the silky feel of her hair and the warmth of her body.

"Oh, Austin, I've been so frightened. I wish I hadn't remembered all those horrible stories I've heard about ships going down and people drowning and I—I—"

"Shh—Come here." He led her to the only chair in the cabin. "Sit down with me. I'll hold you until the storm passes."

Knowing she should say no, Cheval snuggled tighter into the warmth of Austin's arms. Not even the damp shirt could pry her away. Tonight she didn't want to think about what was proper, she only wanted to stay in the security, the warmth and the excitement of Austin's arms.

He sat in the chair and she allowed him to pull her down into his arms. She drew her legs up underneath her and covered them with the skirt of her robe. Austin wrapped his arms around her and rested his chin on the top of her head.

"Your clothes are damp," she whispered.

He stroked her hair with his hand and she found that comforting. "I should have put on a dry shirt before coming in here. Does it bother you?"

"No." She sighed contentedly.

A pleasing chuckle rumbled in his chest. "It

feels good holding you like this. You don't mind, do you?"

"No. I'll get you warm."

Cheval didn't know why, she only knew she wanted to be this close to Austin. She didn't understand her attraction to him, and tonight she didn't want to deny it or run from it. Tomorrow, when the skies were bright with sunshine, she might regret this, but not right now.

"How do you feel now, Cheval?"

"Wonderful, safe."

He chuckled.

In an uncommon gesture, she raised her head and placed her cheek to Austin's. His face was scruffy with a faint beard. She turned ever so slightly so that the side of her lips caressed his skin. It was cold, damp, but it heated her blood. Through her nightgown and robe, she felt the tips of her breasts brush against his damp shirt and harden. His arms tightened around her, and she moaned softly.

Austin moved his head until his lips met hers. Cheval had only been kissed by one other man, when she was fifteen years old. A young man who lived down the street had had her believing she was in love with him. He'd taught her how to kiss. She would have probably married him if he and his family hadn't moved away. He'd promised to send for her one day but never had. She'd soon forgotten about him.

Cheval's lips parted naturally and Austin pressed his lips to hers, softly at first, but when she didn't pull away, he increased the pressure, moving his lips back and forth across hers. Her toes curled; her stomach muscles tightened; her breasts ached to be touched.

She slipped her hands behind his neck, pushing his damp hair aside. As if she'd always known what to do, Cheval opened her mouth and allowed his tongue to enter when she felt it nudging past her lips. His arms tightened. His hands roamed up and down her back, making her skin sing with life. He wasn't just warm. He was hot. His lips were moist, soft, and she loved the feel of them against her own.

The pressure increased. His hands slipped around to cup her face in his palms. His lips left hers and traveled down her neck, kissing her fevered skin. Cheval held each side of his head and gave her body over to the wonderful feelings Austin was creating inside her. She didn't remember the boy down the street ever making her feel like this.

A small tug on the ribbon of her robe parted the bodice and Austin pushed it aside. With nimble fingers he pulled on the neckline of her nightgown, exposing the mere hint of her breasts. His lips moved to the freshly bared skin and he kissed it, licking it with his tongue. His hands slid down her chest and cupped her breasts beneath the cotton gown.

Cheval moaned
Austin groaned.
Thunder crashed.

Cheval jumped.

Sanity returned.

"Oh," she mumbled and scrambled off Austin's lap. She wiped her lips with the back of her hand and swallowed hard. "Yes, well, thank you for making me feel safe. I'm sure I'll be fine the rest of the night." She glanced over to the bed where Bo continued to sleep peacefully.

Slowly, Austin rose from the chair, his arousal showing clearly beneath his breeches. His eyes questioned her, but she remained quiet. She had no answers.

"You're always safe with me, Cheval," he said, then walked out.

Nine

Either the storm had passed them or they had passed through the storm, Cheval wasn't sure which. When she awakened, the first thing she realized was that the ship no longer rocked back and forth. It had settled back down to its gentle swaying. She looked out the porthole and saw light-blue skies and dark-blue water cresting with choppy whitecaps.

Cheval told herself she was pleased Austin wasn't sitting in the dining hall when she and Bo walked in for their morning meal. But she immediately asked herself, if she were happy about that, why did a prickle of disappointment stab through her?

She wasn't sure she was ready to look him in the eyes after their passionate kiss last night. Yet, there was a need, a hunger inside her to see him, to be near him, that she didn't understand. What shocked her more than anything about their embrace was that she wasn't sorry it had happened. She'd wanted to kiss him. She'd been attracted to him since that first night in the tavern when he'd propositioned her and it had fleetingly crossed her mind to consider his offer.

The fluttering desires his kisses had started in her last night were still with her this morning. She hadn't gotten the taste of him out of her mouth, the feel of him off her hands, or the scent of him out of her mind. Austin had stayed with her all through the night.

Reluctantly pushing those thoughts from her mind, Cheval remembered the doubts she'd had, too. She hated the fact that she'd had to search Austin's cabin and lie to Bradley when she'd gotten caught. If only she could make Austin realize the depth of despair Bo's mother had to be in and force him to return Bo. Surely Austin was only thinking of the father.

Cheval led Bo over to the table where they always had their meals. She gasped in surprise. Sitting in front of her was an elaborate checkerboard carved out of cedar. In their proper places sat the game pieces made out of dark and light pieces of corn cob.

She looked up at Jubal with delight in her eyes. "It's so impressive, Jubal. I had no idea you could do such work. Thank you."

A wide smile stretched across his face. His ebony-colored eyes beamed and sparkled with pleasure at her words. "I stained the squares with a mixture of coffee grounds and some red wine Mr. Radcliffe gave me. The captain made the checkers for you."

She picked up one of the round disks and examined the smooth sides. Her heart swelled with appreciation. "He did an excellent job, too. I'm so pleased at how well it turned out. Jubal, thank you. And I'll thank the captain as soon as I see him."

"Can we play now?" Bo asked, looking up at Cheval with expressive eyes lit with excitement.

She looked down at Bo and asked, "Do you know what game this is?"

"Of course. Checkers. I already know how to play. Mama taught me."

Cheval smiled. "Did she, now? Well, tell me, do you usually win, Bo?"

He rubbed his nose as the gleam faded from his eyes. "Sometimes Mama lets me win."

The mention of his mother had dampened his enthusiasm. She had to get it back. "Well, guess what? I'm going to teach you how to win. You'll be able to play with anyone and beat them. How does that sound?"

Keeping his head down, he nodded even as his lips formed a pout.

Cheval's heart went out to him. She knew how much he missed his mother. "Let's eat so we can work on our numbers and letters this morning. Maybe by this afternoon the sunshine will have dried the deck and we'll be able to sit out in the fresh air and play our new game."

"No. I want to play now," Bo said in a petulant tone Cheval hadn't heard him use before.

His display of temper surprised her, and her gaze shot up to Jubal. He was watching her. She took a deep breath. If she let Bo get by with that tone this time, she was afraid he'd use it against her again to try to get what he wanted. Cheval laid a calm, firm hand on Bo's shoulder.

"No, not yet."

He whipped his head up and looked at her with a determined expression on his face and in his eyes. He demanded, "Why can't I play now? I don't want to eat. I'm not hungry."

Quietly, she answered, "No, we're going to eat first, then play."

"Why?"

"Because I said so." She hated relying on that standard line, but she couldn't allow his rude behavior. There was a good chance that if she backed down now, she'd have trouble with his obeying her in the future. She couldn't allow that. But she couldn't alienate him either. He had to trust her completely if she were to manage an escape.

"Why? Why do I have to do it because you said so? You're not my mama." He huffed and folded his arms across his chest.

Embarrassed, Cheval said, "No, but I am in charge here. First we eat, then we play."

Bo started to speak, but she gently placed a finger on his lips to keep him quiet. He brushed her hand aside but didn't try to speak again.

"But," she continued, "I will let you look over the board and game pieces and decide if you want to be the light color or the dark while I get your breakfast ready. Then, we'll have our meal, do our lessons, and this afternoon we'll play. I won't change my mind about that." Cheval kept her voice soft, her tone even but firm.

Bo looked at her for a moment as if trying to decide if he wanted to test her further. Obviously deciding not to, he nodded, and picked up the first game piece and turned it over in his hand, carefully looking at it.

Cheval glanced at Jubal again. "I can't thank you enough for this beautiful checkerboard. I know the time will pass much faster with this game to keep us occupied."

"Yes, Miss. I'm mighty glad you like it."

Later that afternoon, it was difficult for Cheval to look Austin in the eyes when she and Bo made their way on deck with their checkers game. Somehow she had managed to miss seeing Austin the entire morning. When their eyes met, she quickly looked away.

Austin wore the dark breeches and high boots that showed off his muscular thighs. His white shirt, open at the neck, revealed the smattering of hair that covered his broad chest. Her breath grew short just looking at him. Of all the men in the world, she didn't know why fate had decided this man should be the one who could make her tremble with desire with just a look.

It bothered her that she wasn't sorry about what had happened between them last night. Even if she had wanted a few kisses from him, she should never have allowed him the liberties he took with his hands. But at the time, touching and exploration had seemed so right. Just as it had seemed natural for her to initiate the passionate kiss they'd shared and to allow him the freedom to touch her so intimately.

Now she worried what he thought about her this morning. It was ironic that she'd actually done with Austin what Mr. Duncan had accused her of doing to him. She'd allowed too much to happen between them when she'd vowed to stay away from him. That didn't make her happy with herself. How could she have let it happen after what she'd gone through with the Duncans? But she knew the answer even as she asked herself the question. She had never been attracted to Mr. Duncan and had never thought about touching him or kissing him. Mr. Duncan had lied.

Her gaze strayed back over to where Austin stood near the stern with Bradley and Robert. When the tall, lanky lad looked up and saw her and Bo, he came running over to help them set up the make-shift table to put the checkers game on.

"Let me help you with that," the sandy-haired youngster said, grinning at her.

"Thank you, Robert. That would be nice—if you're sure Austin doesn't need you right now."

His brown eyes blinked rapidly, and he brushed his stringy hair away from his face. "No, Miss. I asked him before I came over."

She smiled and nodded. Bo took hold of Robert's hand and pulled him toward the table.

While pretending to be interested in what Bo and Robert were doing, Cheval moved a little closer to Austin and Bradley.

Sunlight brightened the afternoon and skimmed shimmers and glimmers off the dark-blue water. Clear-blue skies had chased away every trace of the darkness of the storm. Looking out over the turbulent water now made Cheval wonder how she could have been so frightened last night.

Her gaze drifted over to Austin again. Why did it please her to just look at him, be in the same room with him, or be near him? He had many good traits, and there were many things to admire about him; but how could she ever get past what he was doing to Bo and Betsy Patterson?

She found herself moving closer to Austin, stopping when she heard their voices.

"My God, we tossed and turned so much last night I thought I was going to be sick," Bradley complained. "Even now, my stomach feels as if it's still rolling from side to side. I don't understand. I did all right the first few days. No problem at all."

"It's not unusual for people to get sick when sailing through the choppy waters of a storm."

"I don't know how sailors stand it day after day on these blasted ships. I think I'm going crazy sometimes. What I wouldn't give to be back at home with Winifred and my practice. Now I remember why I never liked sailing when I was younger."

Bradley continued to talk, but Austin's focus turned to Cheval. She looked especially pretty to him this morning in her dark-gray dress. He wanted to walk over to her and take her in his arms. He wanted to brand her with his kisses so everyone would know she belonged to him. He'd never felt so possessive about a woman. Maybe it was because he had held her and tasted her last night. Maybe it was because he'd seen her with her honey-gold hair flowing down her back. Maybe it was because she was working her way into his heart and life, finding a place to live.

When he'd held her and kissed her last night, he'd felt something different. There was more feeling to his kisses than just the desire to bed her. He hadn't wanted to hurry his time with her; he'd wanted to spend time with her. He hadn't wanted to immediately throw her on the bed, enter her and seek his own release as he had with so many women he'd paid to spend an hour with.

No, he'd wanted to take his time and kiss her slowly. He'd wanted to kiss not only her lips, but her eyes, her cheeks, the base of her throat. He'd wanted to expose her breasts and feast upon them with his eyes, with his hands, with his lips. Because what he felt for her was so different from any woman he'd ever desired, he didn't understand these new feelings.

He only knew that he felt differently about this woman. His heart and his body were telling him this lady was special, but would she ever be his? Would she ever understand and forgive what he was doing on this journey to France? She hadn't mentioned it the last few times they had talked, but he knew it was on her mind.

"Are you going to answer me or just continue to stare at her?" Bradley asked in a quarrelsome tone.

Austin was forced to return his attention to his companion. "I'm sorry. What did you ask?"

"I want to know more about this little boy you're taking to Europe."

"It won't help you to know who he is or to know anything about him."

"Don't be absurd, Austin. I don't want to know because I think it will help me. I want to know so I can help you. You're in real trouble."

"Do you plan on turning me in to the authorities when we return, Bradley?"

"Heaven forbid! But someone might put two and two together and come up with *Aloof* sailing the same night the boy disappeared."

"That's easy to explain. I had to sail to Portugal and Spain to discuss the possibility of building more ships for some of my customers."

"Can you prove that?"

"If I had to, I could call in some favors. Surely, Bradley, you realize the less you know about this, the better off you'll be once we return should there be questions."

"Well, yes, of course you're right about that, however—"

Austin's gaze and thoughts drifted away as Bradley continued to talk. Bo dropped a game piece and Cheval hurried over to pick it up for him. He liked the way she moved. He liked everything about her. From the way she walked and talked to the way she held her head and shoulders so proudly.

"The storm, Austin. Are you listening to me?"

Austin was forced to give Bradley his attention again. "Yes, Bradley, the storm blew us off course, but we should only lose a day or two at the most. We're making excellent time. If the wind holds and we don't have to spend too much time delivering the boy, it would do you just as well to wait for us to resupply the ship and sail back to Baltimore with us. *Aloof* will make better time than any of the passenger ships."

Bradley rubbed his chin. "I've been thinking, Austin. God knows there's nothing else to do on this prison ship. Have you given any thought to dropping anchor in England and allowing me to depart from there? I'm sure I'll be able to find a ship to take me directly back to Baltimore. Then you'll no longer have to worry about me—or your dear sister, I might add.

A pang of guilt assailed Austin. He'd tried not to think about Winifred. He had no doubt she'd be angry and hurt for a long time. There were some things a man just didn't look back on, and making a decision such as this journey was one of those things.

As if with a will of its own, Austin's gaze strayed back to Cheval. It was funny how, if she were in the room, he had to look at her. It had been that way since the first night he'd seen her. "We can't make any stops. I want to get Bo settled with his father as soon as possible."

"You said we were sailing to Europe. Where exactly are we going? You mentioned Portugal and Spain. Won't we encounter Napoleon's warships?"

"I didn't say we were going to either of those countries, and there's always a possibility we might encounter a warship before this journey is finished."

"My word, what have you gotten us into?"

Austin rubbed his forehead, shielding his eyes from the sun at the same time so he could get a better look at Cheval. "Don't be alarmed, Bradley. I've heard rumors about blockades, gunboats, and battleships, but we don't know exactly what to expect. I can assure you I don't plan to be on any coastline any longer than needed to deliver the boy and resupply the ship. If all goes according to what I've been told, we'll be leaving two or three days at the most after arriving, and there shouldn't be the need to put you on another ship."

Bradley's eyes narrowed. "I hear a but in there, Austin. What gives?"

"But if for some reason there has been a mix-up in the plans and no one is there to take the child when we arrive, we might have to wait around. If that happens, I'll look for another ship for you. Because—" Austin stopped.

"Because you can't very well take the boy back to Baltimore with you, right?"

Austin remained quiet. He didn't want to think about that possibility. If Le Camus was wrong and his brother wasn't there to meet him at the *l'Aueerge Guerin*, he didn't know what he'd do.

"That's another thing we need to discuss, Austin. What is going to keep the warships from blowing us out of the water when we get near the coastline? All of Europe is at war, you know."

"I know. It's been taken care of." Austin watched Cheval's movements. If he didn't know better, he'd think she was deliberately moving closer to him and Bradley.

"What are you looking at?" Bradley turned and saw Cheval standing nearby. "Oh, it's *her* again." Bradley sniffed. "I might have known." He looked her up and down. "It appears she and the boy weathered the storm. There's something about kids. This kind of thing never bothers them. My girls could—"

"Excuse me, Bradley. I need to speak to Cheval," Austin said and walked away.

"Wait a minute! What about my question?" he asked, but Austin continued to walk toward Cheval. Bradley followed, huffing. "Damnation, Austin. You haven't let me have a full five minutes of your time since we left Baltimore. How can I be of any help if you don't fill me in on all the details of this mission?"

"Good afternoon, Cheval," Austin said, letting his gaze scan her face. She looked at him, and his stomach muscles tightened. She was so beautiful with the wind blowing loose strands of hair about her face. The background of blue sky behind her made her eyes more brown than green. "I see you and Bo have suffered no ill-effects from the storm."

"We're both fine. Thank you." She turned to Bradley and said stiffly, "Hello, Mr. Thornhill."

"Miss Worthington." Bradley immediately turned to Austin. "You were going to tell me how you're going to assure our safety along the coastline."

Bradley's comment was snide, and Austin didn't like the way he'd snubbed Cheval. "No, I wasn't." He turned back to Cheval. He'd made a crack in her armor last night, and he didn't want to lose the ground he'd gained with her. They had too many things going against them. They couldn't lose touch with the attraction that kept them aware of each other. "I'll ask the cook to prepare a special dinner for us all tonight. I'd like for you and Bradley to join me in my cabin—say six o'clock. We'll have dinner just the three of us."

"Oh, no, I couldn't do that, but thank you," Cheval hurried to say. "I'll have my hands full taking care of Bo this evening."

"Bo won't be a problem. I'll ask Robert and Jubal to dine with him and free you for the evening. You've hardly been out of his sight since we left Baltimore. I think you need a break."

Her gaze darted from Austin to Bradley. "No, really I—"

"I won't accept 'no' for an answer." Austin turned to Bradley. "Assure her we'd like the pleasure of her company tonight, Bradley."

Bradley opened his mouth to speak, closed it, faked a smile, then said, "By all means, Miss

Worthington, please join us. I'm sure you are as eager as I to hear how we're to get in and out of France alive with the madman Napoleon on the loose. Besides, your presence *will* give me another intelligent person to talk to. The men on this ship can't carry on a decent conversation if it's not about sailing, ships, or seas. And I'm bored stiff with that subject."

Austin shrugged. "The men on this ship are here because they are the best at what they do, Bradley, just as you're best at what you do."

Bradley looked out over the water thoughtfully for a moment. "If I have any clients left when I return. Two months is a long time to be gone from one's business."

Another stab of guilt hit Austin, but he quickly brushed it aside. He would have taken Bradley back to Winifred and his law practice if he could have. But once he took Bo on board, there was no turning back and no looking back. He hated disrupting so many lives, even his own; and there would be no mercy for him if he were caught. If there had been any other way out of his vow to Jerome Bonaparte, he would have taken it.

"I think I'll go lie down for awhile. If you'll excuse me." Bradley turned and sauntered away.

Bradley's own foolishness had gotten him in this mess. Still, Austin didn't like seeing him so miserable. He didn't like what Winifred and Betsy Patterson would be going through right now either, but sometimes a choice that was right for one ended up hurting another.

Austin returned his attention to the pretty woman in front of him. "Cheval, you're looking tired. Why don't you let Jubal and Robert look after Bo the rest of the day while you get some rest?"

"Oh, no, Austin, I'm sorry about my uneasiness last night, but I'm really fine today. I don't want you thinking I can't take care of Bo."

He smiled. "Nonsense. I don't think that at all. I'm concerned for your well-being. Minding a three-year-old twenty-four hours a day on a ship has got to be tiresome. I've seen how you run after him, following him up and down the stairs, seeing to his every need."

"Thank you for your concern. I'm fine. Really, I'm not tired. If you insist on my joining you for dinner this evening, I'll have to spend the afternoon with Bo."

"All right." He stepped closer to her. "Did you sleep well after I left last night?"

She moistened her lips. Her eyelashes fluttered. "Yes. I felt safe." She took a deep breath and clasped her hands together in front of her.

Austin wanted to be alone with her, to talk to her. "I had the taste of you on my lips all night."

Cheval gasped and stepped away. "Austin, I'm sorry about last night. Not only for the way I behaved concerning the storm but my forward behavior as well. It was unacceptable. I shouldn't have kissed you."

"Do you regret it?"

Never! Ignoring his question, she said, "My only excuse is that I needed comfort."

Austin lips lifted in a slight smile. She avoided a straight answer. That was promising. "Comfort. Is that what you thought it was? I was trying to show you the desire I have for you. I hoped it was passion I sensed in you when you responded to my touch."

Her face flamed. All the wondrous feelings their kisses had created in her came rushing back to haunt her. Even now she could taste his warm mouth upon hers.

She swallowed and moistened her lips again as she twisted her fingers together in front of her. "I must admit I don't really know what it was. The storm, the danger I felt—maybe it was just the night. I don't know. I was afraid and being close to you offered safety, comfort, and—"

"Passion."

Their eyes met and held. "Yes, even though that bothers me greatly, but I—"

"Miss Cheval, come over here," Bo called interrupting her sentence. "Come see what I've made."

Cheval swallowed hard and took a deep breath. Thank God, Bo called her. She was getting in too deep. "If you'll excuse me I must check on my charge."

"I'll see you at six," he reminded her. "In my cabin."

Ten

Cheval's garnet-colored dress swished across her legs as she walked down the companionway toward Austin's cabin. She'd decided the long-sleeved velvet should keep her warm enough without a wrap. In her hair she'd placed a red-jeweled hairpin that had been her sister's. She didn't know if it were vanity or stupidity that made her do a few extra things with her appearance tonight, like the hairpin, pinching her cheeks for color, and the rose water she'd sprinkled on her neck and shoulders before she'd dressed.

She'd worried all afternoon, not looking forward to dinner with the two Baltimore men. She didn't want to spend time with Bradley because she didn't like him, and she didn't want to spend time with Austin because she did. But what was she to do? she wondered as she walked down the hallway to Austin's cabin. Austin had left her no choice concerning the invitation.

Maybe she would make it through the evening if she stayed as quiet as possible. Bradley could certainly keep a conversation going without her. He'd probably be happy if she didn't speak.

Just before she made it to Austin's door, she stopped. She brushed her hands down the front of her dress and took a deep breath. No matter how many times she told herself it wasn't true and no matter what she thought to the contrary, she wanted to spend this time with Austin.

She walked into the cabin and saw Austin standing in the far corner of the room, a drink in hand, looking deep in thought. Two lamps fastened to the walls flushed the room in a soft, yellow light. One lamp sat on his desk, the other in the center of a small chest.

Austin was handsomely dressed in a white, ruffled shirt with a dark-gray bow-tied cravat. His short jacket had cutaway tails, and his trousers were ankle length. His low-cut shoes were garnished with large, brass buckles. He'd never looked so handsome.

As if sensing her presence, he looked up. Their eyes met. In that moment she wished Bradley weren't going to be joining them for dinner. She would love to have this man all to herself tonight.

"Cheval, come in." He walked over to her and took her hand and gently kissed it. "You look lovely. That shade of red brings out the green in your eyes."

"Thank you," she answered, breathless from the chill of excitement that ran up her arm and settled in her breasts when his lips grazed the back of her palm.

"Let me pour you a glass of sherry."

"No, thank you," she answered, walking into the

dimly lit room. "After working in that tavern, I don't think I'll ever be able to drink spirits." Cheval looked past Austin to the bookshelf, her gaze immediately going to the large book with the gun, before turning her attention to him. A wash of relief settled over her. It was still there. Maybe Austin had accepted her explanation for being in his office.

"That's understandable." He leaned a hip against his desk and studied her face. "I guess you had your share of drinks poured on you."

She saw compassion in his eyes, and it warmed her. "That and more," she said, remembering all the fanny pats, pinches, and lewd comments she'd endured.

"I'm glad you were only there a week. It's no life for a lady."

"It's not an easy life to be sure." If she continued to look into his eyes, she was afraid he'd read what was on her mind. It was ludicrous, she knew, but no matter how many times she told herself he was a deplorable man, she couldn't stop herself from wanting to be in his embrace once again.

Cheval glanced away from him. Her gaze lighted on the table in the center of the room. Something wasn't right. She looked again. There were only two plates sitting on the table. Each plate held boiled sweet potatoes and shredded chicken with flour dumplings. Small side dishes were filled with cooked figs and pears.

"Bradley won't be joining us. Why don't we go ahead and sit down before the food gets cold?"

A prickle of something akin to delight stole over Cheval. She tried to brush it away, but couldn't while her eyes lingered on his face. "What's wrong with him?"

"Sick, I'm afraid." He walked over to the table and pulled out her chair. "He sent word that he couldn't eat a thing and didn't feel he'd be acceptable company for anyone. I hope you don't mind that it will be just the two of us tonight."

Mind? She almost laughed. Hadn't she just been wishing she'd have him all to herself? She wasn't happy Bradley was ill, but she couldn't deny the rush of expectation that surged through her at the thought of being alone with Austin again either.

A short candle burned in the center of the table. The ship rocked gently. The intimate atmosphere was sure to have her thinking of things other than food.

You should leave.

But I want to stay.

No. There's no future for you with him.

I'm only thinking of right now.

You're losing sight of what kind of man he is.

I can handle it.

Denying all the warnings inside her, Cheval took her seat at the table. She waited until Austin had seated himself before picking up her fork and cutting into her potatoes.

It was stupid, silly, outrageous, and appalling but she didn't want to eat. She wanted to look at Austin. She wanted to smile at him, laugh with him. She wanted to lose herself in his company.

"Is Bo settled for the night?" he asked, then put a slice of the tender chicken in his mouth.

"He's dressed and ready for bed, but he won't be going to sleep for a while. Robert is telling him a story about a killer whale that once attacked a ship he was on and almost ate the entire crew for dinner."

Austin laughed. "I remember that story. It was told to me more than fifteen years ago. I've told it myself a few times. The only thing that changes in the story over the years is the young lad's name."

Cheval looked up at him and smiled as she dipped her fork into her dumplings. "Oh, you mean the story he's telling probably isn't true?"

Austin laughed again. "Not if it's about a killer whale. It's a well-worn legend that has been used many times and will be again."

"I had no idea. He seemed to know so much about it, answering all of Bo's questions about the size of the whale and the coloring. I guess he thought it would be a good bedtime story for Bo."

"It will be. He'll have Bo dreaming of heroic feats all night."

The light conversation continued throughout the meal. Cheval enjoyed the banter with Austin. She was glad he hadn't mentioned the storm and her reaction to it, or their passionate embrace. Having admitted she enjoyed the kiss was all she cared to have him know.

The candle had burned low when at last their plates were pushed aside and Austin had finished a couple of his own heroic stories about life at sea. The room grew quiet. Cheval found herself staring into beautiful, gray-green eyes that looked back at her with a questioning clarity. An inner voice told her to take leave, but she stayed.

"What are we going to do about us, Cheval?" Austin finally asked.

Cheval's heartbeat increased. She wasn't sure she wanted to talk about anything as important as what was happening between the two of them, but she wasn't sure she wanted to go, either. Austin had helped kidnap a little boy—something she could never condone, no matter how her body responded to his masculine appeal.

Candlelight threw distorted shadows across the dark panelled walls. The room was cozy and warm. Cheval's feelings for Austin amazed her. She wished she could understand what drew her to him when she was so opposed to what he was doing. It didn't make sense. She should hate the very sight of him; but instead, she found herself wanting to be with him.

She lowered her lashes over her eyes. "Far too many things separate us for there to be anything between us, Austin."

"It doesn't have to be that way."

It did. He didn't know it, but she planned to betray him and take Bo at the first available time. But she'd never turn him over to the authorities. She was sure they would want to know whose ship she and Bo had sailed, but she'd never tell that.

Cheval remained quiet.

Austin rose from his chair and walked over to Cheval. He reached for her hand and helped her to rise. A sense of longing filled her when his hand touched hers. He was warm and she was eager.

Don't let him take you in his arms.

But I want him to.

His embrace will only cause you heartache.

I hurt now from wanting his touch.

This hurt you will get over.

I don't want to get over it. I want to enjoy it.

As Cheval rose to her feet it seemed so natural to go directly into his arms and be held against his chest. She felt his warmth against her cheek, heard his heartbeat against her ear, smelled his scent of shaving soap, touched the coarse cotton of his dinner jacket. How could she not respond to what her body craved? This man.

Cheval stood still with her arms around Austin's neck, her cheek pressed to his chest. His breath stirred the hair on top of her head. He held her, but not too tightly, letting her know that he wasn't going to pressure her into anything she didn't want to do.

"You can't deny what's happening between us, Cheval." His voice was low, inviting.

"I'm not trying to deny it. I've been trying to fight it."

"Because of Bo."

Her breathing became erratic. She swallowed hard, not wanting him to say out loud what lay between them. "Yes, but there are other things too. You are a man of great wealth and I have nothing."

With the tips of his fingers he lifted her chin, forcing her to look into his glazed eyes. "Do you think that matters to me? It doesn't. I desire you like I have no other woman. I've wanted you in my arms since that first night I saw you in the tavern."

He brought her up tighter to his chest, pressing her breasts against him.

"I've wanted to kiss you like this."

Austin bent his head and placed his lips on hers in a long, searing, passionate kiss. His tongue sought the warmth of her mouth, sending tingling sensations throughout her body and leaving her breathless.

"I've wanted to touch you like this," he whispered against her pliant lips.

Slowly he ran his hands up and down her back, over her shoulders, down the front of her dress to place his palms against her breasts. He gently squeezed and massaged her firmness beneath the velvet dress. His hand glided over and around each breast with the lightest of pressure, kneading them seductively. Her breath was so shallow she thought she might faint.

His touch inflamed her, and she yielded to his unspoken command for her to remain passive in his arms and let him love her.

"Cheval, you feel so good. So very good," he said in between delicious, wet kisses. "Can you

fight this? Can you fight how I make you feel?
Can you fight what you know you do to me?"

Push him away before it's too late.

No, go away!

Remember what happened to your sister when she lost her son.

No.

Remember Bo's tears and cries for his mother.

Cheval squeezed her eyes shut and pushed away
from Austin. Sorrow stabbed through her as she
whispered, "I have to fight what I'm feeling for
you."

"Cheval."

He spoke her name so softly she almost gave in
to his seduction.

She looked into the gray-green pool of his eyes
and wished she didn't have to say, "I can't give
myself to a man I have no respect for. I admit
I'm drawn to you as I have been to no other man.
I don't understand it. I don't want it. I don't approve of you, so naturally these feelings I have for
you upset me and cause me great distress."

As the blossom of passion faded from his eyes,
Austin answered, "I can understand all that. But,
Cheval, try to see past the man who's involved in
this kidnapping scheme and—"

"I can't!" she interrupted, making fists with her
hands, trying to tell him so much more with her
eyes. "I see you and I want to touch you, but I also
want to hate you for what you're doing to Bo and
his mother. I look at Bo with his rounded cheeks
and bright eyes. I hold his little hands and comfort

him each night. I know how much he misses his
mother, and I know she must be going crazy wor-
rying about him. I can hold him and kiss the top
of his head, but I can't make up for the loss of his
mother—and neither will his father."

Anger at himself, at Cheval, at Jerome welled
up inside Austin, and he took a step away from
her. His hands remained still at his side as his
eyes drilled into hers. "Aren't you willing to believe there might have been a good reason that
forced me to participate in this madness?"

"No. Nothing—nothing would make what you've
done acceptable," she answered earnestly, refusing
to accept any reason as justifiable.

Austin lowered his hands to his sides and sighed.
"Nothing? Obviously, I don't agree with you."

She swallowed past a tight throat, knowing at
that moment she'd never make him understand
what Bo's mother must be going through. "Obviously."

Cheval turned and walked to the door, but suddenly spun back to face Austin. "I wish things
could have been different between us."

"That doesn't help me much right now."

She understood. It didn't do anything to help
the way she was feeling either, but maybe it would
give her the strength to stay away from him the
rest of the journey.

"Good night, Austin."

Eleven

"Land! Land! Land!"

Cheval looked up from the paper where she was teaching Bo to write his name when she heard the loud cry from above the deck. Frightened excitement coursed through her.

"Land," she whispered. For the first time during the entire voyage, her stomach lurched, tying into knots and making her weak with fear.

After twenty-six days at sea, they would be dropping anchor. The hour had come for her to return to Austin's cabin. Could she do it? Yes, her feelings quickly answered for her mind. She had a seemingly impossible task ahead of her, but she wouldn't back out. She couldn't reunite her sister and her child, but she had a chance of returning Bo to his mother. In this, she wouldn't let herself fail. Bo and his mother had no one to help them except her. She couldn't let them down.

"Will I see Mama, now?" Bo asked, looking up from his paper.

She glanced down at him and gently brushed his bangs away from his forehead. She smiled at him and kissed the top of his head. Considering the circumstances, he'd been a brave little boy.

"Not yet, little one." She wanted to add that he'd see his mother soon. But not knowing how long it would take her to escape with him and get back to Baltimore, she decided it was best not to give him any false hope that it would happen soon.

Her stomach knotted again. She had to get herself together and focus on her plan. The first thing she needed to do was find out where Austin was. She couldn't wait any longer to go into his quarters and take the pistol and look for enough money to get her and Bo back to Baltimore. Too, she had to prepare herself for a confrontation. Whoever took charge of Bo might not want her to travel with Bo to his father's house. Maybe Bo would give her help by crying for her if they declined her offer of assistance to stay with Bo until he settled into his new home.

Cheval heard the shout for land again. She took hold of Bo's hand and said, "Come on. Let's go up on deck. If we're near land, I want to see it, don't you?"

He nodded and scrambled off his chair. Cheval and Bo climbed the steps to the deck. She expected to see a coastline dotted with signs of a city in the distance. All she saw was the dark-blue water and bright-blue skies she'd seen the past three-and-a-half weeks.

"Where is it?" Bo asked. "I don't see land."

Cheval looked all around them, but there was no land in sight. "I'm not sure. Maybe I misunderstood the call." At that thought, a wave of relief washed through her; she had a reprieve. "I thought I heard someone shout 'land.'"

But if she did, where was it? Austin, the captain, Jubal, and several others stood near the helm pointing east, but she couldn't see a thing. Robert turned and noticed them standing over to the far side. After a minute or two, he ran toward them, his sandy-colored hair flying out behind him.

"Is it all right if I take Bo up to the railing and let him watch for awhile, Miss Worthington? I won't let go of his hand with him standing that close to the edge."

"I think that would be all right. As long as you hold tight," she answered, knowing that would give her the perfect opportunity to go down into Austin's cabin for the gun and the money.

She didn't see the land, but she had to assume whoever spotted it knew what they were talking about. Whatever had happened had caused a flurry of activity. When Robert walked up to the edge with Bo, Austin turned around and looked at Cheval standing near the deck house. He started toward her, and her breathing increased rapidly. He was so handsome striding toward her that her whole body cried out to be wrapped in his arms and become a part of him, but she also felt a pang of guilt. She was going to betray the trust he had in her.

He stopped in front of her and his eyes peered down into hers. "You heard?"

She nodded, her gaze searching his face. She

wanted to see some sign from him that he might be thinking about calling off this madness before it was too late to turn back. "I can't see anything that looks like land. Where is it?"

"You can't see it from here. Look up there." He pointed up to the crow's nest, where a man sat, looking through a spyglass. "He can see it."

Her throat felt suddenly dry and tight. Yes, the time had come. "Oh," she said, her heart hammering in her chest. "How long will it be before we actually dock?"

"We're not going to dock, but we will drop anchor about a mile off shore. It will be late this afternoon before we reach our destination."

"I see."

A young man came running up to Austin and handed him a blue flag with a yellow crest on it. "Is this it?" the young man asked.

"Yes. Take it up to him and let it fly."

"What is it?" she asked.

"The flag that will keep Napoleon's warships from firing on us. Now that we can see land, they can see us and no doubt are already on their way to see who we are and what we want."

"We're not in any danger, are we?" she asked as a tense knot of fear settled in her stomach. Now that they were so close, she couldn't avoid feeling the effects of the magnitude of the mission she'd elected.

"Without that flag on our mast we'd not be welcome anywhere near France's shore. That tells Napoleon's men that someone whom Napoleon respects and wishes to enter France is on board. We'll have no trouble once they know we're carrying Jerome's child."

Cheval stiffened. "Yes, Napoleon would want to see that his nephew is kept safe from harm."

"Napoleon couldn't care less about Bo. He annulled Jerome's and Betsy's marriage knowing Bo existed, remember? He's only humoring Jerome because he married the princess Napoleon wanted him to marry for political reasons."

"It's hard to understand how Jerome could have allowed Napoleon to take his wife and son away from him."

Austin looked out over the water. "No, it's easy, really. Jerome chose power, fame, and fortune over love. He wanted to wear a crown and rule a country."

In a desperate need to understand Austin, she took an imploring step toward him and asked, "Why? Austin, can't you tell me why you agreed to do this for Jerome? What hold has he over you? What has he promised you?"

His somber gaze swept across her face. "It's a matter of honor, Cheval."

"Honor? I think not. What honor is there in stealing a child from his mother's arms?"

Austin looked away and for a moment she thought he was going to reveal his inner thoughts, but instead he asked, "If you knew why I was doing this, would it make any difference in your feelings?"

Cheval thought she heard anguish in his voice. Words she wanted to say choked in her throat.

Unable to get the affirmative answer that he asked for past her lips, she reluctantly remained quiet.

"I thought not. You told me nothing would make this act I'm committed to acceptable to you. And I agree. I can only tell you that right or wrong, I did what I had to do. No apologies, Cheval."

As if the dawn had just broken, she understood for the first time. He had to bring Bo to France, just as she had to try to find a way to get him back to Baltimore.

She felt as if a fist had closed around her heart, forever sealing her away from Austin. "And now, even as close as we are to France, you can't be persuaded to change your mind, can you?"

"No, Cheval. Nothing's changed."

She'd understood that almost from the beginning, but it didn't make it any easier to bear. She felt as if she'd just lost a part of herself and would never get it back.

"I wish this could be different," he continued. "As soon as the anchor goes down, Jubal and I will row to shore and find the man we're supposed to meet. If everything goes according to plan, we'll bring him back with us and he'll take Bo away."

"You and Jubal are going ashore without Bo?"

"Yes. You'll remain here with Bo. I'm not going to let Bo off this ship until I'm satisfied that I'm handing him over to the proper people and that he will be all right."

"That's good. I'm glad." She could hardly speak. The idea of leaving Bo in this foreign land with strangers was almost too much to bear.

She looked into Austin's eyes. No, she didn't like what she was going to have to do. She didn't want to do it because looking at Austin now she realized, God help her, she'd fallen in love with him. And now she had to betray him. A physical pain struck her and she winced.

Austin touched her arms. "Cheval? Are you all right?"

She took a deep breath and faked a smile as she pulled her arm away him. "Yes. I'm fine. I— I'm going to miss Bo." *And you.*

"I know. I've seen how fond you are of him."

"Yes." Her voice had turned husky.

That he was being so cautious pleased her. He might be doing wrong, but he worried for Bo's safety. "Looking out for him is the least you can do."

"Right."

"What if you don't think they are right and that you decide at the last minute you can't leave Bo with them?" she found herself asking.

He smiled indulgently. "Then we'll row back to *Aloof* and get the hell out of here. But, Cheval, don't expect that to happen. Le Camus was very specific with his plans. Jerome wants his son."

"What would we do if they came after us?" she asked as the beginning of a new plan started forming in her mind.

"Cheval, *Aloof* was built for speed. We can outrun any of their warships. And there is no way they will fire upon us with Bo on board or as long as that flag flies. You don't have to worry."

She nodded. "Is Bradley going with you?" she asked, her plan continuing to form as she gathered this information that would be crucial to her.

"No. There'll be no need. If Le Camus's brother can take Bo immediately, we'll remain only long enough to resupply the ship for the return; then we'll be on our way. I can get Bradley back faster than any of the passenger ships. If, however, there's been a change of plans and we have to wait until someone can come from Westphalia to take Bo, I'll try to secure Bradley passage on another ship."

"If we have to outrun the French ships, where would we resupply for the journey home if not here?"

"Don't worry, England is less than a day away. And an American ship shouldn't have any problems entering at Dover."

Cheval stored all this information.

"I know you and Bradley don't get along, but you're not afraid to be alone with him, are you?"

"Certainly not. I just know how anxious he is to return to his wife."

"I think we all want the journey to be over and begin the return."

She nodded, feeling guilty for what she had to do, yet knowing it must be done. It would have been so much easier if she'd hated Austin. Loving him made this deceit doubly hard.

"I want you to know I'm pleased with the way you've taken care of Bo. Knowing he was in your care, I haven't worried about him."

"Thank you." Her words were almost a whisper. She didn't want his praise. They had to be enemies.

"I know." He looked away for a moment, then said, "I'll settle payment on you when we return."

"That's fine," she said, not wanting to talk about the future. If she accomplished her plan, he wouldn't want to pay her for caring for Bo. She hated lying, but what else could she do? She couldn't reveal her plans.

He smiled at her, but she couldn't repay him with one of her own. Too many things had happened and too many things were about to happen.

"When we return, you can live at my town house with Thollie until you find other employment. I'll be going immediately out to my mother's estate in the country. Feel free to live there as long as you like. We could consider it part of your payment for this job."

"Thank you, but I don't think it will take me long to find a place to live," she lied. In truth, she couldn't think past returning Bo to his mother. "I really don't want to think about all that until we're on our way home. Do you mind?"

"No, I understand. It will be a long trip back for you."

She looked wistfully at the horizon where the coastline had yet to appear. "Yes, it will be." *And I'm going to miss you terribly.*

Cheval had asked Robert to take Bo to their schoolroom cabin and keep him there when the

French naval ships flanked *Aloof* as the coastline came into view. Cheval hadn't expected to see jagged cliffs and trees as they floated in the water off the coastline of France. She'd expected the landscape to look more like Baltimore, with buildings and lights.

Austin hadn't revealed their exact destination, but knowing they could reach England in less than a day gave her a pretty good idea of where they were.

She stood on deck watching Austin and Jubal rowing to shore, her plan now firmly in her mind. Austin and Jubal had left with swords hanging by their sides. If Austin carried the pistol she had found hidden in the book, it must have been safely tucked away in his jacket because she hadn't seen it when he boarded the small boat.

Her plan was risky, she knew, but after much thought she decided that getting a gun and forcing the captain to sail to England where she and Bo could escape was a much better plan than trying to talk a stranger into letting her go with Bo to his father. Her plan meant leaving Austin in France, a hostile country, without the very person he came to deliver. That thought had caused her much duress, but in the end Bo's best interest won out. She hated doing this to Austin, but he was a strong man and could take care of himself. Bo couldn't.

As she stood and watched Jubal and Austin rowing in the choppy waters, she wondered what the French would do to Austin if her plan succeeded.

Would they punish him for her deed? She didn't want Austin in trouble with that madman Napoleon, but Bo had to come first.

In order for her plan to work, she had to have a pistol. She prayed Austin had left one somewhere in his cabin.

It was now or never, she told herself when Austin and Jubal's small boat neared the shoreline. She looked around. Bradley and Captain Hammersfield were on deck. Before she could dissuade herself, she spun around and hurried down the companionway and into her room, where she grabbed a kitchen knife from under her nightclothes and slid it into the pocket of her dress. She needed it to get into the locked drawer of Austin's desk. She prayed she'd find Austin's money in there. With hurried steps and short breaths, she strode into Austin's cabin.

The room smelled of wax, of wood, of Austin. No, she wouldn't let herself think of him. She couldn't. If she did, she wouldn't go through with this and leave him behind. Quickly throwing those softening thoughts of him aside, she went straight to the bookshelf.

A moan of despair flew past her lips as soon as she lifted the book. It was lighter than she remembered. Her fingers felt cold and trembly as she opened the cover. The gun was gone. Anguish filled her and she moaned again. What was she to do? She put the book on the desk and ran her hands down her side, stopping abruptly when she came to the knife in her pocket. Her heartbeat increased. Was the knife dangerous enough to use as a weapon against eight men? She looked over the thin blade. No, but it would get her into the captain's cabin. Surely he'd have a pistol.

Cheval took the knife and worked on the locked drawer. It wasn't easy with her hands trembling, but she continued to work until she heard the lock snap. The sound was so loud she dropped the knife and it clattered to the floor. Cheval froze with her eyes on the door, fearing that at any moment someone would come and investigate the noise. When there was no sign of anyone, she left the knife where it lay and pulled open the drawer.

An audible sigh of surprise skimmed past her lips. Yes! A pistol with a silver handle lay beside a leather money pouch. She went weak with relief. Thank God, Austin had more than one gun. First, she picked up the pouch and opened it. A quick glance told her there were more than enough coins to secure their passage back to Baltimore. She closed it and stuffed it into the pocket of her skirt.

Carefully, she picked up the gun. It was heavy. Cold. The barrel was long and shiny, like new metal. With trembling fingers, she looked at the weapon, realizing she knew nothing about weapons. She had to assume it was loaded with powder and a ball. Austin didn't appear the kind of man who kept an unloaded gun under lock and key. The only thing she knew to do was point the barrel and press the trigger. God help her, she hoped she never had to do that! She had to be careful with it so she didn't end up shooting herself.

She was going to try not to worry about stealing the money or the pistol. It wasn't that she wanted to do any of this. She had to. Austin's previous actions had predestined it.

Taking a deep breath, she hid the pistol in the folds of her skirt and calmly walked up the stairs to the deck. Three crewmen were busy working, well out of her way on the other end of the ship. Captain Hammersfield and Bradley stood at the helm, watching Austin and Jubal make their way to shore.

The captain turned to her and smiled. "Oh, Miss Worthington, come join us."

Bradley turned and looked at her but didn't speak.

She felt as if her heart would stop, it beat so fast. For a moment she wanted to back out, fearing she wasn't up to the job, but the memory of her sister flashed across her mind, removing the doubt. She spread her legs to give her body more support. Without batting an eyelash, she pulled the gun from the folds of her skirt and raised it with both hands, pointing it directly at the captain's chest. Both men gasped, wide-eyed, open-mouthed.

"Miss Worthington, what are you doing?" the captain asked in a shocked tone.

Cheval remained calm. She had to. "I'm holding Austin's pistol on you."

"Ah—where did you get it?" he asked, still surprised by her actions.

"From the locked drawer in his desk. Don't make any sudden moves. It's loaded," she assured him, although she wasn't sure it was.

"Yes, I'm sure it is."

His eyes blinked, slowly, steadily. "Miss Worthington, what are you doing with Mr. Austin's pistol?"

That the gun was aimed at the captain's chest didn't go unnoticed by either man. "I intend for you to give the order to hoist the sails and head to Dover."

"You must be mad!" Bradley spoke up sharply for the first time, taking a step toward her.

Cheval swung around and pointed the pistol at Austin's brother-in-law. "I realize this pistol has only one shot and it doesn't matter to me which one of you gets it if my orders are not followed." She willed her voice and hands not to tremble. If either man saw her weaken, they'd take the advantage and test her.

"I can't do that, Miss. Austin's about to reach shore. We can't get word to him."

"She knows that, Hammersfield," Bradley said. "That's what she wants."

The captain turned to Bradley. "I don't care what she wants." His gaze shifted quickly to Cheval. "Now put that gun down before you hurt someone. A woman doesn't know how to properly handle a big pistol like that."

Cheval kept her eyes and hands steady. "I know

where the trigger is. I have two fingers on it right now. That's all I need to know, and I'm prepared to squeeze it."

Bradley scoffed indignantly, then sniffed. "She's bluffing, Hammersfield. Go ahead and rush her. She won't shoot you."

The captain's eyes widened and he glanced at Bradley. "I don't trust her. If you don't think she'll shoot, you take that gun away from her."

"It's not my ship," Bradley argued. "And she's not my problem. You do something. You're the captain."

Cheval's gaze darted from one man to the other. She strove to remain calm. She couldn't let their nit-picking fluster her. And she couldn't give any indication that she would hesitate to pull that trigger. No matter what they did or said, she had to keep the pistol pointed at one of them.

"I don't have time for your bickering. Give the order to pull anchor and hoist the sails."

"The captain's right," Bradley said in a more cajoling tone. "We can't leave Austin in France. It's a hostile country. We don't know what they might do to him."

"That's not your problem. I am. Hoist the sails." She couldn't let them see what it was doing to her inside, betraying Austin like this.

"I don't think you've thought this through," said the captain. "Austin could be in real danger. I don't think you want his death on your conscience."

"No more than I want a little boy's kidnapping on my conscience. I don't think the French will

Wish You Were Here?

You can be, every month, with Zebra Historical Romance Novels.

AND TO GET YOU STARTED, ALLOW US TO SEND YOU

4 Historical Romances Free

A $19.96 VALUE!

With absolutely no obligation to buy anything.

YOU'RE GOING TO LOVE GETTING
4 FREE BOOKS

These books worth almost $20, are yours without cost or obligation
when you fill out and mail this certificate.

*(If the certificate is missing below, write to: Zebra Home Subscription Service, Inc.,
120 Brighton Road, P.O. Box 5214, Clifton, New Jersey 07015-5214*

Complete and mail this card to receive 4 Free books!

Yes! Please send me 4 Zebra Historical Romances without cost or obligation. I understand that each month thereafter I will be able to preview 4 new Zebra Historical Romances FREE for 10 days. Then, if I should decide to keep them, I will pay the money-saving preferred publisher's price of just $4.00 each...a total of $16. That's almost $4 less than the publisher's price. (A nominal shipping and handling charge of $1.50 per shipment will be added.) I may return any shipment within 10 days and owe nothing, and I may cancel this subscription at any time. The 4 FREE books will be mine to keep in any case.

Name _____

Address _____ Apt. _____

City _____ State _____ Zip _____

Telephone ( ) _____

Signature _____ LP0195
(If under 18, parent or guardian must sign.)

harm a man who was trying to deliver Napoleon's nephew to his father."

"What!" Bradley's mouth gaped again.

Too late, Cheval realized her mistake. Bradley didn't know who Bo was, but she couldn't let that distract her. "I assumed you knew. Bo is the son of Jerome Bonaparte and Betsy Patterson."

"Damnation! The fool's in worse trouble than I thought. The Pattersons are the wealthiest family in Baltimore. Hellfire! I'll never get him out of this."

"Miss Cheval! Miss Cheval!"

Cheval's heart jumped up in her throat as she heard Bo calling to her. She glanced aside long enough to see Bo running toward her. Out of the corner of her eye she saw the captain make a move toward her. She sidestepped toward Bo. Hammersfield's hand grazed her arm, but he couldn't hold on. Bo grabbed her around the legs and held on tight.

"Bo, come here to me," the captain called.

"Stay were you are, Bo." Cheval pointed the pistol at the captain again. "I swear I'll shoot you next time, captain. Now, you're wasting my time and I'm getting edgy. Give the order to sail." Her voice was trembling as bad as her hands. A roaring started in her ears. Fear forced her to remain calm.

"Are you going to listen to her?" Bradley asked the captain before turning back to Cheval. "I want to return as soon as possible, too, but I don't want to leave Austin at the mercy of the French. My

God, there's a war going on. Napoleon is angry with everyone. Austin could get killed!"

Bradley's earnest pleadings caused her to reconsider leaving Austin, but only for a moment. Just as quickly, she remembered a little boy who wasn't ready to be separated from his mother. Maybe years from now when Bo was a young man, but not now. She had to forsake Austin and leave him in France. She had the chance to return Bo. She had to do it. She had to right Austin's wrong.

Feeling Bo's little arms around her legs, Cheval said, "Sail."

"You have nerve holding that gun on everyone as if you'd really use it. I guess I'm going to have to take the damn gun away from her and tell Austin—"

Tired of his whining, Cheval pulled back the hammer and cut Bradley off in mid-sentence. The click sounded all over the ship. Even the men on the other end of the deck had heard Bo and had turned to watch them.

"Don't think for a moment I won't use this. I suggest you don't try my patience or you won't live to see your wife again. I don't intend for anything to stop me from getting this little boy back to his mother."

"I don't believe you'll pull that trigger."

"Don't dare tempt me, Mr. Thornhill. You haven't given me any reason to be kind to you or to like you, and I don't. I won't blink an eye at pulling this trigger if you come near me."

Bradley's freckles seemed to become one big red

spot as a flaming blush crept up his neck and fused his cheeks. "You don't know anything about guns."

"Don't be stupid, Bradley," the captain said in an irritated voice. "How much does she have to know when her trembling fingers are on the trigger? We can't chance rushing her and possibly hurting that boy." He turned to the men who stood behind them and yelled, "Let the sails fly!"

Three French soldiers met Austin and Jubal with muskets drawn as they pulled the small boat up on shore. Austin knew they would be waiting. He'd seen one of the men signal to shore. The soldiers looked over-dressed in their fancy red coats and blue breeches. Their tricorn hats had ridiculously long plumes sticking out the right side.

Austin was tired from the rowing, ill from what he was about to do, and didn't take kindly to being greeted with three muskets pointed at his chest.

"Your ship flies Napoleon's flag," the ranking officer said in broken English. "Who are you?"

Austin didn't want to give his name. "I'm here as an emissary to meet a Monsieur Alexander Le Camus for Napoleon's brother, King Jerome Bonaparte of Westphalia."

"The dark man?" the officer said, pointing his musket toward Jubal.

"He is my manservant. He will cause no trouble. I'm responsible for him."

"Where are you to meet Monsieur Le Camus?"

"*l'Aueerge Guerin,*" Austin said.

"We know where it is. We will escort you."

Austin nodded and started to follow the Frenchman when Jubal said, "Mr. Radcliffe, look."

Austin kept on walking. "We don't have time to look at anything right now, Jubal. I'm in a hell of a hurry to get this over with."

"I think you're going to want to see this. Somebody has hoisted the sails on *Aloof.*"

Austin felt as if a ball had hit him in the chest. Spinning around on the rocky shore he looked out over the water. All of *Aloof's* three sails were flying."

"Damn," he whispered to himself. "What in the hell is Hammersfield doing?"

"I don't know. But I think she's moving, sir," Jubal said.

Fear like he'd never known rose up so fast in his chest that he choked. "No!" Austin shouted.

His blood pumped. He started running back toward the water. His booted feet caught in the rocky sand and he staggered. Muscles jerked in his legs, he stretched them so far. In a near panic, he ran past their small boat and splashed into the cold water.

When the water reached his chest he started swimming with all his might. The muscles in his arms and legs burned. His lungs ached for him to slow down. Fear kept him going.

Two hundred meters out he stopped and tread water, so tired he could hardly keep his body afloat. He looked at *Aloof.* She was sailing away.

The two French ships flanked her as she maneuvered out of the shallow water heading west.

"No, goddammit! Come back!" he shouted to the ship as his fist hit the water, splashing his face with the chilling wetness.

"Bradley must have found your other gun."

Austin didn't know that Jubal had followed him into the icy water until he spoke those words. He turned and looked at his friend. Water clung to his tightly curled hair. His lips had already turned a deep purplish-blue from the chilling water. But Austin didn't feel the cold.

"It's not Bradley. Dammit!" He hit the water with his open palm. "It's Cheval."

Part Two

The Return

Twelve

Jubal's eyes widened. "Miss Worthington? No, sir." Jubal shook his head as his arms moved at his side, keeping him afloat. "She doesn't know how to do anything like that."

"Yes, dammit, it's Cheval." A chill shook Austin as his arms plowed through the cold water and his legs kicked beneath him.

"She's going to get herself and everybody else killed. The French gunboats are following her. They're going to fire on *Aloof!*"

"No. Not as long as that flag is raised. Besides, Hammersfield should start pulling away from the other ships any minute now. And they'll turn around and come back when they see she's leaving the coastline."

"Why is she leaving us? What is she going to do?"

"What she's going to do is get herself thrown in prison for the rest of her life." Austin groaned inwardly as he said the damning words aloud.

"Prison, sir?" Jubal's words trembled and his teeth started chattering as he continued to tread the icy water.

"Jubal, she's headed back to Baltimore to return Bo to his mother. Dammit, doesn't she know that if she returns Bo they'll assume she was party to his kidnapping and throw her in jail? Dammit. Goddammit!" He slapped the water with his fist for the third time.

What in the hell was he going to do? There was no way on earth he could make it back to Baltimore before she did, even if he stole one of Napoleon's ships and started today. The larger ships wouldn't outrun *Aloof*. How could he have misjudged her?

"You're cold, sir? Let's go back to shore."

Austin kept his eyes on his fast-fading ship. Yes, he was cold, and there was a knot the size of a cannonball in his stomach. He'd never be warm until he held Cheval in his arms again. And that wasn't likely to happen. She obviously didn't know it, but she was sailing her way to life in prison.

Austin sipped the French wine. It was dark and heavy, befitting his mood. Jubal was having a meal in the back room of the inn, but Austin refused to eat. He couldn't think about food until Le Camus arrived and he'd secured passage on a ship away from France and back to America.

He'd wring Cheval's beautiful little neck, if he were ever fortunate enough to see her again, for this foolhardy stunt. Thank God he'd had the good sense to put a few coins in his pocket. Otherwise he and Jubal would still be wearing wet clothes.

He'd felt more kindly toward the French soldiers when he and Jubal had come out of the water and the men hustled them to a nearby cafe. The soldiers were able to tell the innkeeper that they needed dry clothes and a bed for the night.

Now he waited for Le Camus.

The room was shadowed by dim, smoky light. A snub of a candle burned on his table and all the others had burned equally low. Only three other men, including the owner, were in the low-ceilinged room. They talked in quiet tones, for which he was glad. He really didn't want to be disturbed by gaming and raucous behavior.

There was no use lying to himself: Austin had mixed feelings about what Cheval had done. A part of him wanted to swear at her and call her a fool and demand she get what she deserved for her damning actions, while the other part of him admired her courage and strength to take on Hammersfield and the French Navy in her determination to get Bo back to Betsy Patterson.

He also had to admit that it stung to think that she'd duped him. He'd had complete trust in her, never once suspecting she'd attempt something like this. That was not an easy thing to admit to himself.

When he got back to Baltimore, he'd have to find a way to convince the authorities that Cheval had nothing to do with the kidnapping; but since she would be the one returning the child, he wasn't sure he could talk them into believing she was completely innocent.

Another thought bothered him. One that excited, yet angered, him. He had a feeling that Cheval wouldn't mention his name when she returned Bo. It was crazy, he knew. She detested what he'd done; she'd made that clear numerous times. Still, he had the feeling she'd keep his name out of the story. She might not have admitted it to herself, but he knew she had strong feelings for him. He not only sensed, he felt it every time she looked at him.

He sipped the wine again.

"I can't believe you got him all the way here only to lose him after you rowed to shore. Fool, why didn't you bring him with you?"

The tone of the sharp European accent brought Austin to his feet in a flash. He stared into the eyes of a man he recognized immediately. Alexander Le Camus looked just like his brother, Auguste, the one who'd set up this damn kidnapping.

Austin's eyes narrowed. He leaned toward the man. "I don't like your tone. Change it or I'll change it for you."

The Frenchman's ruffled sleeve fanned the air as he made a motion to dismiss Austin's threat. "You're right, of course. As you can understand, I'm highly agitated by this news."

"I'm not crazy about it myself."

"Sit down. Finish your wine." Le Camus pointed to Austin's chair, then seated himself on the opposite chair. "How did it happen that your men disobeyed your orders and sailed without you?"

There was no way Austin would tell this man about Cheval in case the French decided to seek revenge for this action. "Who knows what makes a man turn on his master? Obviously, someone on board figured out who Bo was and decided he could make quick money by returning the boy to his mother." His lie sounded convincing to his own ears.

"That could be, but it might be they are seeking a ransom. King Jerome is a wealthy and powerful man. He could pay much for his child."

Austin nodded, he might as well go with the idea since Le Camus had brought it up. "If the kidnappers are after a ransom, you'll know within a couple of weeks."

"This is going to bring such sorrow to all of Westphalia. King Jerome has dreamed of being united with his son. Now, I must give him the news of this delay."

Austin set up straighter. "Delay? I don't think so. Not if you're thinking of counting me in those plans. My part in this scheme is over. No doubt I'll spend the rest of my life rotting in prison because I thought to honor my debt to Jerome."

"King Jerome," the Frenchman reminded him in a stiff voice. "Your vow was to do him a favor in likeness to the one he did for you."

"And I did." Austin rose and leaned over the table. "I was asked to bring the boy to France. I did. It was beyond my control that someone else kidnapped him from me the hour I arrived."

"We never saw Bo. We don't know that you even brought him."

"Have I not better things to do with my time and my ship for such a fool's errand as to sail to France without the boy? Tell *King* Jerome I consider my debt to him paid. If he wants to try to recapture his son, he'll have to find another lackey. Now, tell me where I can find a ship to take me back to America?"

Cheval felt like a free woman as she took hold of Bo's hand and stepped out of the row boat and set foot on English soil. She was surprised at how quickly they'd made the trip to England. By the time Captain Hammersfield dropped anchor, Cheval had the rest of her plan firmly in place.

The short trip to shore had been choppy. At first she worried that Bo might be frightened or become ill so close to the water. But to her surprise, he loved the bouncing ride across the rough sea.

Vagrant wind blew wispy strands of hair across her face as she looked around the port. The sky was a murky shade of gray, hiding all traces of sunshine. The shoreline was dotted with dark buildings and piers that ran out into the water. Small and large boats were docked side by side. An ominous feeling stole over her, that same unwelcome feeling she'd had the night Mr. Muller threw her out of the tavern. There were several men around the docks. Some working, others standing around, talking. If she hurried, maybe they'd have enough time to locate a ship bound for America, and find lodging before darkness fell on the streets.

"Thank you for rowing us to shore, Robert," she said as they waded out of the ankle-deep water and onto the rocky beach.

"Yes, Miss," he said with a reluctant look in his dark brown eyes.

That he was disappointed in her behavior was evident in his expression. It wasn't easy for any of the men, she knew. No one liked having a gun pointed at them. "I'm sorry we're not parting under better circumstances, Robert. You've been a great help to me with Bo. And although it probably doesn't matter to you, we will miss you."

His eyes brightened. "No, Miss, that's not true. I will miss you, but not just yet." He looked around the area. "I think I should stay with you until you find a place for the night."

"There's no need. We'll be perfectly safe," she answered in a voice that sounded stronger than she felt.

Robert shifted awkwardly from one foot to the other. "I—I don't know why you had to leave *Aloof*, Miss. We can get you back to Baltimore faster than any other vessel. And it shouldn't take the captain more than a day or two to load supplies."

She smiled comfortingly at him. "I know all that. I simply can't trust Captain Hammersfield to take us to Baltimore rather than back to France to get Austin. Not only that, I wasn't comfortable holding that pistol on him, you know."

"I guess not." Robert settled the heels of his palms on the back of his hips and looked directly into her eyes. "I could be a big help to you with Bo, if you'd let me stay with you. I don't think Mr. Radcliffe would be happy with any of us leaving you here to find your way back to Baltimore by yourself."

"Mr. Radcliffe won't hold any of you responsible for what is only my doing. Now, it's getting late." She reached out her hand. "I'll take the satchel."

Reluctantly, Robert picked up the small case and handed it to her.

"And, Robert, please tell Austin I've taken his money and his pistol. I'll return both to his town house as soon as I can."

"I know I have no right to ask you again, Miss, but I wish you'd reconsider. I'd like to stay and help take care of you and the boy. I don't like leaving you here alone in this strange country. Begging your pardon, Miss, but I agree with the captain. Mr. Radcliffe would want one of us to stay with you. And if I don't row back to *Aloof,* they'll know I've stayed with you."

"Let him go with us," Bo spoke up for the first time as he pulled on the tail of Cheval's skirt.

"Not this time, Bo," she said without looking down at the boy. "Your offer is kind, Robert, but no. We're going to be all right. Goodbye, Robert."

With Bo holding one hand and her satchel in the other, Cheval started up the beach toward the buildings and shipping activity. Bo waved to Robert until the young man was out of sight.

Cheval was truly on her own and it was an awesome, yet intimidating feeling. At least she was in an English-speaking country. If she'd had to escape from France, it would have been more difficult. She knew very little French.

"Are we going to find Mama?" Bo asked as they walked along.

She looked down at him and smiled. "Soon, Bo. Soon." It felt wonderful to be able to say that to him. "We are away from the people who took you from your mama. Now all we have to do is find our way back home."

The gray sky made it feel colder than it actually was, especially since her feet were wet. But the pleasure she felt at having accomplished her goal of getting Bo away from Austin put a light bounce in her step. Now, all she had to do was find a ship heading for Baltimore and, with as many of the vessels as she saw lining the coastline, that should be no problem.

Cheval tensed when they passed several derelict-looking men, but when the dock-workers paid the two of them no mind, her tension eased. In the distance along the boardwalk she saw a handsomely-dressed man hurrying their way. When he drew nearer, she stopped him and asked, "Excuse me, sir, could you tell me where I can find a ticket office for passenger ships?"

He placed a finger on his lips, his mustaches twitching. "Humm—I'm in a hurry, but let's see, you go about two miles down into that area over there," he pointed with his walking stick to a group of buildings. "Then go about three streets over from the south. Yes, that should get you there. Just ask anyone once you get in the area." He tipped his hat. "Good day."

"That man wasn't kidding when he said he was in a hurry, Bo," Cheval said as she watched the older gentleman continue his fast pace. "Well, we've no time to waste either. About two miles, he said. Maybe we should take a carriage."

Cheval considered the transportation, but quickly decided she'd do well to save the money and the walk would do them good. "We should be able to walk that in no time. And we certainly need the exercise after being on that ship for so long, don't we?"

Bo nodded.

He and Cheval began their journey.

Not fifteen minutes later, Cheval wished she'd taken one of the carriages she'd seen when they'd come ashore. Now she was beginning to think the money spent would have been well worth it. What on first glance appeared to be a very safe walk into an acceptable neighborhood had turned into a seedy part of the docks. The large two- and three-story buildings rose like dark, threatening clouds. Night seemed to be descending much faster than she thought it should.

Rough and surly-looking men stood on the corners, leering at them as they passed. This was not a position she wanted Bo to be in, even though she felt sure no one would bother a woman with a small child. Still, she picked up her pace.

"I'm tired," Bo complained as he pulled on Cheval's arm, wanting her to slow down or stop.

"I know, but we have to hurry. We don't want to be caught in the dark around here. You've got to be a young man about this and keep up with me. All right? Can you do that?"

She chanced a glance down at him. His head was bobbing up and down in agreement as his short legs worked to match her longer stride. Bo had to run to keep up with her, and the satchel she carried grew heavier each minute. Cheval would have felt better if Bo had been a little bigger, a little older, if the sun had been shining to make the day brighter. If only she'd taken a carriage, she told herself time and again. There was no way the three-year-old would be any help should they be accosted by hoodlums.

At one point, she wondered if she should stop and take the pistol out of her satchel, but how could she hold to it, the satchel, and Bo? No, it would probably be best for them to hurry along and find their way to the ticket office.

A stitch developed in her side; her toes felt numb from the cold, wet shoes she wore. About every fifteen or twenty paces she had to stop and change the heavy satchel from one hand to the other, then take Bo's again.

When they finally arrived at the area the man

had pointed to, Cheval slowed her step and looked around. The streets were deserted. She was beginning to think the man had sent her in the wrong direction. They seemed to have turned away from the shipping area. She shivered and decided to take the first street to the left, hoping to find someone who could give them better directions.

Garbage and trash littered the sides of the dingy, aged buildings, giving off an offensive odor. A short distance down, Cheval realized she was in an alley, not a street. She stopped and looked down the long, narrow passageway, trying to see the end. It wasn't in sight. Maybe she'd turned too soon, she thought, or maybe the nicely dressed man hadn't known what he was talking about.

Cheval's hand tightened on Bo's when she heard footsteps behind her. Her stomach muscles knotted with fear and her throat grew tight. She wondered if she should look back or continue farther down into the labyrinth of semi-darkness. Would they fare better to try to run forward or to go back?

Suddenly a young man ran past her and stopped in front of her. Two others ran up behind her. She swung around, looking from one to the other as she backed away from them all. Fear gripped her so strongly she held her breath. What was she to do?

"Hullo there, young lady. You and the little buggar out for a stroll, are you?"

"My you're a pretty one," another man said.

Her gaze darted from one man to the next. All

three were poorly dressed and scruffy. One wore a straggly beard, but all had long, unkempt hair.

She turned to go back the way they had come, but the two young men closed the distance between them, blocking her way. Cheval squeezed Bo's hand tighter when she felt his other arm slip around her legs. She was furious with herself for getting them into this position. Why hadn't she taken the carriage? This was all her fault.

"Let us pass," she said on a breathy note, finding her voice and her courage. Bo was her responsibility. Her only thought was to take care of him.

"Listen to that, boys. She's American. Wonder what she's doing here?"

Cheval's gaze continued to dart from one to the other. Bo whimpered, but she didn't dare take her eyes off the young men.

"If you don't let us pass, I'll scream," she threatened.

All three men laughed, but one said, "I like to hear my women scream."

They laughed harder.

"Who do you think's going to hear you way down here? You're not in the heart of the city, love."

There was no talking her way out of this. She had to think of something fast if they were going to get away. She'd have no chance of getting the pistol out of her satchel. Why hadn't she taken it out when she'd had the opportunity? Why hadn't she taken the carriage? How could she have been so stupid for the sake of saving a few pennies?

Her fear was so great she couldn't breathe. "I beg you, for the child's sake, let us pass. You're frightening him."

"Then let's move the little buggar out of the way. You're the one we want."

The man standing by himself reached for Bo, but she quickly snatched him behind her. Without hesitation, Cheval tightened her grip on Bo's hand as she brought the satchel around, swinging with all her might. The case whacked the man on the side of the head with a dull sound. He fell against the wall and to the ground.

Cheval dropped the case and started to run, but one of the other men grabbed hold of her skirt and jerked her back. She stumbled and fell to the ground. Bo was torn from her grasp. She heard him scream as she landed hard, her cheek scraping the rocky dirt.

"Bo!" she cried and quickly scrambled to regain her feet. "Run!"

She was grabbed from behind and slung around. She kicked and dug her fingernails into the arms that held her. An open palm slapped her across the face. Twinkles of lights and tiny stars swam before her eyes. She fought to stay conscious.

Through her blurred vision she saw a wide board crack against the head of one of the men. He crumpled to the ground. Robert yelled and charged wide-eyed toward the man holding her, the board raised to strike.

Seeing the danger, the man shoved her to the

ground. But he wasn't quick enough. The board Robert was holding landed across his face, knocking him to the ground.

Cheval jumped to her feet and grabbed Bo's trembling hand.

"Let's get out of here!" Robert yelled as he grabbed the satchel and Bo's other hand. With the small boy between them, they fled down the dark alley to the street.

Thirteen

Austin's first step off the plank pulled a gut-wrenching cramp from him. He half-expected the authorities to be waiting for him when he placed his first foot on land. After a quick look around the docks and seeing no unusual activity, he knew something was wrong. Could it be that Cheval had somehow managed to get Bo back to the Patterson house without being caught? That seemed impossible.

What then? Had he somehow managed to make it back to Baltimore before Cheval? That appeared more likely. But damn! There was still another explanation that he wouldn't allow himself to even think about right now. He'd just keep telling himself that Cheval and Bo were safe.

He wasn't happy he'd underestimated Cheval. He'd never expected she'd try something so stupid. But he should have. All the signs had been there. He had been too caught up in his feelings for her and so he'd missed what she was planning.

And even though he worried about her, he admired her for sticking to what she believed to be right. Just as he had to take Bo to France for

Jerome, Cheval had to kidnap Bo from him and risk their lives.

A man carrying a small chest on his shoulder walked by.

"Excuse me," Austin said, stopping the stranger. "Can you tell me if the ship *Aloof* arrived?"

The bearded man squinted against the spring sunlight. "Aye, I've heard she's in," he said, then kept on walking.

Austin decided the best thing to do would be to go to Bradley's office. If *Aloof* had made it back, Bradley would know what had happened to Cheval and Bo. Besides, what else was a lawyer for if not to give legal advice? He sure as hell was going to need it.

He and Jubal hailed a carriage and headed for Bradley's office. Austin noticed Jubal had been especially quiet since land had been sighted. Austin sensed a fear inside the large man.

"Everything's going to be all right, Jubal. You aren't in any trouble. Just me. Whether Cheval turned Bo in to the authorities or returned him to his mother, by now someone could have talked her into telling who took Bo to Europe."

"If she tells on you, you will go to jail."

"I know," he said without any real emotion. He really didn't think Cheval would tell about his involvement.

"I go where you go. If you go to jail, I'm not letting you go alone."

"No. I'll need you to look after Mama. I'll make sure the authorities know you had nothing to do with this, and they'll let you go. I'll have to know that someone is looking after Mama, and you're the only one I trust to take care of her."

Jubal's dark eyes searched Austin's face. "What about Miss Worthington?"

Austin swallowed hard. An ache started in his chest whenever he thought about her, which was most of the time. He didn't care what she'd done. He longed to see her. On the tiresome voyage home, he'd realized why he felt differently about her than he had about any other woman. Now he knew why he couldn't get her off his mind or out of his thoughts. He loved her. He wasn't exactly sure how he knew this, because he'd never been in love before. He only knew that he'd wanted her the first night he saw her. She'd haunted his dreams. It hurt knowing how much he wanted her to belong to him and that it would never be. Jerome Bonaparte had settled that. What he had done for Napoleon's brother couldn't be undone and Cheval would never understand his reasons for doing his best to fulfill that fateful vow.

When they reached Bradley's office, Austin told Jubal to wait with the carriage while he spoke to Bradley alone. As he walked up to the door, Austin remembered the last time he'd approached Bradley's office. The sun had been shining on Bradley's nameplate that day, too. He paused longer than necessary, hating to go inside, fearing he might hear Cheval was in jail.

He would have liked to believe that Cheval had

somehow managed to get Bo back to his mother
and somehow escaped without anyone knowing
about it. That was simply too unlikely for him to
accept.

Without further thought, he opened the door
and stepped inside.

"My God!" Bradley rose from the chair. "You
made it back." A big smile stretched across his
freckly face. He moved from behind his desk and
met Austin with outstretched hand. They shook
hands and Bradley clapped Austin on the shoulder with the other. A wide pleasant smile lit his
face. "Damn, it's good to see you. I've worried
about you day and night, wondering if those
French bastards would let you leave or even if
they'd let you live seeing how you lost possession
of the treasure you carried to them."

Bradley knew how to make a man feel worse.
"Cheval, where is she?"

"Oh, *her*." The smile dropped quickly from his
face. "I might have known she'd be your first concern. Not how are you, Bradley? Or how is Winifred, who, by the way, gave birth to my son while
I was on that disastrous fool's errand. No, you
don't even bother to ask about your dear mother,
who has been worried sick about you. You have
to ask about that little twit who almost got all of
us killed trying to escape with the little boy *you*
helped kidnap."

Angered by Bradley's choice of words, Austin
grabbed Bradley by the lapels and jerked him up
close to his nose. "Stop the prattling, Bradley. I've

got eyes. I can see that you're doing fine, and I assume that if you are, then Winifred and Mama are doing all right, too, or you wouldn't be in your office greeting me with a smile. You'd be tending them or at least be worried. Now, tell me where the devil are Cheval and Bo?"

Bradley turned his head away from Austin's glare in a show of how he felt about Austin's distasteful aggression. "I don't know where they are."

Austin's hand tightened on Bradley's coat. His insides trembled with fear for Cheval's safety. "You left France with her. You'd better come up with a better answer than that."

"As far as I know, she's in no danger. I'll tell you what little I know if you'll let go of me. You're wrinkling my jacket."

Realizing his frustration had gotten the better of him, Austin let him go and stepped away, calming himself. What was he doing trying to manhandle Bradley? He should be ashamed of himself, but in truth, he was desperate for news of Cheval.

"I don't know where she is, and that's the truth."

"Bradley." His voice was low and meaningful. "I have no patience left."

"You don't know what that little hellion put us through, Austin. She held a gun on us, for God's sake."

"Dammit, Bradley, just start at the beginning and tell me what happened."

"All right, but let me fix us a drink. You look like you could use one, too."

Bradley walked over to the sideboard and poured a small amount of brandy into two glasses. "It all happened about the time you reached shore. As you know, Hammersfield and I were on deck watching you. We turned around and *she* stood there with a pistol—your pistol, might I add—pointed directly at the captain's chest. Later we found out she had broken the lock on your desk and stolen the gun and your money pouch. Real lady, that one." He handed Austin the drink.

"Cut the snide remarks and get on with what happened and where the hell she is." Austin took a generous swallow of the strong liquid, accepting its burning sensations.

"Well, you can imagine, can't you? I told Hammersfield she wouldn't shoot him, but he wouldn't chance rushing her. I think he really believed she'd pull the trigger. That weak-knee ninny of a captain did exactly as she asked and sailed away to England. Hammersfield can give you the details as to where. Once there, she departed with that little boy and the cabin boy—Robert. We resupplied the ship and set sail for Baltimore. The captain decided it would be better to sail back here rather than risk all our lives trying to get back to France. He knew you could handle yourself. I arrived home two weeks after my son, Bradley *Austin* Thornhill was born." He ended the sentence with a sniff.

Austin made no comment about the arrival of his namesake. "What happened to Cheval?"

"We left her in England, of course."

Damn! Austin couldn't believe Bradley and Hammersfield would leave her. If anything had happened to her, he'd smash both their faces.

"I have no idea where. She had the gun, so she did the talking. She insisted Robert be the only one to row her and the boy to shore. She said she didn't trust Hammersfield to take her back to Baltimore and she'd find her own passage back. Hammersfield took the cabin boy aside and told him to follow her and find out where she went and what ship she booked passage so we could tell you. We waited a week. The youngster never came back. The captain and some of the crew asked around the docks, but no one remembered seeing a young woman with a boy."

"I don't believe this. He just left her." His anger grew. His hand tightened around the glass, till he thought it would break. "And you—you let Hammersfield leave without finding out what had happened to them?"

Bradley's face reddened. "No, we did try to find out. The captain and his men walked the docks for two days trying to learn something about her after—" He stopped short.

Austin knew immediately Bradley had just said more than he wanted to. "After what?"

"Nothing," he said quietly and went back to his chair and sat down.

Setting down the empty glass, Austin placed

both hands on the desk and leaned toward his brother-in-law. "Tell me now."

"Well." A vein worked in Bradley's throat. His face flamed red. "There was a double murder down at the docks the afternoon Cheval arrived."

For a moment Austin thought he was going to be sick from fear. He felt the color drain from his face. "A woman?" he asked hoarsely.

"Oh, god no! Two young men. Both their heads bashed in from a board or something like that. Hammersfield didn't want to leave but finally decided she must have booked passage immediately. There was a ship that left only hours after she arrived, and the three of them could have gotten on it immediately. It set sail that very night, but it was going by away of some islands. Guadeloupe and Martinique, I think. In any case, if that's what happened to them, it would take them longer to get here than it did us, even with waiting the week. I can only assume that's what happened because she's not here."

Austin said a silent prayer that she was on that ship. "Didn't you wonder why Robert never came back?"

"Of course we did," Bradley defended. "The captain worried enough for all of us. He finally decided Robert must have talked her into letting him go with her and help her with Bo. The captain had given him some money. He might have had enough to pay his fare."

He was sick with worry, and the brandy lay heavily on Austin's stomach. He straightened.

"You should have never let her off the ship in England."

"Begging your pardon, Austin, but there was the little matter of her having the pistol. With Bo by her side, none of the men would have chanced trying to get it away from her."

"The gun in my desk wasn't loaded, and I doubt Cheval knew how to load it."

Bradley blanched white, causing his freckles to stand out. "She must have loaded it. I'm sure she said it was loaded. Hammersfield thought it was loaded, too."

Austin shook his head. What would he do if Cheval didn't arrive in Baltimore soon? He'd have to sail to England himself. "What's the scuttlebutt on Bo?"

"Oh, that's an interesting bit of news. My word, Austin, what were you thinking to get mixed up with Napoleon's brother?"

"Cut the lecture," Austin snapped, "and tell me the news."

"That's just it—there is none."

"What do you mean? How did you find out Bo was Jerome's son if not by news of the kidnapping?"

"Oh, that, well, *she* let it slip when she took over the ship. When we returned, the papers had no mention of a kidnapping. I made discreet inquiries about Bo and found that the word is out that the boy and his mother have an illness that's keeping them in bed most of the spring. The family is afraid it might be contagious, so they're not allowing visitors."

Something close to relief settled over Austin for a moment. "So they've decided to hide the kidnapping from the world until they see whether or not the child shows up in Jerome's custody." Austin ran both hands through his hair and sighed.

"Or until they receive a ransom note. Really, Austin, you outdid yourself this time. Kidnapping Betsy Patterson's son and taking him to France. My God—you are an American!"

"I'm also a man of my word. And, I've had enough lectures about it. Damn it, I wish I knew for sure Cheval had made it onto that ship."

"I think it's safe to assume she made the ship that was on its way out of port."

Bradley sounded more confident than Austin felt.

"What you need to worry about," Bradley continued, "is how you'll defend yourself if she returns and tells the authorities you are the one who left the country with Bo."

Austin thought back to the day she'd told him she wouldn't turn him in to the police. He'd believed her. "I'm not worried about me. I'm worried she'll try to return Bo by herself and the authorities will arrest her as an accomplice."

"If she tells on you, you'll go to prison. You know that, don't you?" Bradley's voice was serious.

"I know. I knew there was a possibility I'd be caught when I agreed to do this. The important thing is that Cheval doesn't suffer from this in any way."

"Well, that's enough about this for now. We'll talk more about it after dinner, after you've had time to digest what I've told you. A good meal will make you feel better, no doubt. That ship had the worst food I've ever tried to eat. Besides, your sister will be happy to see you. Say you'll stay."

Austin didn't want to believe any harm had come to Cheval. He couldn't. He'd give her a week. If she hadn't arrived by then, he'd go to England and look for himself. He wouldn't rest until he'd found her.

"All right, I'll stay for dinner, but I need to go out and tell Jubal to go on to the town house."

"I'll tell cook to prepare another place at the table and send word to Winifred we'll be having a special guest for dinner." Bradley paused. "But after dinner, Austin, we need to do some serious talking about what you did and how we'll counter it when and if Cheval returns with Bo."

Cold eyes stared at Bradley. "There is no 'if.' She'll return."

Austin walked out to where Jubal stood beside the carriage talking with the driver.

"Jubal, Cheval isn't here. It's a long story and I won't get into it right now. I want you to go on to the town house and eat and rest. I'll be there later. Then we'll make plans. We'll need to watch the docks twenty-four hours a day, checking every ship that comes in. I'll take the time to go and visit Mama for two days, then I'll be back to take up watch with you. We've got to stop Cheval before she does something stupid like try to give Bo back to his mother."

"You're not going to try to take him back to France again, are you?"

"No. But there are safer ways of getting Bo back to his mother than walking in and saying here he is. We'll talk about them after I see Mama tomorrow. She needs to know I'm safe. In the meantime, I want you to meet every ship that comes into the harbor. If Cheval and Bo are on it, I want you to take them directly to the town house and keep them there until I return."

"Yes, sir."

Austin paid the driver and watched him drive Jubal away.

Damn, he was worried about Cheval. He'd never forgive himself if anything had happened to her. He wanted to hold her again. He wanted to talk to her. He wanted to love her.

"And you think my new grandchild resembles Bradley, not Winifred? Why?" Beatrice asked her son as they sat in the reading parlor of the Radcliffe's country estate.

"He had that pink, reddish cast to his skin that Bradley always has."

"Oh, no Austin, he definitely favored Winifred with all that dark hair on his head. And . . ."

Austin only halfway listened to his mother. He was happy his sister had a baby, but he didn't want to talk about the little fellow. In fact the country house was the last place he wanted to be right now. But he had had to let his mother know he'd returned safely and spend some time with her.

As soon as dinner was over, he'd ride back into town and join Jubal down at the docks watching every ship, praying for Cheval's safe and quick return. If what Bradley and Hammersfield had suspected were true, that she was on a ship returning via the islands, Cheval should be arriving any day.

Right now he wanted to think about Cheval. He remembered the night he had held her in his arms and kissed her and how she had responded so lovingly. He remembered how soft her cheeks were, how sweet her mouth, how firm her breasts. He remembered each little contented sound she had made as he had drawn her up close to his chest. He—

"Austin, dear, I'm happy to see you and that you've come for dinner, but I don't feel you are really with me. Something *or* someone else is on your mind. You're distracted."

Glancing up from the half-empty glass he'd been staring into, Austin put a smile on his face and looked at his mother. He wouldn't be able to enjoy anyone's company until he knew that Cheval was safe. He'd not wait more than a week for her to return before he'd set sail for England.

"Mama. You're right. I've been gone a long time, and I should give you my undivided attention." But how could he when he was worried to death about Cheval? He couldn't get her off his mind.

Beatrice brushed her skirt in an unhurried fashion before acknowledging Austin's comment. "What's troubling you? Does it have anything to do with the sudden voyage you just returned from? And I never did get a good explanation as to why Bradley accompanied you at the last minute. That was strange."

Austin hesitated, rubbing his chin. The clock chimed five o'clock from the hallway where it stood by the fireplace. Two more hours before dinner would be served.

"I really can't get into all that, Mama. What Bradley told you was the truth. I was making an emergency trip to Europe for a friend, and Bradley came on board to get some details from me and fell asleep in my cabin waiting for me. By the time he awakened, we were too far out to sea to return."

"Then there has to be more to your long face than that," Beatrice offered. "It must be a woman causing your dour expression."

He chuckled for the first time in weeks. His mother was sharp.

"How can you tell a woman has anything to do with what has me preoccupied?" he asked, trying to make his mother happy by taking more of an interest in the conversation. "It could be business."

The pleased smile on his mother's lips told him she was happy with his response. "It's not business. I see it in your eyes. They have a sparkle that hasn't been there before, even though your expression is one of worry. Things aren't going well between the two of you, I see. Who is she?"

Seeing no harm in discussing Cheval with his mother he said, "Cheval Worthington."

Beatrice put a finger to her lips and pondered. "I don't recognize that name. Do we know her family?"

"No. She comes from a good family, although there's no money there. She's a governess."

"Oh." Beatrice's eyes blinked rapidly, and her pale cheeks flushed a shade of claret. "Well, I see." She touched her hand to the chignon at the back of her head. "I mean, I guess the important thing is that she comes from a good family." She looked down at her glass of sherry, composing herself, before turning her face to Austin again. "After all, you have enough money. You don't really need a dowry, do you? Heavens knows what you'll do with all the money you and your father made in ship building anyway."

His mother's reaction didn't surprise him at all. It was only natural for her to want him to marry a woman in his own social and financial class. But he was proud of her for trying to remain calm about his news. He sipped his drink, wishing he knew Cheval was all right, wishing he knew where she was.

"I didn't expect you to be so generous about her lack of prosperity."

Beatrice shifted her glass from one hand to the other. "Five or six years ago, I wouldn't have been.

But I've mellowed since I lost your father. Besides, after all these years of watching you attend parties and not showing a bit of interest in any of the young belles paraded before you, I'd almost given up hope that you'd find anyone in my lifetime."

"Mama, I'm not that old. Are you rushing me?"

"Oh, heavens no. It's just that Winifred doesn't visit as often as you do. And I'd like to think that if you married, you and your family would spend more time here."

Austin felt a twinge of guilt. No doubt his mother became lonely at times with only her servants to talk to. It's true he could have married years ago, but he was waiting for just the right woman before he considered settling down. Cheval was the woman he wanted. The trouble was that she didn't want him because of what he'd done for Jerome. But he wasn't going to let that keep him from trying to win her hand in marriage.

Still flustered, Beatrice asked, "Do you think you've found someone, dear?"

Austin nodded, remembering Cheval's lips upon his. He wanted to know that she was all right. His insides twisted at the thought of not finding her safe. He was angry at himself for not realizing her intentions. He'd been too besotted by the way she made him feel to see that she was making her own plans.

"Did this young woman, Cheval, have anything to do with your taking the voyage? Were you following her or was she with you? What does she look like? Who—"

"Mama, please," Austin held up his hand. "One question at a time, and don't expect them all to be answered. I'm not sure I'm ready to talk about her in any detail."

"Then tell me what makes her so special that she's caught your eye."

He remembered their fiery kisses and passionate embrace. How could he tell his mother that his whole body burned like liquid fire when he touched Cheval. "She's beautiful, circumspect, intelligent—"

"Don't give me that runaround," Beatrice interrupted with a smile. "Every young woman you have danced with at all the parties you've attended these past fifteen years has been beautiful and circumspect. And I don't think intelligence is that important."

He laughed again, before finishing off his drink. "Take my word for it, Mama. Intelligence counts for a lot to me. Cheval's independent and honorable, too. That sets her apart from other women. Like me, she has a strong sense of what's right and wrong and is willing to fight for what she believes in." He turned somber. "I don't know what it is. There's something about her. It's almost as if she's bewitched me. I can't explain it. She's different, special."

"Then what's the problem? Bring her here and let me meet her."

He wiped his brow with the palm of his hand. "That's not possible right now. Some things have happened, important things. Things I can't discuss. We might never get together. I only know that I wanted to be with her the first time I saw her. That hasn't changed."

"And?"

He questioned her with his eyes. "And what?"

"How does she feel about you?"

Should he be truthful? Why not. "Therein lies the biggest problem."

She looked at him with that soft, understanding expression that only a mother could give her son. "Can I help?"

"Rest assured, if I find a way you can be of assistance, I won't hesitate to ask you."

Beatrice reached over and placed her glass on the table by the lamp. "Can you tell me what it is that separates the two of you?"

He couldn't tell his mother about Bo. "Because of something that happened, Cheval lost her respect for me and she thinks I have no honor."

His mother's face turned serious. "I can't believe anyone would doubt your honor."

"It's a story I really don't want to get into, Mama."

She reached over and covered his hand with hers. "All right; but Austin, can you love a woman who'll deny you respect and honor?"

Austin glanced at her affectionately, then looked at the painting of his father that hung over the mantel. His parents had had a good marriage rooted in trust and mutual respect. Austin rose from his chair and walked over to the fireplace.

At last he turned to his mother and admitted, "I've wondered about that myself?"

"And?"

"I understand why she feels the way she does."

"Is that enough?"

"I don't know."

Fourteen

Tired and not feeling well, Cheval stood on deck of the *Packard* and rubbed the back of her neck as she watched their approach to Baltimore Harbor. It was the most beautiful sight she'd ever seen. There were many times on the voyage she'd wondered if they'd make it home.

The hot sunshine was buffered by the cool May breeze that whipped at her cheeks and hair. White, puffy clouds dotted the light-blue sky. Leaning a hip against the railing, she kept her gaze riveted to the shoreline.

On the long voyage back to America, it had been easy to tell herself she'd deal with getting Bo back to his mother when land was in sight. That time had come. There was no use telling herself she was too tired to think about it. She had no choice.

The best plan seemed to be for her to take Bo to police headquarters and send him inside by himself. As soon as he told them his name, they'd return Bo to his mother. If she took him to his mother or the police, they would ask questions she didn't want to answer. What Austin had done wasn't right, but she'd never tell on him.

There was cause to worry, too, that Bo might be able to tell them enough to make them suspicious of Austin. Not only did he know her first name, he knew Jubal's—and Robert's, too. Her name and Robert's were common. But if Bo told them about a large Negro man named Jubal, that could be enough information to send the police straight to Austin's door.

She glanced a few feet away where Bo played checkers with a dark-haired boy who, with his parents, had sailed with them on the journey back to America. Having the older child as a playmate to Bo had been a life-saver for both of them. The two months she and Bo had spent traveling together on ships showed in their dispositions. Both were ill-tempered and teary-eyed at times. Even Robert had failed to produce his friendly smile on occasions when Bo got fussy. She didn't know how she would have made it without the young man to help her.

Cheval sighed and watched the buildings get closer. It seemed so long ago that they'd left England. The trip through the Caribbean waters and stops at two islands had added fifteen days to their voyage.

Turning her face back into the wind, Cheval thought of Austin. It staggered her when she thought about how much she'd missed him during the past month. She not only missed him as a friend, a comforter, and a protector, she missed him as a lover. And mostly, she had to admit to herself, she thought of him as a lover.

When she lay in her bunk at night with Bo's little body snuggled next to her back, Austin was the one she thought about, dreamed about, longed for. She'd spent many sleepless nights remembering his kisses, the taste of him. Her body cried out for his touch. She wanted to know what went on beyond the kisses and caresses they'd shared on the ship that night. She wanted to know what delicious pleasures came after that, for surely it could only get better once they lay in each other's arms.

Cheval closed her eyes and breathed deeply while the sea air whipped against her cheeks and the ship slipped quietly through the dark-blue waterway.

Yes, she thought back to that stormy night when she and Austin were alone in the cabin on board *Aloof.* She remembered the comforting tone to his voice and the softly spoken words that eased her fears and calmed her. Austin had held her tenderly, yet protectively. She remembered warmth coming from his body and the thrill that rushed through her as her untutored hands discovered and explored the firm muscles in his arms, his back, and his hard chest.

Oh yes, even now she could feel the pads of his fingers on her neck as he pressed his lips to hers. His tongue in her mouth had sent ripples of desire clamoring through her. When his hands caressed her breasts, delicious little feelings of delight sprin-

kled through her. She liked the way it made her
stomach muscles contract with desires that were foreign to her, yet welcome.

And oh yes, and how could she forget how he
clutched her hair in his hands, palming it, gently
tugging on it just enough to let her know he was
the stronger of the two. It was only proper that
she put an end to the kiss, the embrace, before it
went any further, but she didn't want to.

*And oh yes, dear Austin, your touch, your taste, your
scent is still with me.*

Coming out of her daydream, Cheval's eyes fluttered open. Quickly she glanced at Bo, making
sure he was still all right, before gazing at the
harbor in the distance.

She loved Austin. Of that there was no doubt.
Maybe she had from the first time she'd seen
him in The Boar's Head Tavern. There had been
something there between them even then. She'd
felt it and so had Austin, she was sure. But whatever had developed between them could never
be.

Austin's crime against Betsy Patterson and her
own need to right his wrong would always be
between them. She loved him. She wanted him.
But would she ever be able to forgive, understand, and accept his participation in the kidnapping of a small child? It seemed impossible. As
she had told him from the very first, nothing
could justify what he had done. And nothing
would have stopped her from trying to right his
wrong. Even if she'd found it within herself to

forgive him and understand what he'd done, how could he forgive her for betraying him by returning Bo to his mother?

Her gaze centered on the landscape and she scanned it. "Oh, yes, Austin," she whispered aloud into the wind. "I love you, and I'll miss you all the days of my life."

Austin stood on shore, in the late afternoon, wind whipping a strand of hair across his face, watching the passengers slowly leaving the *Packard*. Word had it that the big ship was coming in from Martinique when she'd dropped anchor a couple of hours before.

His stomach muscles twisted into firm knots. His throat ached and tightened with fear when he thought about the real possibility of Cheval's not being aboard. He had *Aloof* ready to set sail should Cheval not be among the passengers. He'd waited long enough for her return. He'd have to sail to England and find out what had happened to her. But somehow though he felt sure she was on this ship. It was as if he sensed she was near him.

After he'd returned from visiting his mother, he'd questioned Hammersfield. The captain had told the same story Bradley had a few days before. And although Hammersfield never said it, Austin knew the older man had great admiration for Cheval for having the courage to steal his ship and force them to leave him on the beach in France.

A nerve in his eye twitched. His heartbeat increased. He spotted her at last. She wore a long cloak, and a wide-brimmed bonnet covered most of her face, but he recognized her. Bo stood by her side. He, too, was clothed in a long coat and an oversized cap that covered most of his face. Robert stayed right behind them. Relief washed over him like a cleansing waterfall. The sight of her was so sweet to his eyes, his legs almost buckled beneath him. He took a deep, steadying breath and let his eyes feast upon her approaching figure. How he'd missed her!

Even at a long distance and despite the shapeless cloak she wore, the first thing Austin noticed about her was the way she carried herself with poise and grace. She had a beauty that seemed to glow from her inner self. And even though she must have been tired from the long journey, she didn't let that keep her from holding her head high.

There was a slight swing to her shoulders and an attractive swish to the skirts of her dress as her legs carried her along. Her cloak looked soiled and wrinkled, but that didn't surprise him after the two incredible voyages she'd endured. The smile was gone from her face, but he understood that, too. She walked with impatience, obviously wanting to get where she was going quickly. Something told him she was heading directly to the authorities.

"There she is, Mr. Radcliffe."

"Don't point, Jubal. I see her."

"Sorry." The Negro lowered his arm. "What do you want me to do?"

Austin didn't take his eyes off her. He couldn't. Watching her made him sure. He needed her. He wanted her. He loved her, and he wouldn't be whole without her in his life.

"We need to intercept her before she walks too far. The fewer people who see her the better. Although the kidnapping's not in the papers yet, I'm sure the family has people stationed all over town."

"It's been more than two months now. Do you think they're still looking for the boy?"

"I'm sure." The odd thing that struck him was that he wanted Cheval to succeed in her plan. He wanted her to see that Bo was returned to his mother. But he also wanted it done in a way that would keep anyone from knowing who had been involved.

Austin dragged his gaze away from Cheval and made sure his and Jubal's post was secure behind the crates and barrels where they stood. Not more than twenty-five feet away, the carriage and driver were in place.

He turned to his trusted friend and stepped farther back behind the crates. "As soon as I grab her, you take Bo's hand and Robert and rush them to the carriage and get them inside as quickly as possible. If Cheval screams or causes any disturbance that might bring the police or anyone else to her aid, don't wait around. You know where to take them."

"Yes, sir. I know what to do."

Austin gave his attention back to the line of people filing past the crates. He tensed. Waited. The hem of her blue cloak came into view. Austin stepped in front of Cheval, picked her up in his arms and swung her around, laughing.

"I'm so glad you're home," he said loud enough for anyone passing by to hear.

The startled expression on her face told him all he needed to know. She hadn't been expecting him. He set her feet on the ground, wrapped his arms fully around her and pulled her up to his chest as he lowered his lips to hers, claiming her mouth in a passionate kiss.

Being so close to her was like stepping into heaven. The mere touch of her aroused him immediately. The kiss and embrace were supposed to catch her off guard, all for show to give Jubal time to get Bo into the carriage; but how could he not be affected by touching her, kissing her, holding her against him? He couldn't. Especially when she didn't fight him as he'd thought she would.

Like him, she instantly warmed to the power of their kiss. Her arms went around his neck; her mouth opened to receive his thrusting tongue. He couldn't get deep enough. He couldn't get enough of her. Her hands slid up the back of his neck and into his hair, sending chills of desire straight to the center of his being. He pulled her up tighter to his chest, crushing her, wanting desperately to take her into his body and to give her his.

Their kiss was hungry, their embrace desperate with neither of them breaking the contact. But somewhere in the fog of his mind, rushing past the feral feelings Cheval aroused inside him, was the snickering of laughter. They were making a spectacle of themselves, putting on a show for the dock-workers. But he didn't want to let her go. How could he let her go when she tasted so good, when she was so warm, and so receptive, when he thought he might never hold her like this again?

He tore one hand away from her back and motioned for the driver to bring the carriage closer. Because Cheval was small, he easily lifted her off the ground and started walking with her to meet the carriage. When the door swung open, he tore his lips away from Cheval's, reached down and scooped her up in the crook of his arm, and lifted her into the carriage. He quickly climbed in after her. He shut the door with a bang, and the carriage took off.

Robert and Bo sat on one side of the carriage, and he took the seat beside a surprised Cheval.

"You tricked me! How dare you do that, then throw me in this carriage as if I were a sack of potatoes?" Eyes shooting furious sparks at him, she reached for the door handle.

"Don't touch that." Austin grabbed her hand and shoved her back against the seat, pinning her there with his chest, and holding her shoulders with the palms of his hands. His gaze met hers. "I had to. I didn't want you to make a scene."

"And kissing me like that in front of Bo and Robert wasn't causing a scene?" she asked angrily as she squirmed to break his hold.

"I had to catch you off guard."

"How dare you—"

"How dare you steal my ship?" he countered as angrily as she'd spoken to him. It hurt that her kiss had been so warm and inviting and now she was talking to him as if he were a lackey. "You have no right to question anything I do."

He heard Bo whimper and knew he was frightening the little boy, but he couldn't let Cheval think she could out-maneuver him as she had Bradley and Hammersfield. She had to know that he was in control. He looked into her sparkling eyes, and the waning light of day couldn't hide the dark circles underneath her eyes. She was exhausted.

"I—I didn't steal your ship," she said breathlessly. "I merely borrowed it."

Her eyes seemed to be searching his for any sign of weakness she might use against him. "Holding men at gunpoint and forcing them to do your bidding is borrowing?"

"I—I asked the captain to return your ship to you as soon as he docked."

"And my gun and my money?" He dared not remove the fierce expression from his face even though Bo continued to whimper and he desperately wanted to take her in his arms and love her not scold her.

Her eyes softened. "Yes, I took them. I'll return
it all as soon as—" She stopped.

"As soon as what, Cheval? As soon as Bo is returned?"

Her gaze held steady on his. "Yes." Her chest
heaved.

She touched his heart, but he wasn't ready to
let her see him soften. She was warm and soft
beneath his palm. He couldn't stay angry with
her. He wanted her too badly. Bo whimpered
louder. For now he could relax. The carriage
moved along at a brisk pace, taking them to the
safety of his town house. He let go of Cheval and
sat back against the seat.

"W—what are you doing? Where are you taking
us?" She looked frantically about the carriage as
if searching for a way to get out.

Her beautiful eyes were tired, sad. Her face was
flushed. Her lips looked so pink and thoroughly
kissed that he longed to take her in his arms and
cover her lips with his again and again. He wanted
to say to hell with Bo, the police, and everything
else and take her to bed.

"My town house." He turned to Bo and Robert,
who sat looking at the two of them. The kiss and
their argument had obviously stunned more than
him and Cheval. And he had to admit that there
was something distinctly pleasing about seeing
that little boy back in Baltimore.

Although he was proud of her courage, he
couldn't condone what she'd done. It had been

foolish, dangerous. Too many things could have gone wrong.

"Hello, Bo."

The little boy moved closer to Robert and said, "Don't hurt her."

The small boy's soft whimper softened his heart. How could he hurt Cheval? He loved her. He ached to hold her and comfort her.

He swallowed and said hoarsely, "I won't hurt her." He turned to the young man. "Robert, I trust you did a good job of taking care of Miss Worthington?"

The young man's eyes widened with fear. "Yes, sir. I followed her just like the captain told me to. I had to hit a couple of men who were—"

"Robert," Cheval interrupted him. "I'm sure Mr. Radcliffe doesn't want to hear about that. And it's not necessary to tell him anything."

Austin threw a glance her way, but kept his attention on Robert. "She's wrong. I do want to hear, but you can tell me later. Report in to Captain Hammersfield first thing tomorrow morning. I'll see you're rewarded for returning them safely."

A shy smile eased across the young man's face. "Thank you, sir."

Cheval sat on the edge of the bed and gently brushed Bo's hair away from his forehead. A short candle burned on the night table, casting the room in a dim glow.

Bo slept peacefully. She allowed her fingertips

the pleasure of trailing down his soft cheek and over his chin. His chest rose and fell evenly with each breath. He was now less than two months from his fourth birthday. She'd watched him grow taller and learn how to be a friend these past weeks. She was so fond of him.

When they'd arrived at the town house, Thollie had started preparing a hot meal of roasted chicken, stewed sweet potatoes, and cornmeal gravy. After accepting that she couldn't return Bo to his mother immediately, Cheval had decided to make him as presentable as possible. While the chicken had cooked, Thollie had washed both of them a change of clothes. When the time came, she wanted to present Bo to his mother in clean clothes. She refused to believe that she'd come this far only to be stopped now.

Bo had stood as still as a tree on a windless day while Cheval clipped his long hair to an acceptable length. Then she'd filled a tub in the kitchen with warm water and given Bo a good bath, washing his hair twice and scrubbing under his fingernails. He had enjoyed the water so much, Cheval had let him stay in the tub and play long after the water had turned cold. As soon as the clothes had been washed, Thollie had taken one of Bo's nightshirts and hung it close to the cook fire so it would be dry by the time he'd finished with his bath and dinner.

It would be hard to give up the little boy, now that she'd grown so fond of him. Soon she would have to tell him goodbye. Forever. She could never be a part of his life again. In a way, she wished she could keep him.

Austin. He'd put a quick stop to her plans to take Bo directly to police headquarters. That his mother had to wait even one more night to hold her sweet son, cover his face with kisses, and know that he was all right was a torture Betsy Patterson shouldn't have to endure.

As her fingers sifted through Bo's shiny hair, she studied her predicament. She knew that Austin planned to stop her from returning Bo to his family and that he would take him back to France. Why else would he have accosted her as soon as they'd stepped off the ship? She should have known Austin would have made it home before her when she decided to board a ship that was taking the long route to America. At the time, she just wanted to get away from the dangers at the docks. If only the French soldiers had held him a bit longer!

She sighed wearily. It didn't matter how much she loved Austin and wanted to be with him, she couldn't let him take Bo back to France. Her reason for all the chances she'd taken so far was to return Bo to his mother. That, she still had to accomplish. And she knew it would be hard to do stuck in Austin's town house.

Having a few quiet minutes to herself, she pondered a plan to get Bo away from Austin. She'd just about used up all her courage, all her strength, but she couldn't let that stop her. In order to get out of the house, she had to catch Austin unawares.

She'd have to slip out of the house with Bo after Austin went to sleep.

Cheval forced her mind away from those raw feelings that plagued her and remembered events of earlier in the evening as she brushed Bo's hair away from his forehead. She was glad Austin hadn't asked her to wait and have dinner with him. She had been too tired and too dirty to sit at anyone's table. Besides, she hadn't seen him since Thollie had met them at the door and he had given his housekeeper instructions for the hot meal and baths. She thought he'd left, but Thollie had told her he was in his office catching up on his paperwork.

She'd noticed that Jubal was stationed at the back door when she'd thrown out Bo's wash water. When the time came, the front door would be the one she'd have to use even though it was closest to the stairs. She shuddered inwardly at the thought of slipping out. She was tired of plotting and planning escapes, but what else could she do?

For more than one reason, Cheval had lingered over her own time in the washtub, soaping her hair several times and rinsing it thoroughly before she finished. She knew the time would come when Austin would seek her out and want to talk to her. He was simply giving her time to eat, wash, and get Bo put to bed. But what could they say to each other that hadn't already been said? She thought Bo belonged with his mother and he believed his father had rights.

Thollie had brought her a nightgown and robe

and when she'd questioned the housekeeper about it, Thollie had told her it was Austin's mother's. Beatrice hadn't visited the town house in more than a year, but Austin always kept clothes available for her should she ever come to town and discover she had to stay overnight. Even though the nightgown was a little too tight and too short, she didn't care. The material was soft, fresh, and clean.

Cheval squeezed her eyes shut for a moment. Her head and her heart were heavy. There was no way she could have prepared herself for the rush of emotion that had flooded her when Austin had picked her up in his arms, swung her around, and kissed her so passionately. She should have immediately screamed, or kicked, or run, something. But no, her body and her mind had betrayed her. She'd hungered after his touch, his embrace, his kisses so many nights that she hadn't been able to deny herself. She hadn't meant to kiss him so hard, so hungrily, as if she needed his touch or his taste to breathe. But those few moments had felt wonderful. Wonderful. How could she not have responded to him when she loved him so completely? And why, after all that had happened, did she still want to be in his arms, in his bed? His bed. Did she dare let herself think about that possibility?

She hadn't come to her senses until he'd deposited her in the carriage. Then, when she'd realized what had happened, she'd become angry with herself for not realizing Austin was tricking her and angry with Austin for allowing the kiss to become so heated.

All Austin had to do was touch her, and she was lost to the magic of his embrace, forgetting everything and clinging only to him. She sensed the feeling was mutual. It appeared she had as much power over him as he her.

It pained her to even think about it, but she would be forced once more to take Bo away from him. No matter how much it would hurt her.

Austin wouldn't take Bo to France again. She'd make sure of that. She smiled at the sleeping Bo and reached over and kissed his silky, soft cheek. He stirred, rubbed his nose, and settled back down to his sleep.

Her stomach muscles tightened as she watched Bo. Their only chance of escape was stealing away in the night. And in order to do that, she had to wait until Austin was asleep.

Cheval was acutely aware of possible flaws in her plan. Jubal blocked the door. Austin might not go to sleep; then there was the possibility that she might fall asleep herself. She was so tired from the journey, it would be a risky thing for her to lie down on the bed. Her body not only craved Austin's touch, she craved sleep and rest as well. But she couldn't wait until morning. By then it might be too late for Bo.

"Cheval."

Her hand stilled. She turned and looked at Austin standing so tall, so handsome, so proudly in the doorway. *Oh, how she'd missed him. Oh, how she wanted to rush into his embrace.*

His gaze raked down her face, over the rise and fall of her breasts and back again to her face, awakening flames of desire within her.

"We need to talk," he said.

Fifteen

Cheval knew what she wanted and it wasn't to talk.

No, tonight she didn't want to talk. She didn't want to hear his excuses for taking Bo back to France to be with his father. Looking into his eyes, she knew that the only thing she wanted from Austin tonight was his touch, his kisses, his love. If she denied them this one chance to be together, she knew she'd regret it the rest of her life. He might forgive her for taking Bo away from him once, but never if she did it twice.

"Not in here. We may wake Bo." She paused to catch her breath. Her heartbeat was hammering so fast it frightened her. Her stomach jumped. There was no more time to think about what she was going to do. Tomorrow Austin would be lost to her forever, so why shouldn't she love him tonight?

"Let's go to your room."

Before she could give herself time to back out, she hurried past him and forged her way down the hallway and into Austin's room. She stopped by the foot of his bed, grabbing hold of the cannonball bed post. She leaned against it, letting the wood take all her weight as her gaze quickly scanned the semi-dark room.

A large lump formed in her throat. She felt weak with fear that he might reject her. Didn't he know how her body yearned for him? Did he know how much she wanted to be with him? Could he feel what was burning inside her?

Austin stopped in the doorway and watched her. A shaft of bright light from the hallway lamps silhouetted his body, making it difficult for her to see his features clearly, but she didn't miss the questioning look on his face that caused a wrinkle to appear on his forehead. From his eyes, from his expression, she knew he comprehended what she was doing.

"I'm not sure this is a good idea, Cheval," he said, remaining not quite inside the boundary of his room.

"I'm not either." She hated the trembly sound to her voice.

"We can talk downstairs. Thollie has retired for the night," he said.

He was giving her the opportunity to change her mind, a way out. She appreciated that about him and for a brief moment considered it. But no. She needed tonight, and by the frantic working of the muscle in his jaw, she could tell that Austin did, too.

Cheval stood still, never taking her gaze from him. Her eyes continued to search his face. The rise and fall of his chest became more pronounced. So many emotions warred inside her. Loving Austin and wanting him. Hating what he'd done. How could she have these desirous feelings for him when she knew him to be an untrustworthy man? It confused her, worried her; but as she looked at him, she knew that for tonight she had to forget what he'd done.

The past and Bo had to be left outside that door if Austin chose to come inside and meet her halfway. There would be no room in his bed for her if she brought those nagging feelings of unease and distrust with her. If he stepped across the threshold, those had to be denied. Her love had to be unconditional.

She swallowed hard. "I'd rather stay here," she whispered softly, "if you don't mind."

After a moment, after his gaze raked up and down her body, after a sigh of indecision, Austin moved just inside the room. He stopped as if waiting for her to protest. When she remained still and quiet, watching him, making no sound, Austin closed the door.

The click of the door shutting jarred her as if the slight sound had been the crack of a whip. Cheval's heartbeat increased again; her muscles tightened.

Austin moistened his lips and studied her. He blinked rapidly several times before asking, "Do you know what you're doing, Cheval?"

Letting instinct take over, she quietly murmured, "I only know that I've missed you and even

after all that's happened between us I'm so happy
to see you."

He took a step closer. "Do you mean that?"

She pushed away from the bed post and straightened her shoulders. "Oh, yes. As much as I'd rather
it were different, I can't deny my feelings for you."

His gliding steps toward her were so effortless,
Cheval thought he must be walking on air. He
didn't stop until he stood so close to her she felt
the warmth of his body, heard his quiet breathing,
smelled the clean scent of shaving soap which
clung to him.

As his gray-green eyes looked down into hers,
Cheval blocked out everything except her need to
love this man. Tonight there would be no other
people, no other world except theirs.

"Don't tempt me, Cheval," he said in a ragged
voice.

Austin's breath fanned her lashes, and she welcomed the hint of brandy that clung to his breath.
"Why not? You tempt me."

"There's a difference. I'm capable of going
through with anything I suggest. I'm not sure you
are."

Was he challenging her? "I am," she said again
and as if it were a natural part of her everyday
life to disrobe in front of this man, Cheval slipped
out of the cotton robe and stood before him
dressed only in the long-sleeved white nightgown.

Aware of nothing but the two of them in the
room, she stood still, listening to their shallow
breaths. Austin's eyes shimmered in the semi-

darkness of the pale moonlight. She sensed he was unsure of her actions and knew he was wise to be cautious. She had tricked him once before, and she was sure he didn't want a repeat of that.

Hoping to put his fears to rest she said, "I know many things need to be settled between us, Austin, but right now my body is telling me the most important one is physical." She lifted her arms and reached for him.

He hesitated.

Fear of rejection surfaced from within her and she was sure it showed on her face. Was he going to deny them this night together?

"Do you know what you're agreeing to?" he asked in a hoarse whisper.

She nodded.

"If I come to you, Cheval, I'll have to have all of you."

Calmly she said, "I wasn't planning on anything less. I've dreamed of your touch and your kisses night and day since I left you in France. Can't we put all that aside for tonight and just be happy to have this time to be together?"

He took his thumb and ran it over her lips, touching her nowhere else. "Yes."

Cheval craved to be snuggled deep in the circle of his arms, but he only touched her lips with the pad of his thumb. She yearned for so much more of him. All of him.

She pursed her lips and kissed the pad of his thumb as it raked back and forth across her mouth. The scent of shaving soap assailed her again and filled her with a wondrous feeling. As with a will of their own, her lips parted, her mouth opened, and she gently took the tip of his thumb into her waiting mouth. She sucked lightly. She tasted his slightly salty skin. Her stomach muscles contracted with wanting.

Flames of desire lit in his eyes. She felt him tremble. She heard his intake of breath. Relief settled over her. She relaxed. He wanted her as much as she wanted him.

Love for her flooded him. Austin felt his willpower spin out of control, out of his reach, out of his mind, chasing away his doubts and filling him with tenderness as Cheval's beautifully shaped lips closed around his thumb and gently pulled on it.

Never in his life had a woman seduced him like this one, and never had he fallen so easily for a woman's seduction. He couldn't forget that she'd duped him once, but right now that was getting harder to remember. She was wrong. They needed to talk. They needed to talk now and settle things between them before they came together, but how could he deny her? How could he deny himself when he'd wanted this since the first time he'd seen her in the tavern?

His lower body tightened with hunger, with the need to possess this bewitching woman before him. He placed an open hand against the back of her head and pressed her against his chest. He encircled her with the other arm, pulling her tightly against him. He wanted her to suck his thumb deeper into her mouth, into her warmth.

Closing his eyes, Austin savored the feel of her warm, soft body against him. He shuddered, thinking how close he came to losing her. How he still might. But like her, he didn't want to think about that right now. He didn't want to give up tonight.

"All right," he bent his head and whispered against her ear, drinking in the scent of her fresh-washed hair, "We'll wait and talk tomorrow. But, Cheval, we have some tough decisions ahead of us." He slid his thumb from her mouth and wrapped his arms so tightly around her, he thought she might cry out from the force of his strength. He kissed the top of her head. Somehow, holding her sealed so tightly and so securely against him gave him the feeling he would never have to let her go.

"I know," she answered softly.

Tomorrow they would figure out a way to get Bo back to his mother without either of them getting caught, but not tonight. No, this night would be for just the two of them.

Austin slowly loosened his grip and lifted her chin with the tips of his fingers as he lowered his face to hers. When their eyes met in the darkened room, he smiled. He saw she was feeling the same things he felt. Anticipation shot through him, causing his legs to go weak and his manhood to swell. He hadn't been alone with his feelings. He'd been right. She wanted him, too.

He closed his eyes and placed his lips upon hers

in a soft, exploring kiss that was meant only as a prelude for what was to come. He didn't want to scare her. For all her brazenness in fleeing into his room and reaching out for him, he knew she'd never lain with a man. He had to be gentle with her, even though his throbbing manhood told him to throw her down on the bed, shove her night-gown up to her neck, and drive himself deeply into her womanly secrets while he suckled from those softly firm breasts.

But deep inside himself Austin had no desire to treat Cheval in such an uncaring manner. He wanted to take his time, take the night and lie with her and love her. He wanted to enjoy her touch and the feel of her soft body beneath his hands. He wanted to hear every little sound that passed her beautifully tempting lips and watch every move she made. He wanted to breathe in the tantalizingly fresh scent of her hair and her skin as his tongue caressed her and bathed her with all the passion he was feeling.

Without realizing it was happening, letting nature take its course, his kiss deepened. His tongue parted her lips and thrust past her teeth into the depth of her slightly open mouth.

It was warm. It was good. It was exciting.

He swelled inside his breeches, straining the cloth. The teaser kiss had outlived its time, and now his lips demanded a response to his invitation as they pressed harder against hers and his tongue probed inside her mouth.

His hand left the thickness of her hair and

slipped down to cup her breast. His hand tingled as he explored the shape, the weight, the firmness and the softness of her breast. He yearned to cast the nightgown aside and pull the nipple of her breast into his eager, waiting mouth.

Desperate to feel her hands on his hot and fevered skin, he tore at the buttons on his shirt. Cheval must have realized what he needed for she helped him unbutton the shirt, pull it from his breeches, and slide it down his muscled arms.

He heard her soft moan as she ran her hands up his chest, over his shoulders, and down his back. He answered with a passionate groan of his own. It had never felt so wonderful to have a woman touch him.

Not wanting to waste another moment of his time with her, Austin picked up Cheval in his arms and gently laid her upon the raspberry-colored, goose-feathered bed covering.

"Shouldn't we push the bedding aside?" she asked as he worked the buttons on his breeches.

Austin looked at her golden-blonde hair spread out on the purplish-red material. He found the prim and proper white nightgown she wore seductive. "Hell, no," he muttered passionately as he left his breeches unfastened and struggled to stand on one leg while pulling off a boot. Damn, the things were as tight as his breeches, and *they* were killing him.

Slightly parted drapes allowed a streak of light into the room. Moonlight and starlight cast the room with a romantic glow.

Cheval's gaze swept over the well-defined muscles working in Austin's chest, arms, and upper back as he strained to remove his knee-high boots. As she watched him, she couldn't help but smile. She had no doubts about what they were going to do. She had no doubts that she loved Austin Radcliffe with all her heart, and she wanted this night with him.

When the boots were finally discarded, Austin, with the waist of his breeches falling open, exposing his abdomen, climbed on the bed and straddled her hips.

She looked up at him and smiled.

He looked down at her and smiled.

"Kiss me."

His eyes glowing, he gave her a daringly sensual look. "How?" His voice was low, sultry. "Where?" He placed his fingertips on her lips. "Here?" He moved his hand down to the base of her neck. "Here?" Sliding his open palm farther down, he covered her breast and gently squeezed. "Here?" His hand moved still lower to her abdomen and rested there a moment. "Here, or—" He swung his arm behind him and quickly bunched her nightgown up her legs and touched that warmest part of her between her legs. "Here?"

Cheval gasped, trembled. The heat from his fingertips sent flames of fire leaping to her cheeks. His words, his touch had her wound so tight all she could whisper was, "Yes. Anywhere. Just kiss me."

"Oh, yes, Cheval. I'm going to kiss you."

He untied the ribbon holding the bodice of her nightgown together and worked it up her body and over her head. Then he threw it to the floor. She lay invitingly against the dark-red bedding. His eyes fell immediately to her breasts. They were more tempting than he'd imagined. He liked the dusty-brown color of her nipples, and he ached to pull all of it into his mouth and taste her.

He liked the way her waist nipped in at the sides and the slight flare to her hips. He ran an open palm over both her breasts, gliding from one to the other and back again, letting the pert nipples tease his heated skin and tighten his stomach muscles.

Yes, he wanted to kiss her. Everywhere. But he also enjoyed simply looking at her as he was now. She was so beautiful. He wanted her so badly, he had to remain perfectly still for a few moments and get his emotions under control before he could continue.

"Do I look all right?"

His gaze left her breasts and shot up to her face. He saw concern in her expression. He smiled. "Oh, yes, my love. You are the most beautiful woman I have ever seen. You're so perfectly shaped, so lovely it takes my breath away. I'm trying to get it back before I continue."

Austin rose to his knees and, hooking his thumbs under his waistband, slid his breeches down as far as they would go. He watched Cheval's worried expression change to one of surprise as she stared at his engorged member.

Her innocence made him grow harder. Damn, he

didn't know how he'd gotten so lucky as to have Cheval in his bed and wanting him. He had to take her at her word and believe that she had missed him and wanted him as much as he had missed and wanted her.

There was no way he was going to hurry this night; but with every heartbeat, his throbbing manhood was telling him to stretch out on top of her and make her his, quickly, before she had the chance to change her mind.

By holding himself up on one knee at a time, he stripped the breeches from his legs and cast them aside, then gently settled his buttocks down on her thighs again. He was going to have a hell of a time waiting long enough to see that Cheval enjoyed her first sexual experience.

"I want you to lie still and let me love you," he whispered as his hands caressed her breasts.

Cheval nodded.

He reached down and kissed her softly on her forehead. From there he let his lips glide down to each eye, her nose, her upper lip, then her lower one, nipping them lightly. He kissed each cheek before starting down her neck, then over each shoulder. He kept his kisses short and moist, moving until he closed the rosebud of her breast into his mouth. He sucked gently, stroking the firm nipple with his tongue, bathing it with his taste. He grew harder.

Austin kissed the valley between her soft breasts before moving to her shoulder. His hands slid down to her waistline and rested there while he kissed the hollow at the base of her throat.

Cheval gasped and arched her chest upward. Her lower body thrust forward, too. Never before had she been so aware of a person's touch or scent. How could she not move when her hands itched to touch his skin and her lips ached to kiss him?

Ignoring his command for her to lie still, Cheval threw her arms around his neck. His skin was warm, damp with need. She dug her fingers into the back of his hair and pressed his head closer to her breasts. Although he hadn't said it, she instinctively knew that her touch gave him pleasure, too, and she wanted to please him.

She couldn't get close enough to him. His hands caressed and explored her waist, her hip, between her legs, but he wasn't touching her hard enough, long enough. She wanted more.

Holding nothing back, he bent to kiss her breasts again. Her breath shortened and became shallow; her eyes glazed. "Yes!" she whispered as Austin lifted his head and gave her a hard, demanding kiss on her lips. His heart beat wildly against her chest, her breasts. The urgency she felt inside dominated her feelings and made up for her lack of experience. She didn't know how they'd managed to wait so long to come together like this. Everything about the night seemed right.

His fingers danced; his palms caressed all the way down her body, giving her sensations she'd never experienced before. She held her body so tight she thought she might break in two for fear of losing the feelings he created inside her.

"Love me, Austin," she whispered into the mouth that covered hers.

A broken gasp slid past his lips. Covering her with his arms, his chest, and his legs, he settled his body over hers. Instinctively, Cheval slid her hand between their damp, heated bodies and closed her fingers around his pulsing manhood. He jerked, gasped, but allowed her the freedom to explore his length and his hardness.

When Austin couldn't wait any longer, he gently removed her hand and said, "I'm going to be as gentle as I can, but this might hurt."

With the way she was tingling with discovery, Cheval didn't know how anything could hurt. She felt his probing at the same time he covered her lips with his in a searing kiss. She stiffened when the probing turned to pushing and a slight burning pain developed inside her and at the same time she felt hot and full.

"Don't lie so still, Cheval. Move with me and it will be easier for you. It will feel better, too."

She did as he commanded, gently raising her hips to meet his. He was right. Within moments he was going deeper, filling her with himself, increasing his tempo. Thrilling excitement built so quickly in her chest and lower abdomen she felt as if she were going to explode. Her breathing became so shallow it frightened her. She wondered if what she was feeling was natural.

"You feel so good." His voice was throaty. "So damn good. So damn hot and tight."

He moved exquisitely slow. So slow she was almost begging for more. She gasped as the tightening in her body mounted until she writhed beneath him in a spasm of something so wonderful she couldn't explain it.

Austin continued to move as Cheval arched to meet him, matching his thrusts. When a breathless cry escaped her parted lips and her body went still, he knew her moment had come.

He smiled to himself and concentrated on his own fulfillment. Aware of nothing but the ecstasy of filling her soul and her body, Austin yielded to his body's clamoring for release. He moaned softly into her shoulder, shuddered, and went still.

They lay together, panting.

A few moments later, conscious thought returned to Cheval and she realized she was out of breath and out of energy. Her eyes were heavy with sleep.

"Is it over?" she asked, not sure what would come next.

A low chuckle rumbled in Austin as he lay on top of her. "No, Cheval. That was only the beginning."

"Thank God," she whispered and threw her arms around his back and held to him.

Austin chuckled again.

She was tired but, like Austin, didn't want the night to end too soon. Daybreak would be soon enough for what she had to do. She kissed the base of his neck and shoulder while her hands moved languidly over his back. Heat radiated throughout her body.

After tomorrow she would never have another opportunity to lie with him like this, and she wasn't going to miss making the most of the night no matter how tired she was, because by dawn she'd be on her way to Betsy Patterson's house.

Sixteen

Her eyes grew heavy. Cheval's body was so tired, so languid, so satisfied, all she wanted to do was snuggle against the back of the man who lay beside her and sleep. Maybe a quick nap would be all right, her mind told her as her eyes closed against the darkened room.

But no, her lids flew up seconds later as Bo's sad little face flashed across her mind's eye. She stiffened. She couldn't sleep. Not yet. Remembrance of how the little boy had cried for his mother the first few days of their voyage to France lay heavily upon her. All the risks she'd taken since she'd invaded Austin's cabin and taken his pistol were so she could return Bo to his home. If nothing else would keep her exhausted body awake, remembering that would.

How could she rest again until she'd delivered Bo to his mother? She was so close to accomplishing that goal! She lay still. When sleep threatened and her eyes tried to close, she held them open, willing Austin to fall into a deep sleep so she could slip out of the room before dawn crested on the horizon.

Austin. Yes, thoughts of him and her love for him could keep her awake, too. She slowly turned her head toward him and saw that Austin slept peacefully by her side. She didn't want to leave his bed, his house, but she had to. Last night she had known they would have only this one night together. She hadn't known it would be so difficult to leave.

Smiling to herself, she was tempted to reach over and run her hand over his shoulder, down his back, and across his hip one more time. She wished they'd had longer together. Leaving his bed would be hard; knowing he'd never forgive her a second time broke her heart.

He had wanted to hold her close and snuggle her in his arms after their last lovemaking, but she had known the danger in being wrapped tightly in his arms and told him she was hot and needed to cool off for a few minutes. She'd encouraged him to go to sleep, promising she would snuggle against his back when she had cooled down.

It hurt, but she couldn't afford to keep that whispered promise. It would be impossible to get out of the bed without waking him if she were tied up in his arms. Even with being inches from touching him, it would be difficult to leave the bed without waking him.

Cheval lay on her back watching the spring breeze from the open window stir the drapery panel. A slice of moonlight filtered in, filling the room with a faint, white glow. From her position on the bed she could see Austin's black dress jacket hanging on the wall. His shaving plate and mirror sat on the tall chest. How she would love to wake in the mornings and watch him as he tended to that daily routine. She breathed deeply, knowing the scent of shaving soap on his face and neck would always be her reminder of Austin and how she desperately wished things could have been different for them.

She had no idea of the time but knew daylight couldn't be far away. While Austin breathed so evenly would be the best time to slip off the bed and out of the room. She hated leaving his warmth, his loving. She hated to leave him for she knew that if she succeeded, he'd never forgive her. She prayed that one day he would realize she loved him with all her heart and that she would never be complete or whole without him.

The time had come. She could wait no longer. Taking another deep breath, she raised slightly. Her movements were so slow and carefully planned; her muscles ached from the strain as she eased from the bed. Her feet touched the floor. Her weight left the bed. Austin didn't stir.

She looked around the floor and spotted her robe. Quickly, she grabbed it up and shoved her arms into the sleeves. Cold fingers closed only the button at her breast to hold the robe together as she tiptoed to the door. Her clothes and shoes were in Bo's room. If she made it that far, she'd have to take time to put them on.

Getting the door open without making a sound would not be easy. But she knew if she could get out of the bedroom without waking Austin, she'd have a good chance of getting out of the house. Her prayer was that just maybe he was as tired as she and the soft sounds that she made wouldn't disturb his sleep.

Cheval placed her hand on the cold doorknob and turned it while keeping her eyes trained on the sleeping form lying on his side. She turned the knob so slowly she had plenty of time to look at Austin. A strip of moon and starlight lay across the lower half of his body, giving her a perfect view of his lean hip, rounded buttock, and handsome, muscular thigh. She enjoyed looking at his body. Even now, she wanted to run back to the bed and caress his muscled skin one more time.

A slight clicking sound startled her as if it had been a loud shot in the dark. Cheval held her breath. Her gaze flew up to Austin's head and shoulders. He didn't stir. Her heartbeat speeded up so fast she thought she might grow faint. All she had to do was open the door enough to squeeze through. She pulled. Another creak. Again, she held her breath. Austin didn't move.

Holding in her stomach and chest, Cheval slipped outside into the hallway; then grabbing the knob on the outside, she held tight until she had pulled the door shut. Slowly, quietly, she released the knob and let the latch slide back in place.

She stood a moment in the semi-dark hallway, afraid to believe she'd actually made it out of the bedroom without waking Austin.

Fear of being caught spurred her feet and she

rushed the short distance down the hallway and into Bo's room, thankful Austin had left Bo's door open when he'd followed her into his room. Cheval quickly dug into her satchel and yanked out her dark-green dress, taking no time to bother with a chemise. The shift-like style of the dress made it easy to slip over her head.

She worked the buttons at the back of the high-waisted dress while stepping into her shoes without benefit of stockings. There would be time to properly don her clothes after Bo had been delivered to his mother. She grabbed the small drawstring purse and stuffed it into her dress pocket, praying she'd be able to find a carriage driver who knew how to take them to the Patterson house.

Without slowing her movements, Cheval reached one arm under Bo's head and the other beneath his legs and picked him up. She didn't want to wake him until they were away from the house because he could be cranky when he first awakened in the morning.

Cheval had no trouble getting out of Bo's room and down the hallway. Thank God, he was a small child or she'd never be able to get down the stairs with him. When she had made it to the top of the stairs, she groaned. Moonlight lit the foyer and showed Jubal sitting in a chair beside the front door. A quick assessment told her he was hard asleep. His hands lay folded in his lap; his head hung awkwardly to one side, and a stuffy, snoring sound escaped his lips.

Frantic that Austin might pop out at her any moment, Cheval slipped one hand down and clutched at the folds of her skirt, lifting the hem so she wouldn't trip over her dress as she descended the stairs. Her skin prickled and her stomach quaked. How was she going to get down the stairs and out the back door without waking Jubal, Bo, or Austin?

Knowing she couldn't waste time with indecision, Cheval took the first step. It was difficult to walk down the stairs with Bo in her arms. His little body grew heavy quickly and she had to help support him by resting one arm on the bannister, letting it slide along the varnished wood with each step she took. To keep from screaming from the nerve-racking tension filling her, she counted the steps as each foot silently landed on the stairs. Five. Six. Seven.

Her movements were painstakingly slow and difficult down the twelve steps. She was physically and mentally fatigued. Putting one foot in front of the other was a major task. Halfway down, Bo almost slipped from her hold. Her chest tightened. The muscles in her arms starting quivering from weakness. She was forced to rely heavily on the bannister to guide her the rest of the way.

Keeping her gaze on Jubal at the bottom of the stairs, she continued to move slowly down the hallway toward the kitchen and the back door. She held her muscles so tight she couldn't have hurried if she'd wanted to. Her arms ached from the weight of the child and the tension in her body.

When she rounded the doorway into the kitchen, she whispered a sigh of relief, seeing that Thollie's bedroom door was shut. Twilight lit her way to the door. She dropped her skirt and grabbed hold of the handle, sensing freedom was just beyond that one opening.

It was locked! She whirled around, deliriously thinking Austin must have beat her down the stairs and locked the door. But quickly realizing she was being irrational, she worked her fingers down below the handle, praying the key had been left in the keyhole, but finding nothing. She shifted the sleeping boy in her tired arms and looked frantically around the small room.

Her fear mounted. Her frustration spiraled out of control. What was she going to do? She wanted to sink to the floor on her knees and cry out at the unfairness of that locked door. But she couldn't. She was too close to give up now. Freedom for Bo lay just beyond that door, that wall, that window.

Window?

She whirled back around and stared at the curtainless window. It wasn't a large one, but maybe it was wide enough for her and Bo to crawl through. She looked back at the doorway into the kitchen. She had no choice. She couldn't chance trying to get out the front door with Jubal's chair beside it, no matter how soundly he slept.

With jerky unsure movements, the first thing she did was lay Bo on the floor. He stirred and stretched, but didn't make a sound. Next she removed the kettle and milk pitcher that sat on the table in front of the window. Now came the hard part. Opening the window and crawling out before they were discovered. Looking out, she saw that it was a five or six feet drop to the ground.

"No," she whispered into the darkness.

Cheval winced as she looked from the doorway and back to the sleeping boy. She couldn't do it. It was too difficult. She'd gone as far as she could go. She was too tired, too exhausted to go on. Maybe Bo was supposed to be with his father. Every time she had thought she was close to getting Bo home, something had happened to thwart her. There was nothing left to do but accept defeat and go back upstairs to the man who had given her a glimpse of heaven earlier in the night.

"Yes," she whispered to herself, feeling light-headed, feeling as if she suddenly had all her problems worked out.

This idea of getting Bo back to his mother was madness. Why hadn't she thought of this before? What would be the harm in Bo's living with his father? Napoleon had made Jerome Bonaparte a king. *A king!* Bo was a prince. Didn't he belong with his father and all the inherited title offered? Why hadn't she stopped to think about what she was denying Bo? All she'd thought about was her own feelings and his mother's feelings. A calmness settled over her.

"Yes," she murmured aloud again, rubbing her aching arms. What had she been thinking? Now she understood why Austin had agreed to take Bo to France. Of course he would be better off with his father. She couldn't deny Bo the chance to be King of Westphalia one day. It was his birthright.

She moved to pick up Bo and take him back upstairs to his bed but stopped abruptly when her sister's face appeared before her. Cheval gasped.

Big tears rolled down Loraine's face. Her nose was reddened from crying. "I want my son," she mumbled past blue, trembling lips. "Bring me my son. My son."

"Loraine!" Cheval whispered earnestly, her throat so tight she barely got the word out. Loraine's face turned swimmy and distorted.

Cheval reached to make contact with her sister to comfort her but grasped only air. Cheval stepped back. Loraine wasn't there. She was gone as quickly as she'd appeared.

Cheval trembled from cold, from fear. She felt as if her heart might explode in her chest, her body might break in two if she tried to move. She must have gone mad for a few seconds. Loraine had seemed so real. She'd thought her sister had come back to her. She'd thought she could touch her.

Taking a deep breath, Cheval tried to calm her racing heartbeat and moisten her dry mouth. She tingled as if the blood had drained from her body for a time and was only now returning.

Thinking more clearly, Cheval realized she'd allowed stress and her emotional fatigue to addle her for a few moments. No, Bo was not old enough to be turned over to his father.

Knowing what she had to do, Cheval turned

quickly to the window. She had precious little time. Already the moon had faded and the sky had turned pink. She'd have to raise the window, lower Bo to the ground, then jump out.

The wood was cold to her shaky fingers as she pulled upward on the window. It was stuck. She pulled harder. A creaking, scraping sound pierced the quiet like the shriek of a wild animal.

Cheval froze and turned toward the doorway. She heard the shuffling of feet coming from the front room. What was she to do? The noise had awakened Jubal. He was coming to investigate. She looked around and, picking up the lid to the iron kettle, she flattened herself against the wall at the entrance to the kitchen. Holding the cold metal with both hands as Jubal walked through the doorway, she raised the lid.

Jubal saw her and tried to react, but Cheval brought down the lid. It struck him across the side of his head. Jubal groaned and fell to the floor with a resounding thud.

Cheval cried out as she dropped the lid, hating herself for what she'd had to do to the man who'd always been so good to her. But there was no time to fret. She would have the rest of her life to do that once Bo was safe.

She glanced up at the window, open only about four inches. If Austin had heard the commotion they'd created, there was no time to get out the window. He'd be down the stairs in a flash. Frantically, she searched the pockets of Jubal's waistcoat and found two keys.

On shaky legs she hurried to the door and tried the first key. She glanced over her shoulder to Jubal, who lay on the floor, groaning. Her gaze darted up to the doorway.

The lock wouldn't turn.

She dropped the key. It clanged on the wooden floor.

Trembly with fear, she stuck the other key in the small keyhole and it clicked. She turned the knob and jerked the door open. The early dawn air hit her in the face like a bucket of cold water.

Cheval rushed back to pick up Bo.

Austin's eyes popped open. Had he heard a creak, or thud, or something falling? Seconds ticked by while he listened. He heard movement. His arms swung out behind him, reaching for Cheval, but only meeting an empty bed.

He jerked, twisted over, and jumped out of the bed all in one easy motion. His feet tangled in some clothes lying on the floor by the bed and he stumbled. Realizing it was his own breeches that halted him, he snatched them up and stomped into the legs as he yanked the bedroom door open.

His heartbeat increased as he hurried, barefooted, down the hallway to look into Bo's room.

A stab of fear hit him in his gut. Bo was gone. The open satchel and discarded robe lay on the floor at the foot of the bed. He knew last night that Cheval would try again to escape with Bo, but he'd allowed his love for her to cloud his wisdom, his instinct.

Why had he been fool enough to think one night in his bed would change anything between them?

He darted away from the door and ran down the staircase. He had to stop her. The early morning afforded him a little light in the house and he saw the empty chair where Jubal was supposed to be keeping watch. He prayed that he'd find Jubal, Cheval, and Bo making morning tea.

He hurried into the kitchen so fast, he didn't see anything on the floor. He kicked something, then stumbled and fell, hitting his knee and sprawling to the floor, hitting his elbow hard as his eyes caught sight of the open back door.

Rage tore through him as pain shot through his arm and knee. "No!" he yelled. "Cheval, come back!"

He scrambled to his feet, groaning as pressure sent more spirals of pain shooting up his leg. When he made it to the door, he saw Cheval running toward the front of the house, with Bo jiggling in her arms.

With her carrying the boy, Austin knew he could catch her. "Cheval! Stop!" he called, racing after her as fast as his injured knee would allow him.

Damn! He shouldn't have trusted her, he told himself as his bare feet hit the rocky ground.

Damn! He shouldn't have become so sated with her lovemaking that he'd fallen asleep.

Damn! She ran fast for a slightly built woman carrying a thirty-pound boy.

Forcing aside the pain in his body, the burning in his lungs, he pushed harder and quickly gained on her. She reached the main street and almost flew down it, she ran so fast, but with her burden she was no match for him. Out of breath and his knee throbbing with pain, he reached out and grabbed hold of Cheval's shoulder.

"No," she screamed, trying to wrench away from him and continue her flight. Bo struggled and cried in her arms; still she held him tightly to her chest. Her eyes were wild with fright; her chest heaved with each breath, and her face flushed red from exertion.

Damn! He hated frightening her. "Promise you won't run and I'll let go of you," he managed to say between labored breaths.

She nodded as Bo continued to whimper and try to raise up in her arms. He wanted to take the child from her and let her rest, but he knew she wouldn't give Bo up willingly.

In the distance he heard the approach of a carriage and wanted to get Cheval and Bo away from the street before the carriage passed. Still gasping for breath he said, "Step over here with me." He pointed to a clump of trees just beyond the road.

She shook her head.

"Dammit, Cheval, someone is coming. I don't want them to see the boy, now—"

A quick glance in the direction of the carriage gave her enough time to shoot past him and start running again. Austin knew she had no energy left. She was running on fear. He easily caught her in only a few steps. Jerking her around to face him almost stripped Bo from her arms.

"No—, let me go!" she pleaded. "I—I have to g—get him back t—to his mother."

Bo cried louder.

If he didn't calm them both immediately, all his neighbors would be in the street.

He held tightly to her upper arms, shaking her gently. "Stop this madness! You can't take Bo back. They will assume you helped kidnap him and put you in jail."

"No. How—could they when I return him? Let me go!" she whimpered. "I have to do this. I have to do it for my sister."

"Your sister?" he asked, confused by her words.

"I couldn't help my sister, but I can help Bo's mother."

Understanding dawned. It was too late for Cheval's sister, but not for Betsy Patterson. He relaxed his grip. His love for her overflowed. He wanted to hold her, reassure her of his love and his commitment to her.

Austin softened his voice and said, "I'll help you return Bo to his mother."

She shook her head. Her eyes glistened in the early light. "I don't believe you."

The carriage came closer.

"I promise to return him to his mother," he said, still speaking softly. "Cheval, you have to trust me on this."

She sniffled. Tears rolled down her cheeks. Her lips trembled. "I don't trust you to keep that promise."

Her words hurt. He flinched. "Why don't you trust me? I love you. I want to marry you. Didn't what happened between us in that bed mean anything to you?"

Fresh tears streamed down her face. She was visibly shaken. He could see his words of love and marriage had touched her heart.

"Yes. Yes, it meant everything to me." She choked on a sob before continuing. "I love you, but I don't trust you. You have different values than I. You've done something I could never condone. How can I marry you, even though I love you, when I can't accept what you've done to this little boy and his mother?"

Her words cut through him like a sword, but he had no time to react. There was precious little time left before the carriage came upon them.

"Cheval, come back inside and let's discuss this. Let me prove to you that I am an honorable and trustworthy man. Bradley can arrange the return of Bo so no one will ever connect either of our names to this."

"No!" She jerked out of his grasp. "Do you think I'm going to trust you and Bradley to give Bo back to his mother. I'm not crazy."

Austin grabbed her again and she struggled. Bo fought them both.

"Here, here! What's going on here? Unhand that woman, sir," a well-dressed older man said, stepping out of his carriage. The gentleman's driver, a tall, portly man, set the brake on the carriage and jumped down beside his master.

Cheval stopped struggling and looked at the outraged gentleman with bulging blue eyes. Even Bo sensed something had happened and quieted.

Austin knew the two men meant trouble. He had to think fast. He smiled and said in a friendly voice, "There's no problem here we can't handle, but my thanks for stopping. My wife's a bit miffed because I didn't come home last night. She thinks to take my son and leave me, but I'm trying to tell her she has nowhere to go."

The man twisted the brass handle of his cane in his hand as he considered what Austin had said. By the look in the older man's eyes Austin knew he'd done a good job convincing him, but so did Cheval.

"No, that's not true," Cheval said, stepping forward, her voice stronger than Austin thought it should have been under the circumstances.

"Cheval, don't," Austin warned.

"This man has held me against my wishes in his house. I am not his wife and this child is not his son." She moved closer to the well-dressed gentleman.

Austin tensed. "Don't do this, Cheval." He spoke quietly, but firmly. "I love you. You have to believe me when I say it will be better for both of us if we let Bradley handle this for us." He glanced at the stranger and added for his benefit,

"He'll take care of everything and keep us out of trouble."

Her lips trembled. Her eyes teared. Austin saw the indecision in her face. He also saw that she was exhausted, frantic, and on the edge.

"I can't. I don't trust you or Bradley." She turned to the stranger and said, "Please take me to the police headquarters. I need to—"

"No!" Austin stepped forward and grabbed Cheval's arm. She cried out, and the older gentleman struck Austin across the head with the handle of his brass cane.

Pain sliced through Austin's forehead, and he fell to his knees. Twinkling lights flitted across his eyes as he saw Cheval's surprised expression. She cried out for the man not to hit him again. Austin struggled to maintain consciousness. Cheval and Bo swam before him. He had to stop her.

He tried to reach for her again, but he couldn't focus on where they were. He fought to keep control. Through blurred, distorted vision he saw the man hustle Cheval and Bo into the carriage and shut the windowless door behind them.

Struggling to get to his feet, he tried to call her name, but couldn't. The world around him spun. "N—no—" He tried to say the word but wasn't sure he did.

The driver swung the back of his arm through the air, knocking Austin to the ground. A muffled cry broke past his lips. A booted foot caught him in the ribs, lifting him off the ground, robbing him of breath. Twice more he jerked and moaned from the blows the driver dealt before climbing back up on the carriage and driving away.

Austin held his ribs and tried to rise. The pain was so great he couldn't. He fought for consciousness, but darkness crept up on him. He had to stop the carriage. He had to stop Cheva—

Seventeen

With a heavy heart, Cheval stood in front of police headquarters and waved one last time to the older gentleman who'd helped her as he climbed back in his carriage and rode away.

She was angry with herself and the man who had struck Austin with his cane. It was her fault for telling the stranger that Austin **had held** her against her will. For a moment, she'd been torn between seeing if Austin was badly hurt and getting Bo away from him as quickly as possible. Knowing she would check on Austin and Jubal after Bo was safely back with his mother, she'd stepped inside the carriage and left without seeing about Austin.

Her shoulders sagged with the weight of everything that had happened over the past weeks. What kind of person had she turned into? Holding men at gunpoint, hitting Jubal on the head—all because she didn't believe one parent had the right to steal a child from the other parent. Was she attempting to control fate? Was she playing God?

"No," she whispered confidently to herself. She

was merely following her motherly instincts. And that couldn't be the wrong thing to do.

Cheval glanced at the police headquarters, one of the newer-looking stone-and-wood buildings in the downtown section of Baltimore. Early morning sun shone brightly against the face of the building, glaring at her with its warmth. As she stared at the building, it seemed to loom before her, growing smaller and larger until she felt as if the building were swaying. She quickly looked away. She was obviously feeling the effects of her tiresome journey from Europe and lack of sleep.

The street was quiet except for a street vendor setting up his cart on the corner and a shopkeeper who swept the boardwalk in front of his store.

"Why are we here?"

Peering down into the dark-blue eyes of the little boy whose hand she held, Cheval answered past a lump in her throat. "I'm trying to get you home."

"Home? Is that where Mama is?"

She smiled. "Yes."

"Are you going with me?"

Cheval bent down in front of Bo and started straightening his clothes. She suddenly realized she was reluctant to let him go. How could she give him up? She'd taken care of him and loved him for over two months. She'd fed him, washed him, combed his hair, trimmed his nails. She'd taught him his letters and how to spell his first name. With Jubal's and Robert's help she'd taught him the beginning moves in chess. How could she give him up? When he laughed, it delighted her. When he cried, she cried inside, too.

Reaching over, she kissed his soft, rounded cheek. His short arms went around her neck and held her tight. She pulled his little body to her. She couldn't give him up. He was hers. She'd keep him and run away with him. No one would find them. But as the irrational thoughts coursed through her mind, her sister's face swam before her.

"No," she whispered, but knew she had to give him back to his mother. Her sister's pale, drawn face had appeared to her, telling her she had to let Bo go. He didn't belong to Cheval.

Denying her own pain of loss, Cheval pushed away from Bo. She looked down into his little-boy face. He trusted her, and she couldn't let him down. If she were ever lucky enough to have a son of her own, she'd want him to be as brave and as trusting as Jerome Napoleon Bonaparte.

"Out of the way! Coming through."

A man pushing a milk cart headed toward them, so Cheval and Bo moved farther away from the street and closer to the steps that led inside the police building. In just the few minutes they'd stood there, the day had gotten busier and more people dotted the street and walkways.

Now that she was here, it wasn't as easy as she'd thought it would be to boldly walk into the police hall with Bo as she'd once planned. Now that she'd had more time to think things through, she knew taking him inside was a risky and foolish idea. She had to say goodbye outside and let Bo go through the door alone. He could tell them his name, and they'd see he was returned home. This way no one would have to know of Austin's involvement in the kidnapping.

A heartbreaking thought tore through her and caused her to wince. Once Bo walked inside that building, she would never see him again. She was sure of that. His mother would see to it that he was protected from any other possible attempts at abducting him.

She bent in front of Bo again to get on his eye level. She had done the job Austin had hired her to do. She had taken care of Bo. Not the way he'd wanted her to, that was for sure. And she'd done the job she felt compelled to do: Return Bo to his mother. It was still unbelievable to her that fate had been with her and she'd gotten as far as she had.

Austin crossed her mind again. She hoped he was all right. As much as she'd rather not, she would be forced to go back to his town house. All the clothes she had in the world were there. But besides that, she was sure Austin and Jubal would have a few things to say to her. Things she didn't really want to hear.

What would she do now that her mission was over? She had to find work as a governess somewhere. That was really all she knew how to do, and she loved working with children. She prayed she wouldn't have to go back to tavern work, back to the stench of tobacco and dried ale on her clothes. Cheval shuddered. She remembered the pats, pinches, jeers, and laughing she'd endured. How could she go back to that?

Cheval straightened Bo's coat again, feeling the effects of her sleepless night catching up with her. All she wanted to do was curl up and go to sleep and dream about her wonderful night with Austin.

"Now listen to me," she said. "We're here where the police work. They will take you back to your mama."

"I want you to take me back," he said, rubbing his nose.

Her heart went out to him. It had been two-and-a-half months since he'd seen his mother; it was only natural he would be a little frightened.

She took a deep breath. "You're a smart young fellow and a big boy for your age. You can handle this by yourself. All right?"

"I want you to go with me."

His eyes teared and Cheval almost relented. It wasn't going to be easy leaving him on his own. "I can't, love," she whispered.

"Why?"

"They'll ask me too many questions. Questions I can't answer. You'll be safe with these men. I wouldn't leave you if I weren't positive you'd be taken directly to your mother. All right?"

He nodded.

"I'm going to miss you, little one." She felt her own tears and knew the time had come. She had to send him on his way now before he saw her cry. "I want you to go up those steps; and when you get inside, go up to one of the men and tell him your name. That's all you have to do."

"I want you to go with me," he said again, his bottom lip trembling.

"I can't, but I'll wait until you—" A large hand clamped down on her shoulder. Cheval froze.

She looked up and into the face of an older man wearing a police uniform.

"Would you and the boy come with me, Miss?"

Cheval's eyes rolled back in her head. Her neck seemed no longer capable of holding up her head. Her hands and feet felt numb from lack of use and the cold room. Each breath was slow and labored. Her tongue and mouth were so dry she couldn't moisten her lips. She was too tired too think, too exhausted to be afraid. She had to sleep.

The sharp crack of a leather strap on the table jerked her head up, and her eyes fluttered open. She squinted from the bright light that shone in her face. Why wouldn't they let her go to sleep? She didn't know how much longer she could hold herself up in the straight-back chair. Shivering, she wrapped her arms around her chest. She didn't know why it was so cold in the small room.

In front of her, she saw the shadows of three men sitting around a table; but with the glaring lamp light in her eyes, she couldn't see the men's features. The windowless room stifled her, and she longed for fresh air. The stench of stale tobacco and heating oil filled the room, making her stomach roil.

So far, she hadn't been hit with the short leather strap one of the men held. Every time she heard the crack of the whip, she jerked to a rigid upright position, afraid she was going to be flogged with it. Now she was too weary to be frightened of the beastly thing, even though the noise managed to keep her awake.

"Sleeeeep," she managed to say past a dry mouth and a thick tongue. Why wouldn't they let her have rest, food, or water? What had she done wrong? She'd returned Bo so he could be with his mother. What else did they want from her?

"You can sleep after you tell us who was in on this kidnapping with you? We don't believe you acted alone. Tell us the names of your accomplices."

No, not even if they decided to use that awful-sounding whip on her would she implicate Austin in Bo's abduction. She had to protect him at all cost. If they were this mean to a woman, she didn't even want to think about what they'd do to a man. Austin's name would never escape her lips. What he'd done was safe with her.

Cheval shielded her eyes with a shaky hand, wanting to see who questioned her. She didn't know which of the three men shadowed by the bright lamp sitting on the desk had spoken to her.

"This will go much easier on you if you will cooperate and tell us everything we want to know," a different man said. "We know you didn't act alone in stealing this child. Tell us who helped you, Miss Worthington."

She wasn't so tired she couldn't repeat the same story she'd told them when she first sat down in the chair hours ago. "I had nothing to do with kidnapping Bo. When I discovered who he was, I did everything in my power to get him back to his mother."

"So you didn't know who he was until after the kidnapping had taken place?" the man with the softer voice asked.

She remained silent.

"Where were you when you discovered the true identity of the boy?"

All day they'd tried to put words in her mouth when what she needed was water and warmth. She tried to swallow again, but it was no use. Her head fell to one side, but she managed to ask, "Did you take care of Bo? Has he been returned to his mother?"

"Why should we tell you what you want to know, Miss Worthington, when you refuse to tell us what we want to know?" one of the men barked sharply. "You're not doing yourself any favors by remaining silent."

Cheval shook from the angry tone, from the cold room, from being too tired to go on. It seemed like hours ago she stopped asking for water, realizing they wouldn't give her anything she wanted until she told them what they wanted to know; but she had still had strength then. She couldn't go on any longer. "Sleep. Water." She managed to say again.

"I don't think you realize how much trouble you are in. You could very well spend the rest of your life in prison," the man with the petulant voice remarked. "You're a young woman, and I don't think you know what prison would be like."

"Maybe we should let her spend a couple of days in the hole," one of the other men said. "I suspect she'll be ready to talk after a few days in the hellhole."

It was quiet for a moment, then she heard whispers among the men. They were wrong if they thought jail would frighten her. She didn't care where they put her as long as she could lie down and sleep.

She slumped in the chair, thinking now she could rest. The whip hit the desk with a resounding slap. She forced her eyes open, but quickly closed them when she found it impossible to focus on the men. It was impossible to keep her eyes open against the glaring light.

The sharp crack of the whip sounded on the table again, but this time Cheval ignored it. Let them beat her. She didn't care anymore. She had to sleep. She'd tried to stand, but her legs were too weak. She heard muffled voices as she fell forward to the hard floor.

* * *

Austin's body cried out in agony. Each breath brought a burning pain in his side. His head felt the size of a barge and pounded with a throbbing ache. God, what had happened to him! He hurt so bad he couldn't open his eyes. He tried to focus his mind. He knew his name. That was a good sign. Now, where was he? He listened. There was no sound. He was warm, and what he lay on was too soft to be grass or the ground. He had to be in a bed, but was it his bed?

All of a sudden he remembered Cheval and Bo getting into the carriage and the beating from the driver. His eyes popped open, and he tried to rise. He mumbled a curse and fell back against the pillow, panting. The pain was so great, it took his breath. For a few seconds, he thought he might pass out.

Damn! He tried to cough to clear his throat and lungs, but his side hurt too bad. Damn, that bastard had done a job on him before driving away. Austin had been in fights before and had had sore ribs, but this time he might have cracked a rib. He'd never felt this bad.

Austin had to push the pain aside and think. At least he was alive and lying in his own bed, but where was Cheval? How long had it been since she'd climbed into the carriage with that stranger? By the light in the room, he judged it to be midday.

He tried to turn his head to look out the window. It hurt. He'd be sore a week, he thought angrily. He had to get up, no matter how bad it hurt him. Not only did he have to find Cheval, if he didn't start moving, he would only get stiffer.

He tried to rise again, slower this time, but the pain stabbing through his side and mid-section was so great he almost passed out before he could lie back down.

Thollie or Jubal would know what was going on. Slowly he turned his head and looked toward the door. Thank God it was open.

"Th—Thollie. Jub-al." His voice was so weak no one could have heard him in the next room, let alone downstairs where they would be. He had to do better.

Taking a deep breath he yelled, "Thollie! Jubal!"

He heard the running of feet on the stairs. Seconds later, Thollie rounded the corner, wiping her wet hands on her apron. Surprise showed in her eyes as she stopped beside his bed.

"You're awake!" she exclaimed, smoothing her apron down the front of her dress. A broad smile sliced across her face; her dark eyes sparkled. "We was beginning to wonder if you were ever going to wake up."

Austin tensed. "H—how long have I been asleep?"

"Two days now."

"Damnation!" he muttered, managing to raise himself on his elbow.

"Course the first time you woke up, you were

in such a bad way the doctor had to give you this here medicine. He said it would make you sleep for awhile, and it has." She picked up the jar of white powder and looked at it.

He didn't care about that right now. "Cheval? Where is she?"

Thollie peered down at him. "We don't know for sure. Jubal told me to tell you when you woke up that he be down at the police building waiting to see if she goes in or out of there. I don't know why he thinks she be there. I asked him, but he didn't answer."

Damn, his head hurt so bad he could hardly think. If that man had taken Cheval to the police, there would have been news of her story. "Has there been any word of a kidnapping in the papers?"

"Kidnapping?" Thollie wrinkled her face, pursing her lips. "What you talking about?"

Surely it would be all over town by now if Cheval had managed to get Bo back to his mother. "Have you heard anything about a little boy being kidnapped?"

"Now you know I can't read, but Mildred next door, she does. She hasn't mentioned anything about no kidnapping to me. I think I better call the doctor."

His head pounded. Austin tried to think. Each breath hurt. The damn bastard must have cracked a rib. What had happened to Cheval? Where was she? Bradley. He'd know what the hell was going on.

Austin looked up at his housekeeper. "Thollie, I want you to go get Bradley. Don't walk. Take some money out of my pockets and take a carriage. Tell him I need him to drop everything and to come immediately."

"Don't you want me to bring you some hot tea or broth first so you can—"

"No!" he answered, sharper than he wanted to, but this was too important. Cheval's life could be in danger. "I want you to get Bradley over here; then find Jubal and get him here. Go *now*."

"My God, you look like two dock-workers beat the hell out of you," Bradley said upon entering Austin's room.

"One did."

"My word! Is that true?"

"Close enough."

"That's a nasty cut over your eye. When did this happen? Why haven't I been informed before now?"

Austin wasn't surprised Jubal and Thollie had kept his condition secret. They knew he would want to talk to them before they said anything to the family.

Fighting the pain, Austin forced himself to raise on one elbow again. It pleased him that it seemed to be a little easier this time.

"I don't want to talk about that right now. Have you had word from Cheval?"

Bradley slid a chair over to the bed and sat down. "Certainly not. As I told you, the last time I saw Miss Worthington, she had a pistol pointed at my chest. If I never see her—"

"Something's happened."

"Quite obviously, Austin. You look terrible, and I can see you're having trouble breathing. What in God's name happened?"

That's exactly what Austin wanted to know. He groaned inwardly and took a steadying breath. He had to make it short. He could fill in details later. "As you know, Jubal and I watched the port. When Cheval returned from Europe, I waylaid her and brought her and Bo here. Sometime during the night, she hit Jubal over the head and tried to escape."

"That doesn't surprise me."

Austin ignored his caustic remark. "I was trying to stop her from going to the police when a knight in shining armor decided to come to her rescue."

"So you were beaten up because of her?" Bradley sniffed.

Austin again ignored his brother-in-law's implied *I told you so* and said, "I don't know where Cheval and Bo are. Has there been any word about either of them in the papers or on the street?"

The cockiness faded, and a worried expression settled on Bradley's face. "No, nothing. I would have already been over to see you had I heard anything about Bo's being returned."

"Dammit, where could they be?" Austin hit the bed with his fist. "Where could that dandy have taken them?"

Bradley crossed one leg over the other and pondered for a moment. "Where was she heading when you stopped her, or tried to stop her?"

"The authorities. I heard her ask the man to take her to the police." Austin tried to rub his forehead to ease the pounding over his eyes, but the touch of his fingers only made it worse.

"Surely she wouldn't just walk into the police building and hand the boy over to them. That would be suicide."

"I don't think she was thinking about anyone or anything except getting Bo to his mother."

"All right, let's just say she did take Bo to the police and all is fine."

"Why haven't we heard anything?"

Bradley sniffed again. "Well, from the beginning they've kept this kidnapping a secret."

"But once Bo was returned, what would be the purpose of not talking about it?"

"Good question. Unless—" Bradley paused. "Unless, Miss Worthington simply dropped him out front and ran away. Would she have come back here?"

"Probably not," Austin said, denying the feelings of hurt that resurfaced when he thought of

Cheval's last words to him. "But if Bo had been returned, wouldn't there be news of it?"

"Not necessarily. As I said, the family might want to continue the secret. I think it's safe to assume she dropped the boy at the police and ran. I doubt you'll ever hear from her again, Austin; and once you've had a good look in the mirror, I think you'll say, 'good riddance.' "

Bradley's words angered Austin. "What if she went in with Bo and they are holding her in jail?"

Shaking his head, Bradley said, "I don't think that's very likely. There would be some news. Something."

"Find out."

"How?" he argued. "I can't very well go to the authorities and start asking them about a woman who *might* have brought in a little boy that *no one* is supposed to know has been kidnapped. There's not been one word about it in the papers. They'll have me in jail, too."

"So you think she's there."

Bradley rose, almost knocking over the chair. "No. It's my guess she dropped the boy off and now she's run away where you'll never find her. You know, Austin, she ran off and left you in France and it appears she's done it again. She obviously doesn't care a whit for you—"

"That's enough, Bradley." Austin's voice was deadly calm. He didn't know which possibility was worse. That Cheval had run away and he would

never see her again, or that she might be in jail.
He didn't like either thought.

"Go to the jail and see if she's there."

"But—"

"You're my lawyer. I don't care how you do it,
Bradley, just do it and do it now," he finished in
a loud voice.

"Be reasonable, Austin. I just explained to you
why I can't do that. If she's there, chances are
that she'll tell what she knows, if she hasn't already. And at least one of us has to stay out of
jail."

Austin's head was pounding. "You're good at
talking your way around things. Think of a way."

Bradley rubbed his chin and paced the room,
mulling over his thoughts. "Well, I suppose I
could tell the guards that I received an anonymous
note asking me to come talk to Miss Worthington
and that I have no idea what she might want."

"Fine. Just do it," he said, wanting to get
Bradley out of his room so he could rest a few
minutes before he tried to walk. Austin was shaking from fear for Cheval. If she were in jail, he
had to go there and get her out. It didn't matter
that she was the reason he was lying in bed with
his head and side throbbing with pain.

"Austin, just keep in mind that if she walked
in carrying that boy—there is nothing I can do for
her. She sealed her own fate."

No, he wouldn't believe that. He kept his expression straight as he said, "On your way out,

tell Thollie to bring me some soup and strong coffee."

Bradley turned to walk out and Austin said, "I need to know as soon as you find out anything."

Tight-lipped, Bradley said, "No need to worry. I'll come directly back here."

Eighteen

"Who helped you kidnap the boy?"

"I didn't kidnap him."

"How did you get into his bedroom?"

"I didn't."

"Where did you keep him hidden all these weeks?"

"I only wanted to get him back to his mother."

"Who helped you?"

"You must tell us!"

"Who helped you?"

"No! No! No one!"

Cheval screamed and jerked awake. She shivered, yet she felt that she was burning up. Shaking in the cold, dark cell of the jail house, she scrambled to the top of the straw mat nestled in the corner of the small room and huddled there against the stone wall. She coughed, thanking God it was just another bad dream. The guards hadn't dragged her back into that horrible room with the glaring light and faceless men.

She pulled the worn, foul-smelling blanket up around her shoulders and tucked it as best she could underneath her legs, thinking she'd never be warm again, never stop shaking. How she wished for her chemise, her stockings, and her cloak to help keep her warm. All those things she didn't take time to put on when she escaped with Bo.

With trembly fingers, she managed to place her long hair around her neck and shoulders to give her more warmth. She ached from the chills and coughing that had racked her whole body for the past two—or was it three?—days that she'd been here? She could no longer remember how long they'd kept her locked in the cold, dark room.

Her small cell had no window to let her know if it were night or day. The only light in the room came from a tiny opening in the top portion of the heavy, wooden door. And that light, which came from the lamps in the hallway, was too dim to be of much help.

The first day, she was too tired and sleepy to realize how cold she was. She only knew that when she finally awakened she was chilled to the bone and hadn't been warm since. She'd asked for an extra blanket several times, but the guards merely ignored her as they had whenever she tried to question them about what was going on outside that locked door. The men had been trained well. They remained silent, not even telling her the time of day when they brought her meals. It didn't take long to realize they didn't care about her welfare. She wondered if they knew why she was in jail?

She wondered why it was so damp and cold in the cell with the season already half-past the month of May. Summer was almost upon them. She longed to see the sunshine and feel its warmth.

A chill shook her body. She closed her eyes and tried to rest, but another coughing spasm started. It took her a few moments to catch her breath. Her throat felt raw and her chest ached. Her breathing was labored. She felt so bad she couldn't even cry. How could she when she knew that she'd done the right thing? She'd never be sorry she'd returned Bo to his mother.

Maybe it was better that she'd lost count of the days that she'd been in jail. What was the difference between three, five, or ten? She might never be allowed out of the tiny cell.

Occasionally she would hear shouts or cries of fear, anger, and rage from other inmates. That helped keep her from feeling so alone. She sympathized with them, knowing their frustration.

Twice a day, the guard brought her a cold cup of gruel. She ate it even though it had no taste. Only one time had the gruel actually been warm, and she'd gobbled it up so fast, she'd been ashamed of herself. When she'd finished the porridge, she'd held the warm cup to her breast until sometime during her sleep it fell from her arms and became as cold as the room.

At least they hadn't broken her spirit, she reminded herself as she huddled her feet and legs closer to her body and rearranged her hair around her chest to help warm her. She hadn't told them one word about Austin and the trip to France on board *Aloof*. And although they wouldn't confirm it for her, she was sure Bo had been reunited with his mother. She sensed it.

"Austin." She whispered his name into the silent room. She prayed he was all right from the strike with the cane and that some day he would find it in his heart to understand and forgive her for all she'd done to him. And Jubal. She hoped he'd forgive her one day, too. She wouldn't have hit him on the head if there had been any other way to get Bo out of the house.

Austin. Yes, thinking of him was the only thing that kept her sane, the only thing that gave her the will to go on when she shook so bad her teeth rattled together. When she could no longer bear the cold and darkness, the loneliness, she'd close her eyes and pretend she was on board *Aloof,* standing on the deck with Austin in the full light of day, the sun warming her face and the gentle wind blowing her hair.

Sometimes she'd think about their night of lovemaking and how warm his body had been entwined so closely to hers. She remembered how desperately she'd wanted to snuggle up against his back and stay there the rest of the night, the rest of her life.

Then sometimes the fairy tale disappeared and she remembered the man who helped take a little boy away from his mother and she'd realize they never could have had a happy life together because of that.

She coughed again, knowing the pain in her chest was not a good sign. But what would the guards care if she had lung fever? She pressed her cheek against the cold stone of the cell and closed her eyes. She had to get warm so she could go back to sleep. Rest was the only thing she could do to help heal her body.

"Yes," she whispered to herself. "I'll think about Austin. About the night he loved me, about what might have been." Oh, how she missed him!

She'd start at the beginning when he rubbed his thumb across her lips and continue until she'd relived every touch, every kiss, and every word he whispered during that wonderful night when she lay in his bed.

With eyes closed, she pretended her head lay on Austin's shoulder rather than against the cold, stone wall. She pretended it was his body that covered her and not the hole-ridden blanket. She pretended it was his rhythmic breathing she heard instead of her own ragged breath, and a peacefulness settled over her.

"Miss Worthington? Miss Worthington? Is it you?"

A muffled cry sprang from Cheval as she startled awake. Someone knelt in front of her, touching her arm. Thinking it was the guard wanting to take her back to that horrible room, she cried out again in a hoarse voice and pushed the man. He fell backward onto his rump, grunting, as she scrambled further into the corner, trying to get away from him.

"Don't be frightened. It's me, Bradley. Bradley Thornhill."

Mr. Thornhill? "Oh, Mr. Thor—" she tried to murmur his name, but a coughing fit attacked her, racking her chest and tearing at her throat. She shivered and grabbed for the blanket which had fallen around her waist.

"My God, that's a nasty cough." He pulled out his handkerchief and gave it to her. "How long have you had it?" he asked when she calmed down enough to hear him.

Cheval placed her hand on her forehead, trying to wipe the sleep from her eyes and dirt from her face, but her hand shook too bad. She couldn't stop shaking. Her lips trembled and her chest hurt from the racking cough.

Bradley picked up the lamp he'd brought in with him and held it up so he could see her. She turned away from the light until her eyes could adjust to the brightness.

"Saints alive! You look terrible. You're worse than Austin."

"Austin? Is he here?" Her heartbeat raced at the thought he'd come to see her, to get her out of this place.

"No. He's not here."

Her hope died.

"He's in bed—where it sounds like you should be. How long have you been sick?"

She coughed again. "What's wrong with Austin?" she asked, her eyes getting used to the light. She pulled the blanket up under her chin to try to keep herself from shaking.

Bradley reached over and felt her forehead.

"You're burning up with fever. What have they done to you? They can't treat you like this. You need medicine. Have they given you anything?"

Cheval never thought she'd welcome Bradley Thornhill's touch, but she did. His palm on her skin soothed her and gave her hope. It was hard to believe he was acting decent for a change.

"Austin. What's wrong with him?" she asked again.

"Nothing a couple of days in bed won't cure. Apparently the man who came to your rescue left Austin with a few bruises."

Cheval winced. She should never have asked that man to help her. But she'd had no way of knowing he'd attack Austin with his cane.

She wanted to ask more about Austin, but all she could do was cough.

"Here," Bradley said. "You're freezing to death. Take my coat."

"No. No, I—couldn't."

"Nonsense. I may not approve of your forward behavior toward Austin and I might have treated you poorly on the ship, but I'm not above a kind act when circumstances call for it. I can see you're sick. I'm not cold; and by the way you're shivering, it looks like you're swimming in icy-cold water. Your lips have no color to them."

He shrugged out of his summer wool coat and helped her slip her arms through the sleeves. It was so warm from his body heat, she felt as if she melted into it. It was such a welcome comfort she wanted him to go away and let her snuggle down into its warmth so she could go to sleep.

"Austin." She whispered his name.

"Don't worry about him right now. Take my word for it, he'll live; and he's not the one in this dreadful place. You are. Bradley took the blanket and folded it, then tucked it around her feet and legs. He set the lamp closer to her for what little warmth the small flame afforded the chilled room. "There. That should help you get warmer faster."

"Thank you," she whispered, although she could see Bradley wanted no thanks.

"Lie back and rest. I have a few questions."

"Did they take Bo back to his mother?" she asked, wishing her thoughts didn't feel so jumbled. "I keep asking, but they won't tell me anything."

"I'm sure they have, but that's something I'll have to check on when I leave here." Bradley settled himself on his knees in front of her. "I had a devil of a time finding you when I got here. At first I was told there was no one here by your name. But something in the guard's eyes made me suspicious, so I lied. I told them I'd received an anonymous message that you were here and you'd asked to see me, so they'd better find you."

She held the coat tighter as she coughed. She desperately wanted something warm to drink to soothe her aching throat.

"I'm sure I'll be questioned before I'm allowed to leave. They are going to want to know why you wanted to speak to me."

She nodded, trying to keep focused on his words when all she wanted to do was sleep.

"Keep your voice low in case they have anyone listening at the door."

"I understand."

"Now tell me how you got in jail. Did you bring the boy inside the building?"

"No, I was telling him goodbye out front when a uniformed man approached us." She coughed. "He asked me to come inside with him. He said they'd been looking for a boy who fit Bo's description."

"What have you told them so far?"

Her head started pounding. Her eyes felt heavy. "My name. I told them my name."

"What else?"

"Only that as soon as I realized who Bo was, I did everything in my power to get him back to his mother."

"And—"

"And, they just kept asking who helped me kidnap Bo. Where I had been hiding him? Things like that. I told them I needed to sleep. I was so tired."

"You didn't mention Austin's name or mine?"

"Of course not." She wished Bradley wasn't so short and to the point with her.

He studied her a moment. "It's my guess they're hoping a few days down here will make you change your mind about talking."

Cheval didn't like the doubt she heard in his

voice. "It won't." She looked straight into his eyes. "I'd never tell on Austin."

"I believe you—about Austin, anyway." He cleared his throat. "They haven't hurt you, have they?"

"Hurt me?" she asked. What did he think? They only brought her a cold cornmeal soup twice a day. She was burning up with fever; she had a bad cough, and they were trying to freeze her to death.

"You know. Have they hit you, or burned you, or—forced you in any way to do anything you didn't want to do?"

She shook her head. "No, nothing like that. At first, they didn't want me to sleep. They tried to keep me awake, but I was so tired from the journey and the night in Austin's be—house that I had to sleep." She glanced up at Bradley, but his expression didn't change. "I couldn't stay awake. Two men came in here and questioned me, but I was coughing so bad they soon left."

"And you're fairly sure you haven't told them anything about Austin, me, or the trip to France."

"I'm certain."

"It's strange," Bradley said, sniffing as he rubbed a hand, over his chin. "This should be all over the papers by now. They should have formally charged you in the kidnapping of Betsy Patterson's son, but they haven't." He rose and looked down at her. "Something's not right, and I intend to find out what's going on here. I'll be back."

"Will you tell Austin I'm so very sorry that man hit him?"

Bradley nodded, but she could tell he wasn't interested in what she'd said.

"You're forgetting your coat." She started to take it off.

He reached for it, then quickly drew back his hand. "No, no. You keep it until they get you another blanket."

"Thank you, Mr. Thornhill. I'm grateful for the use of your coat. It's very warm. And thank you for the lamp, too. It's so dark in here, I never know if it's night or day."

"I probably won't be back today, but I'll be back tomorrow. I'll also see that they get you some medicine. In the meantime, if they try to question you about any of this, don't say a word."

"No, I won't."

The soup had made Austin feel better, stronger. He'd had Jubal help him out of bed and walk him around the bedroom a couple of times, but it hurt like hell. He'd like to find the bastard who'd beaten him up and even the score. The driver would never have gotten the jump on him if that dandy hadn't already stunned him with the brass handle of his cane.

Not only was Austin in physical pain, he was worried sick about Cheval. He was tempted to crawl out of bed and go to the jail and find her himself. What could be keeping Bradley? He'd been gone for hours. Already it was nightfall.

Thollie had been in to light the lamp more than

an hour ago. He'd sent Jubal to see if he could find out what had happened to Bradley. They'd all been on *Aloof,* and they could all end up in jail.

At last, when he thought he couldn't stand the waiting another moment, he heard a knock on the front door. It had to be Bradley. His muscles tensed as he heard Thollie walk to the door and open it. Relief washed over him when he heard Bradley chatting with Thollie. It irritated him that Bradley would take time to talk to her when he must know that Austin was in a state of extreme frustration wanting news of Cheval.

"It's about time you got here," Austin said in a foul temper when Bradley walked through the bedroom door. "Where the hell have you been?"

Ignoring Austin's outburst, Bradley said, "Good evening to you, too. With a disposition like that, do you have to wonder why I stayed away so long?"

Austin wasn't in a mood for Bradley's banter or to apologize so he growled.

"My, my, being bed-ridden doesn't seem to agree with you, does it?"

"Cut the chit-chat and tell me you what you found out about Cheval."

Bradley's face turned serious. He stuffed his hands in the pocket of his ankle-length breeches. "She's there."

His heartbeat increased. "Did you see her?"

"Yes."

Bradley was hedging, but why? "How is she?"

"Not well."

He swallowed hard; the tightening in his side moved to his chest. "What is it?"

"I'm not sure. Maybe lung fever."

"Oh, no!" Austin tried to rise too quickly and moaned aloud as he gasped for breath. Bradley grabbed him by the shoulders and helped him lie back on the bed. He had to remember to move slowly until his ribs healed a little more.

"I have to go to her."

"Not now."

"Yes. Right now."

"Will you just stay in the bed and take care of yourself for the moment? I can handle this. That's why you sent for me, remember? Your ribs and muscles can't heal if you wrench them like that every time you move."

"I've got to go to her," he managed to say again.

"It won't do you any good to go to the jail right now. They won't let you see her. They only let me in because I'm a lawyer."

"I have something better. I have money, and it can out-talk you."

Bradley threw him a sardonic glance. "Are you ready to settle down and listen to me, or do we have to go on fencing for a few more minutes?"

Austin lay back on the pillow and looked up at his friend. "All right. Tell me what you found out."

"I had a devil of a time getting to see her. At first, I couldn't get anyone to admit she was there, but something told me the guard was lying. I told him what we'd discussed about an anonymous letter stating she was there and needed my help. I assured them I had no idea what it was about, and I demanded to talk to her.

"At last, they allowed me into her cell. She was coughing, shivering, and I think she had fever, too. I gave her my coat to help keep her warm and forced the guard to give her another blanket before I left. I wanted to go immediately to get her some medicine, but they wouldn't let me leave until I'd talked with Avery. I believe you've heard of him. He's been put in charge of her case."

"Why didn't you insist they send a doctor to look after her."

"As soon as they let me go, I went to Chadwick's Apothecary and he gave me some medicine for her. That was the best I could do as late as it was in the day. Don't worry, Austin, we're going to get all of this cleared up."

"I want her out."

"So do I. But nothing would make them release her tonight. This has to be handled with care."

"Do you think she's going to be all right?" Austin asked, wanting some assurance that Cheval wasn't in immediate danger of losing her life.

"I think she needs to get out of that cold cell; but, Austin, to be truthful, I don't see that happening in the next few days. They think she helped kidnapped Bo, and they're trying to find some evidence to prove it."

"I knew it. I tried to warn her. I tried to tell her they'd assume she kidnapped Bo. She thought

all she had to do was tell her story and they'd
believe her."

"What story? She has no story. She hasn't told
them anything, other than her name. Cheval's
been very cagy, thank God, and hasn't talked
about any of the rest of us. And, she didn't take
the boy inside. That's in her favor. Someone discovered her with him outside the building and
took them in."

"What?"

"It's true. They kept her awake, trying to tire her
out and force her into a confession or into telling
them something they could use against her; but she
held on and only told them that she was trying to
get the boy back to his mother. Which, thank God,
is true. I plan to point out to the police that she'd
have to be a total idiot to take a child she'd kidnapped so close to their headquarters."

"What did Avery want with you?"

"The usual. To know what she told me and what
I said to her. We played a cat-and-mouse game for
close to an hour. We were talking, but neither of
us was really saying anything. He didn't want to
show his hand, and I sure as hell wasn't about to
tell him all that I know about this kidnapping.
They'd put me in jail, too."

"And?"

"And what?"

"What did Cheval tell you?"

"Nothing, really. What could she tell me that I
don't already know? Besides, even if she'd told me
anything, it would be privileged information."

"Don't play that game with me."

"I don't intend to. I think you're trying to change this conversation from business to personal." Bradley stood up. "Marshal Avery told me they are holding Cheval for a possible kidnapping, but there's been no formal charge yet. I don't know if that is from lack of evidence or something else."

"What else could it be?"

"Not much of anything. I asked him why there had been no mention of any of this *possible kidnapping* in the papers, and he said they were keeping it quiet until they had all their information together; but I don't believe him. Something isn't right about this, and I haven't figured out what it is yet." He smiled. "But I will." He held up his hand. "And before you ask, yes I tried to get them to release her. They laughed in my face. They agreed I could get her some medication and that was all."

"God, I hope she's going to be all right," he murmured more to himself than to Bradley.

"I'm going to leave. I want to have some time to think about this; and I want to visit my son, who—I might add—you've only seen one time, before Winifred puts him to bed for the night."

"I'll be back around to see them. I promise." And he would, but first he had to get Cheval out of jail.

"For some reason they don't want this story leaked to the press. There's a reason and when I figure out what it is, I'll know what to do."

"I don't intend to wait around that long."

Bradley queried him with his eyes. "What are you talking about?"

"I'm going to the jail the first thing in the morning and tell Avery the truth."

"Don't be stupid. You can't tell them what you did."

"I have to. I can't let Cheval stay in jail for something I did when, if not for her, the boy would be with his father today. She did nothing wrong, everything right, and she's the one in jail. They should be thanking her, and I intend to tell them so."

"You can't even get out of bed by yourself."

Austin gritted his teeth. "I'll be better tomorrow. I've already been up once walking around and I'll do it a couple of more times during the night. By mid-morning I should be strong enough to make it down to police headquarters."

"You can't do that."

"Dammit, Bradley, I can't *not* do it. I wouldn't let anyone stay in jail for a crime they didn't commit and surely not the woman I love."

Bradley pursed his lips. "Love is it? Hmm—I should have thought as much. But to turn yourself in is suicide."

"I knew the risks when I decided to take that little boy to France."

"You're being too hasty," Bradley pleaded from the doorway. "Give me more time to work on this. If you go to the police, you'll be thrown in jail and in all likelihood Cheval won't be released.

The authorities obviously can't prove Cheval kidnapped Bo, so we have a chance to get her out. If you confess, we have no chance."

What Bradley said made sense, but— "We don't have time. Cheval is sick. I have to get her out of that place. I'll send her to the country. Mama will take care of her for me. Now, before you go, help me up so I can walk around the room again. I've got to be able to walk tomorrow."

Nineteen

It was mid-afternoon before Austin felt strong enough to make it down the stairs and out of the town house with Jubal's and Bradley's help. It hadn't been any easier getting in and out of the carriage that took them to the police building. He felt every bump in the road the carriage hit on the way downtown. Only now that he'd been sitting in Avery's office for the past few minutes had he started breathing a little easier.

Bradley worried him the way he paced in front of the window. Austin wished he'd sit down and stop mumbling to himself.

At last, the portly Avery opened the door and walked inside. "Mr. Radcliffe, I'm sorry you had to wa—Good Lord! What happened? You look awful." The older man's gaze darted from Austin to Bradley. "I can tell you we'll find whoever did this to you and see they're properly punished."

Austin gritted his teeth and rose to greet the officer. "That's not why I'm here," he told the man with the graying beard.

The police officer looked puzzled. "Ah—er—well, sit down and tell me what I can do for you."

He pursed his lips and pointed to the chair Austin had just occupied.

"No thank you. I'll stand." Austin realized he actually felt better when he was standing up straight. "I'm here about a young woman named Cheval Worthington."

Avery gasped and turned an angry face toward Bradley. "You told him about her. I said this case involving her was to remain an utmost secret." He clamped his teeth together sharply and glowered.

"He didn't have to tell me anything," Austin remarked. "I know why she's here. I'm the one who sent Bradley to talk to her."

The marshal walked behind his desk but didn't sit down. He remained standing like the other two men in the room. "We've been very careful concerning this case. What possible light can you shed on it?"

"I'm here to clear Cheval's name."

"Clear her name? I—I don't understand." His gaze darted again between the two men.

Avery was clearly confused as to why Austin, a well-respected businessman, would know anything about this dastardly deed. His facial expressions changed so rapidly they made him comical. Austin might have laughed if he hadn't been so worried about Cheval.

"I can assure you," Austin said, "Cheval Worthington had nothing to do with the kidnapping of Bo Bonaparte."

Again, surprise showed in the law officer's face. His mouth and his eyes rounded. "How did you know his name? We've not said one word about this to anyone." He turned to Bradley again. "You told him all this, didn't you? I'll have you arrested for—"

"I'm afraid I'll be the one you're arresting, Avery." Obviously the marshal wasn't listening to Austin.

"Austin, as your lawyer, I have to advise you one last time not to say anything about this," Bradley said, speaking up for the first time. "There has to be some other way out of this."

Austin's gaze remained focused on the marshal. "And I'll have to decline, again."

"What's going on here? I don't like being in the dark about this. If Mr. Thornhill didn't tell you about this case, I want to know who did."

"Bradley didn't have to tell me anything." Austin winced and grabbed his side when he moved too quickly. "I know all about the disappearance of Jerome Napoleon Bonaparte from the Patterson house on South Street. I probably know more about it than anyone."

"I have to advise you not to do this, Austin."

The pain in his side did little to help Austin hold onto his temper. "Keep quiet, Bradley."

Stepping closer to him, Bradley said, "No, I won't hold my silence. Not only are you my client, you're my brother-in-law, too. I thought I could stay out of it and let you do what you must for this woman, but I can't. I won't let you do this to yourself."

The reddish-brown freckles on Bradley's face

stood out against his white complexion. His agitated features enhanced the flushed coloring, but Austin ignored his pleadings. "You can't stop me."

"She's not worth it."

Austin grabbed the lapels of Bradley's coat. "The hell she's not."

"What's going on here?" Avery asked, scooting from behind his desk to stand before the two men.

"Is she worth spending the rest of your life in jail? Think about your mother."

"My mother's not in jail. Cheval is," Austin countered, letting go of Bradley's coat and turning toward the befuddled marshal.

Austin needed a moment to catch his breath. He wasn't strong enough for a fight. He walked over to the window and looked out to the busy street below. No, he didn't want to spend the rest of his life in jail. She didn't want anything to do with him because of what he did, but that wasn't going to keep him from getting her out.

It was funny that Bradley should mention his mother. This whole thing started because Napoleon's youngest brother saved his mother's life. He'd felt indebted, honor-bound to return the favor no matter the personal cost to him or others, such as Bo's mother. He was glad the boy had been returned, and he wasn't sorry he'd done his best to fulfill his vow. He had done what was expected of him as a man of his word. Now, he must do that again. Cheval was innocent. He was guilty. Nothing else needed to be said.

In trying to pay his debt to Jerome Bonaparte, he'd ended up being indebted to Cheval. It didn't surprise him that she hadn't breathed one word about his involvement in the kidnapping. He knew she wouldn't. She loved him, she'd admitted as much, but she didn't trust him. She thought he had no honor, and that hurt him even worse. She was right. As hard as it was for him to accept, he now realized they had no future together.

Austin turned back to the two men staring at him. He zeroed his gaze in on Avery. "Cheval had nothing to do with the kidnapping. I only hired her to look after the boy. It was all my idea."

"For God's sake, Austin, confess if you must, but at least get it right." The red-faced Bradley turned to Avery. "The kidnapping wasn't his idea. This entire plot came from Jerome Bonaparte and some man named Le Camus." He quickly turned to Austin. "You only provided the ship, remember?"

"Ship? What ship? And how did you know about Le Camus? Wait. Wait a minute," Avery said. "I think somebody better start at the beginning of this story."

"I'll tell you everything you want to know, but Cheval has to be released first."

"I can't do that," Avery said without hesitation.

Austin tensed. "She had nothing to do with—"

"She had possession of a little boy who's been missing from his mother for over two months," Avery interrupted him.

Austin's breath became shallow, making his side

hurt. "You can't let her go even if I swear to you she had nothing to do with the kidnapping?"

"No."

"What if I told you she kidnapped the boy from the kidnappers just so she could bring him back to his mother?"

"You can and should tell me everything you know about this case, but nothing you can say will make me release Miss Worthington."

Avery was so firm in his conviction it scared the hell out of Austin. "She didn't do anything wrong! The boy's mother should be down on her knees kissing Cheval's feet for returning her son."

The marshal fluttered his lashes over his dark-brown eyes. "And the mother might well do that, but I don't intend to. You obviously know quite a bit about this case, and I intend to find out all you know."

"I won't talk until Cheval is free."

Avery hesitated, then walked over to the door of his office and opened it. "I'm sorry, Mr. Radcliffe, but I can't let Miss Worthington go. I'm going to have to arrest you." He looked out the door and yelled, "Guard!"

"Dammit! I knew this was going to happen," Bradley muttered under his breath.

When Austin awoke the next morning, his side felt better. He felt more mobile and he could breathe much easier, but that hadn't kept him from spending an uncomfortable night in the jail cell. What had made the night doubly bad for him was knowing that Cheval had already spent several nights in this hellhole.

It was no wonder she was sick. The stone walls and windowless rooms held the dampness and cold inside. He had to make them listen to him and get her out. If telling the truth wouldn't get her out, maybe his money would. It was the only thing left to do. He didn't care how many he had to bribe to get it done.

"Cheval." He whispered her name several times into the quiet of the dark cell. He was going crazy with worry, wanting to know if she were feeling better. All night he'd thought about her. His arms ached to hold her. He ached to comfort her and see to her needs.

Austin closed his eyes and remembered Cheval as she'd stood in his bedroom dressed in the long-sleeved nightgown with her hair flowing past her shoulders. He remembered her sweet scent and her outstretched arms beckoning, asking him to accept her, welcoming him into her embrace. He remembered the taste of her and longed to kiss her again. In his mind he lingered over each touch, each caress, each sigh they'd shared. It had pleased him more and more each time he'd brought her to fulfillment.

If he didn't watch it, he was going to drive himself crazy. He had to remember that no matter how much he wanted Cheval, she didn't want him. She didn't trust him. He had to forget all that and concentrate on getting her out of jail. That had to be the only important thing on his mind. He didn't care what they did to him: He was guilty. But he loved her. He had to find a way to get her out and protect her.

Austin grunted as he rose from the knotty pallet that served as a bed. He felt better standing up than lying on the straw mattress that did little to shield his rib cage from contact with the hard-packed earth floor.

As he paced the dark room, he grew angry with himself for allowing Cheval to become involved in this illegal mess. He was trying to uphold his honor when he agreed to do this, but what good would his honor be to him if he didn't manage to get Cheval out of jail?

Honor. Jerome had put him in a no-win situation. He saw that now. What had been right for his honor and for Jerome had been wrong for Betsy and her son.

So many times, a thousand times, he wished he'd followed his first instinct that rainy night long ago and not agreed Cheval could go along with him on the journey to France. He'd realized then she was willing to fight for what she wanted, fight for what she believed in. But selfishly, he'd wanted her to accompany him. He'd been intrigued by her, enraptured by her, bewitched by her the first night he saw her, and that hadn't changed. It had only grown deeper, fuller, and brighter. And now, after teaching her how a man and woman please each other, after loving her, he didn't know how he was going to live without her.

Austin heard the key in the lock and turned toward the door. It swung open and Bradley walked in carrying a bundle of clothes.

"I thought you'd never return," Austin said, taking the clothes from him. "What took you so long? What have you been doing?"

"I—"

"No, don't answer that," he interrupted before Bradley had the chance to respond. "It doesn't matter what you've been doing right now. Have you seen Cheval today? Is she better? Have you found a way to make them release her?"

"Austin, please, one question at a time. Right from the beginning I've told you this would be difficult. All I can report is that I'm working on it."

"That's not good enough," Austin countered angrily, throwing the bundle of clothes to the straw mat in the corner.

"It has to be." Bradley kept his voice low.

"It!" Austin's voice rose even though yelling only made his side hurt worse. "It what? What the hell are you working on, Bradley?"

"Trying to get Cheval and *you* released. If this had been handled properly in the first place, we wouldn't—"

"Save it, Bradley. I'm in no mood to hear it." He rubbed his forehead, then slid his hand through his hair, trying to ease the building tension. He started pacing again. "I don't have to be reminded that the whole damn mess is my fault for agreeing to take the boy to his father in the first place. A man has a right to have his son with him," he said, knowing that didn't justify what he'd done or what had happened since, knowing he wasn't even sure he believed that anymore.

"No. No, he doesn't have the right if he is a foreigner and has to steal the child from the mother, whose father, I might add, is one of the wealthiest men in America," Bradley quipped sarcastically.

Austin tried to calm his breathing. "I know you're right," he said in an attempt at an apology. "I don't care what happens to me. I just want Cheval out of here and taken to my mother. She'll care for Cheval, help her get well." Austin stood close to Bradley and said in a low voice, "I don't care who you have to pay or how much. Get her out today."

Bradley shook his head. "That's not as easy to do as it is to say. And don't be so hard on yourself. Cheval has to take some responsibility for this predicament."

"No."

"Yes," Bradley insisted. "I could have arranged for the child to be delivered without anyone ever knowing Cheval or you were involved in this, if only she hadn't taken matters into her own hands."

"Yes, well, Cheval had reason not to trust me or you when I told her that."

"And on the same subject, there has been a bit of news that is of interest to us. Betsy Patterson Bonaparte and her son Bo were seen in public last night for the first time in over two months. They've both recovered from their long illnesses."

Austin was surprised at the relief he felt. He nodded. "Good. I'm glad to know Cheval accomplished what she set out to do and that the boy is home with his mother." He couldn't keep the pride out of his voice. Cheval was a remarkable woman.

"It seems so, but—"

"But?"

He glanced over at Bradley. "But there's still nothing in the papers or on the streets about a kidnapping."

"Why?"

Bradley folded his hands across his chest and pondered. "If they were keeping the kidnapping quiet in hopes of somehow getting Bo back home safely, that's happened. Why weren't charges filed against the two of you the first thing this morning?"

Austin was beginning to see what Bradley was getting at. "Are you sure no charges have been filed?"

"Positive. Naturally I asked upon arriving here. You can't be charged with a kidnapping if they haven't reported the kidnapping existed."

The hair on the back of Austin's neck stood out. "So what's going on? Why are they still holding us without charging us?"

"I don't know yet. That's what I'm trying to find out. I've asked to speak with Avery. He was unavailable when I arrived, so I came on over here to see you."

"Go back to his office and camp out at his door. Don't leave until you know exactly what's going on."

"I will."

"Have you seen Cheval this morning?"

"No, I wanted to see you first."

"Bradley, this is a hellhole," he said, unable to keep his thoughts from wandering back to Cheval. "I want her out of here. I don't care if you tell them I stole the child from his crib. Just get her out."

"You aren't listening to me or Avery. I can tell them, but it won't free Cheval. Austin, stop thinking about how you feel about her and what you know to be true. The authorities don't know her. It doesn't matter how big or little they think your part in this is. It won't affect what they do to Cheval. Your part in this is just that. Your part. Cheval has to stand on her own. What you did or didn't do won't have any bearing on what they think she did."

"That's not fair."

"For better or worse, that's the way it works."

"Cheval. Cheval."

She heard someone calling her name, but she didn't want to wake up. After she had taken the medicine Bradley had brought her, her coughing had eased a little and she'd slept. She'd finally gotten warm. She didn't want to peek out from under the covers. And every time she woke up, her chest and throat hurt. Every time she sat up, she started coughing. There was a constant roaring in her ears that was driving her crazy. She didn't know what was wrong with her. She only knew that now that she'd gotten comfortable and warm, she didn't want to move.

Something shook her shoulder, but she didn't raise her head from underneath the blankets. "Go away," she mumbled past an achy throat, trying to shake off the offending disturbance.

"Cheval, you must wake up."

"Go away," she said, hoping whoever was bothering her would leave her alone.

"You have to get up and change clothes. Someone wants to see you."

Bradley's voice finally penetrated her drugged mind. Her eyes popped open and her glazed vision landed on Bradley's face. "Austin? Is Austin coming to see me?" she managed to ask in a voice so hoarse it wasn't recognizable as her own.

"You will be seeing him, yes, but there's also someone else who wants to see you."

"Oh," she scrambled to a sitting position and immediately felt dizzy. She forced the feeling aside and started trying to comb her hair with her fingers.

"Don't worry about that right now," Bradley said, taking hold of her hand. "Here, take this. I've brought you some clean clothes to change into and a brush and pins for your hair. Thollie put everything together for you, but they wouldn't let me bring you any water to wash with."

"That's all right, I'll manage." She took the articles, grateful to see that the bundle included a chemise, stockings, and her cloak. How she'd wished for those things since she'd been in jail. Tears welled up in her eyes. Suddenly she felt like crying. "Thank you for the clean clothes and for the medicine. It helped."

"Don't mention it."

She started shaking. "I—I needed fresh clothes, and I—I want to see Austin."

"Please, Cheval, don't do this. I have three daughters, but I don't know what to do when they cry."

"No, I won't cry," she said, wiping the tears from her face.

Bradley touched her forehead. "You still have fever. Are you feeling any better?"

She brushed at her hair with her hand. "My cough is better, I think. My chest and throat still hurt."

"And your voice is almost gone, I see. Let me do the talking. I'll fill you in on what's happened the past couple of days."

"First tell me about Austin."

"He's—in jail."

"Jail. How? Why? How did they find out what he did? I haven't said a word about him." She was too stunned, too distraught to say more.

"Don't get upset. I must admit I might have misjudged you. I—I admire you for remaining so strong in all this. What happened to Austin was nothing you said or did. He did it. He turned himself in trying to get you out."

"But why?" She brushed her hair away from her face. "I'll tell them it was all my doing and that they have to let him go."

Bradley sighed. "That should work. If Austin insists it was all his plot and you insist it was all yours, it'll make my job easy. They'll end up keeping both of you in jail for the rest of your lives."

"What has he said? Why did they put him in jail? Are you sure they'll let me see him?"

"Yes, you'll see him. I'd really like to answer all your questions; but, quite frankly, Cheval, we don't have the time right now. I'm going to step outside the door while you change. We'll talk on the way to the marshal's office. There's someone who wants to speak to you and Austin, and we don't want to keep her waiting."

"Her? Who?"

"Bo's mother, Betsy Patterson."

Twenty

Bradley's comment stunned Cheval so she couldn't speak. Betsy Patterson wanted to see her? Why?

As if sensing her need to be alone for a few minutes, Bradley opened the cell door and said again, "I'll wait out here until you're dressed. Just open the door whenever you're ready."

Cheval's mind filled with all sorts of possibilities as she sat down on her mattress to change clothes. Bo's mother wanted to see her? Why? Did she want to say horrible things to her? Did she want to quiz her about where Bo had been and how he'd been treated? What did the woman want with her?

Cheval tried to slow her wildly beating heart. She tried to will away the pounding in her head and the pain in her chest. Well, it didn't matter, she bravely assured herself. As long as Bo was with his mother, that was the important thing. She could take whatever Betsy Patterson had to say to her. Even after all that she'd been through, she'd do it all again to return Bo to his mother. A peacefulness settled over her. She had not been able to help her sister, but she had helped Betsy.

Her head felt heavy and she had very little strength as she pulled her dirty dress over her head. She shivered as she hurriedly slipped on her chemise and then the long-sleeved green velvet dress Bradley had brought. A weakness in her legs forced her to sit down on her pallet.

She had no strength. She wasn't sure she could hold her head up through a meeting with anyone. Her cough was better, but not gone away. Her whole body ached and she felt as if a cow had kicked her in the chest. Her throat was still so sore she couldn't swallow without a burning pain. She knew she'd feel better if she could just see the outside world, if she could just feel the sunshine on her face.

As fast as her shaky hands would allow, she donned her stockings. After stepping into her slippers, she managed to make some semblance of order out of her hair by arranging it into a bun at the back of her neck. When she finished, she opened the door and stepped out into the hallway. Even the dim light from the oil lamps stationed on the wall every fifteen feet hurt her eyes.

The guard standing beside Bradley stepped forward, holding shackles in his hands. "I'm sorry, Miss. I've got to do this."

She looked from Bradley to the guard. "I—I'm not going to run away."

"I know that, Miss, but it's the rules." He knelt down and placed shackles around her ankles.

She turned to Bradley. He nodded and said, "I've already spoken to him about this. There's nothing to be done. He'll have to put them around your wrists, too."

In all the days she'd been in the jail, this was the first time she'd felt like a criminal. Why were they treating her this way?

While the guard fastened her anklets, she handed Bradley his coat. "Thanks for lending this to me." She coughed. "Even with the extra blanket, I don't think I could have made it another night without its warmth."

"I only wish I had known you were here before you became so ill. Here, take my arm and let me help you walk. It's quite a ways to the marshal's office."

Three or four steps down the narrow hallway, Cheval realized just how weak and unsteady on her feet the illness had made her. She had to rely heavily on Bradley's strength as the guard led them through a labyrinth of hazy halls and darkened rooms. Several times she had to ask them to stop and let her catch her breath and renew her strength before continuing. Her legs were so weak she felt as if she might fall before they led her into a small office and helped her sit down in a chair.

A coughing spasm left her tired and breathless. She felt so bad seeing Bo's mother held no appeal for her as it once would have. She'd wanted to tell the woman how brave her little boy was. Now, all she wanted to do was see Austin so she could lie back down and go to sleep.

"Are you going to be all right?" Bradley asked, placing a cup to her mouth.

She nodded after taking a sip of the tepid water. The brightness of the room and expended energy had Cheval's head spinning and her vision blurred. She'd had no idea she'd been buried so deep within the bowels of the jail house.

The door to the office opened, and Cheval looked up and saw Austin. She smiled and tried to rise, wanting to run to him, but realized that not only was she too weak to stand, but the guard had locked her shackles to the legs of the chair. "Austin," she murmured softly and reached for him.

"Cheval!"

Austin started toward her, but the guard stepped between them and pushed him into a chair on the other side of the room. "Dammit! Let me see her."

"You have to sit down or I'll be forced to take you back to your cell," the burly guard said.

"No, let me go to her," Austin said, struggling against the burly man's hands, which were clamped around his arms like iron bands.

"You have to sit down there, sir. I have to chain you to the chair."

"Austin, sit down," Bradley echoed the guard.

"Can't you see I'm not trying to escape?" Austin argued, still trying to make his way over to Cheval. "I just want to see about her."

Cheval let her gaze feast upon Austin. It seemed

like it had been years since she'd seen him. It
lifted her spirits just knowing he was in the same
room with her. She saw the bruise on his forehead
where he'd been struck with the cane, and renewed anger at herself and the man who'd hit
him surged within her. She noticed that, like her,
Austin had been shackled at the wrists and ankles.
She hated seeing him bound, but she was so happy
to see him it brought tears to her eyes.

"Cheval, how are you feeling?" Austin asked
over the guard's broad shoulder.

His eyes caressed her face with a warm expression, comforting her. She wished she'd had a bath
and her hair had been washed. She wished she
could get close enough to touch him and breathe
in his scent, feel his warmth. As it was, it made
her feel better just to look at him.

"I'm fine," she managed to say past a tight,
scratchy throat. She couldn't take her gaze off
him. She'd worried that he might not want to see
her after all that she'd done to him and Jubal.
Thank God he wasn't so angry with her that he
didn't want to talk to her. She wanted to crawl up
in Austin's lap, lay her head against his chest, and
let the beating of his heart put her to sleep.

"Bradley, tell them I don't want to run away or
try to free her. I just want to be near her," he
said, straining against the guard's grip.

"Austin, the guard can only follow the orders
he's been given." He gently touched Austin's
shoulder. "Sit down and let this man do his job.
We'll see what Avery says when he gets here. He's

allowed to break some of the rules. The guard can't."

"That's easy for you to say," Austin remarked, but sat down in the chair. "What in the hell are we doing in here, anyway? This goon wouldn't tell me anything."

"They're guards, not messengers." Bradley kept his tone level. "Mrs. Jerome Bonaparte or Miss Betsy Patterson—I'm not sure which way she prefers to be addressed these days—has asked to see you and Cheval."

"What? Are you sure about this? Why?"

"I'm sure, and I don't have a clue as to why. Right from the beginning this has been a strange case. Nothing has been handled the way it should have been. I'm as confused about this as anyone."

Cheval tried not to cough, but to no avail. She didn't want Austin to know how bad she felt, but there was no stopping the chesty cough that had plagued her since her second day in jail.

"Let me out of the goddamned chair so I can see about her!" Austin said, struggling against the restraining shackles that held him bound to the chair.

The guard didn't move.

Cheval didn't want Austin to get in trouble trying to help her. "I'm fine, really," she lied. She knew she wasn't. She had no strength. Sheer force of will was keeping her upright in the chair when her body begged to slip quietly to the floor. She prayed that Bo's mother would come quickly and say her piece before Cheval fainted. "My cough is better now, Austin; please do as Bradley asked."

"Would you like some more water, Cheval?" Bradley asked.

"No thank you," she answered, afraid if she put anything into her stomach it would come right back.

The office door opened and Marshal Avery walked inside. Behind him came a tall, slender woman impeccably attired in a chamois-colored dress and matching leghorn hat. Her clothes were exquisite in fashion and fit, and her glowing dark hair perfectly coiffured beneath her straw hat. All eyes in the room turned to the lissome, regal-looking lady. Cheval gasped. Bo's mother was as stunningly beautiful as Cheval had heard she was.

Betsy stood with erect head and straight shoulders as she glanced from Austin to Cheval before turning to Avery. "Leave us. I want to talk to them alone."

"I can't do that," Avery said. "We can't leave you alone with the prisoners."

"Don't be ridiculous, Marshal. I can see you have them both chained to their chairs. I don't think I'll come to any harm." She turned to Bradley. "You, too."

"Oh, I'm their attorney." He smiled at the lovely woman and pulled on the tail of his waistcoat. "Whatever you have to say to them can be said in my presence."

Cheval tried not to cough, but again it was no use. It was embarrassing. She had to make it through this so she could ask the woman about Bo. She knew he'd be happy to be home, but she wondered if he missed her a little, wondered if he'd ever called her name.

"This woman is sick," Betsy said to the Marshal.

"Er—well, we—"

"Let her rot in that goddamned damp cell and didn't do a damn thing for her," Austin said, interrupting Avery.

Betsy walked over and opened the office door. "Leave us," she said again. "All of you. If you're so worried about me, stand outside the door."

Avery and Bradley continued to mumble their objections as they followed the guard out the door. As soon as Betsy had closed it behind them, Cheval asked in a husky voice, "Bo, how is he? Is he all right? Is he happy to be home?"

"She didn't have anything to do with the kidnapping," Austin said. "Tell them to let her go. You can see she's sick and in need of care."

Ignoring Austin's outburst, the woman walked closer to Cheval. Looking down at her, Betsy said, "He's fine. Are you the young woman who took care of him? Miss Worthington?"

Cheval tried to smile, but she wasn't sure her lips managed it. "Yes, he's—" she coughed again. "A very bright young man. I know you must be very proud of him."

A smile graced Betsy's lips, but it didn't reach her eyes. Those alluringly lovely, dark round eyes were sad. They told the story of a woman who'd seen too much, wanted too much, and had been denied too much. How Cheval would have loved to have met this beautiful young woman before Jerome had come into her life.

"Yes. I am proud of him. Bo tells me you were teaching him how to play chess."

She nodded, praying she'd be able to stay alert until she heard what Betsy wanted to say.

"Miss Worthington, did you kidnap my son?"

Cheval hesitated. She didn't want to get Austin in any more trouble, but looking up into this woman's face she knew she couldn't lie to her either. "No."

"Were you in the process of returning Bo to me when you were stopped by the police?"

"Yes."

"I hired her to look after the boy on the voyage to France," Austin admitted.

Both Cheval and Betsy looked his way.

"Austin, no!" Cheval managed to say.

"This woman deserves the truth. Cheval tried to force me to take Bo back to Baltimore the moment she found out he'd been kidnapped."

"Don't, Austin," she pleaded.

"Cheval, I'm not going to let you be blamed for something that I did."

Betsy walked closer to Austin. "I received a letter from Jerome stating that he had taken Bo so that his son might have his rightful place by his father's side in Westphalia. Were you involved in that?"

Austin didn't blink. "Only to the point that my ship was used to take Bo to France."

"And what happened that he wasn't delivered to his father?"

"While I went ashore to make final arrangements and to meet the man who was to take Bo to his father, Cheval took over my ship and through great sacrifice brought him back to America. Her only involvement was in taking the utmost care of Bo and bringing him safely back to you."

"Austin, don't," she whispered, wanting to protect him from himself.

"Cheval, you've done nothing wrong and everything that was right. Bo is back home and happy. I want you out of here. I want Jubal to take you to my country estate so my mother can care for you and make you well." He turned his attention to Betsy. "For reasons of my own, I agreed to take Bo to Jerome."

Betsy's eyes seemed to look through him to a distant place. "Yes, I knew it was Jerome from the moment I found Bo gone. You'll never know the anguish I felt, what I went through that morning. And two days later when I received Jerome's note telling me that he was taking our son, I thought I had no reason to go on living."

Cheval's heart felt as heavy as her head, her chest, and her eyelids. She'd known what Betsy would be going through. She'd watched her sister fight those same feelings. She knew what Betsy was capable of. Thank God she'd returned Bo in time to save Betsy.

Standing straight, still, Betsy spoke again, looking into the past. "I felt it was as if Napoleon had won again. That mighty warrior had struck my breast again and left me bleeding. I once thought I no longer had a heart to be ripped out, but I was wrong. Napoleon!" She whispered the Emperor's name reverently. "I couldn't fight him. I couldn't win. I tried. Oh, how I tried! He was too powerful, too great. I would have been the perfect wife for King Jerome, much better than the woman he now has by his side."

Betsy closed her eyes for a moment, and when she opened them, they were smiling. She didn't look at Cheval or Austin, but appeared to be in a faraway land. "Jerome always called me his Elise. Jerome. A more handsome, polished, and gallant man I never met. His manners were courtly. His clothes elegant, fine. He wore scarlets, purples, and blues sewn with gold and silver threads. His magnificence was overwhelming. He was extravagant in everything he did, and I loved it all. I was proud to be his wife. Jerome with all his glorious trappings was mine. I once told my father I'd rather be the wife of Jerome Bonaparte for one hour than any other man's wife for the rest of my life."

The smile faded from her eyes. "How cruel of fate to call my hand and rob me of the only thing in life I wanted. Dear Jerome. His exquisite manners and smooth veneer could not hide his cowardice, his treachery.

"Oh, but for a time, he loved me above all else, including Napoleon. Some think I hate Napoleon for what he did to me, banishing me from Europe; but in truth, I have grudging admiration for him."

A bitter laugh flowed past her perfectly shaped lips. "Napoleon wouldn't let me step one foot off the ship. Not in France, not Lisbon, not even when we arrived at Amsterdam. He was such a powerful man! It was my tragedy to have crossed paths with Napoleon at a time when he was consolidating his Empire with royal alliances. That was all that mattered to him. Jerome's happiness mattered not at all.

"The Emperor denied me admittance to France, to his family, and to his empire and sent me back to what I hated most on earth—my Baltimore obscurity. Even that condemnation could not destroy the admiration I felt for Napoleon's genius and his glory." Her voice softened further. "If only Jerome could have had some of Napoleon's strength, some of his madness. Everything would have been different.

"When I first arrived back at my father's house, cowardice was the only thing that prevented me from exchanging life for the grave. But later it was Bo. Jerome's son.

"My father wanted me to remarry, but how could I when I am now the wife of a king?" As if sensing she'd said too much, Betsy pulled a handkerchief from inside the cuff of her sleeve and wiped the corners of her eyes.

Too mesmerized by her story to speak, Cheval remained silent, but Austin asked, "What do you plan to do to Jerome?"

Bitterness crept into her voice. "After what Jerome has done to me, all I can possibly do for him is hold my tongue. I knew Jerome wanted his son. He begged me to send Bo to him in Westphalia. He even asked me to join him—but only after he'd made the marriage Napoleon had arranged for him. How childish, how immature, how arrogant of him to think he could have two queens! My sorrow, my cross is that Jerome didn't have the strength of character to stand up to his mighty brother, Napoleon." Betsy turned to Cheval. "I can't have Jerome, the love of my life; but thanks to you, I do have his son. Please accept my gratitude."

Cheval managed a weak nod.

"No matter how diverse your roles in this incident, I must ask a deeply important favor from you both." She looked from one to the other. "I'll see to it there will be no charges brought against either of you under the condition that you never make this kidnapping public."

Cheval gasped.

Austin felt as if his heart might beat out of his chest. Did the woman know what she was saying? Did she have the authority to say it? He chanced a quick glance over to Cheval. He didn't know how much longer she could sit in that chair. She looked as if she were about to faint.

"Cheval can go free?" Austin asked.

"Yes, both of you. But only if you promise complete silence. I can't allow this story to even be rumored. There could be any number of like at-

tempts from fortune hunters. It would be too easy
for someone to decide to kidnap Bo and take him
to his father for favors or hold Bo for ransom.
The next person to try might not have a Miss
Worthington to look after Bo. Someone else might
succeed. Bo will be a wealthy young man one day.
Not only from his father, the king, but also from
my father. I'm certain it would be to Bo's detri-
ment to allow gossip of this incident to flourish."

"We can both go free? No charges? No questions? No answers? No mention this ever happened?"

"That's correct. You must never breathe a word.
The important thing is that I have my son. From
now on, I'll take proper care to see that he's safe
and guarded at all times until he's old enough to
make up his own mind about his father."

Austin couldn't believe this was true. It was too
easy. Silence was all she requested after he'd admitted to taking her son all the way to France. No
anger? No punishment? No revenge? What kind
of woman was she?

Cheval coughed and Austin glanced her way.
There wasn't much time. "I swear we'll not say a
word of this, but what of the marshal and the
guards? What is to keep them from talking?"

"The guards don't know why you're here. And
the marshal and the few others who know about
this want to keep their jobs. As you know, Mr.
Radcliffe, my father is very powerful in this city.
The glory of telling a story such as this dims in

the light of a man facing the desire to feed and take care of his family."

Without further hesitation, Austin said, "Swear to it, Cheval."

Her head hung low as she whispered, "I swear, I'll never breathe a word to anyone."

"I swear we'll take this knowledge to our graves."

The woman's sad, dark eyes rested on his face for a moment. "As soon as I've talked with the marshal, you'll be free to go." She turned and as quietly, regally as she had entered, she walked out.

"Bradley!" Austin called, pulling against the chains that bound him to the chair. "Come in here and get us out of these damned things."

Twenty-one

Sunshine spilling across the foot of the bed was the first thing Cheval saw when she awakened. She lay on her back in the bed in a room she didn't recognize. Slowly she looked around. The room was pleasant to the eyes. A low fire burned in the fireplace, giving her a cozy feeling. Above the mantel hung a round mirror with brass candlesticks mounted on each side. A dusty-pink rose pattern had been stenciled along the top of the wall just below the ceiling. Draperies in the same color fabric hung at the one window. The side chair sitting next to her bed had been covered in a flower-printed velvet.

Cheval coughed, but noticed it didn't rack her whole body. She took a deep breath. The ache was gone. She swallowed. There was very little pain in her throat and the constant roaring had left her ears. She smiled as she raised up on her elbows. Her head felt a bit fuzzy, but the dizziness that had plagued her had vanished. She tried to remember exactly what had happened to bring her to this beautiful room.

Austin. They were sitting in a room talking to

Betsy Patterson. Cheval remembered trying her best to focus on the conversation, willing herself not to pass out. The next thing she remembered was Austin holding her in his arms and carrying her outside the prison.

Oh, yes, she remembered feeling the sunshine on her face, breathing the fresh air, hearing the street sounds of people walking and talking, vendors, horses and carriages. Closing her eyes and sighing, she remembered more. Being held close to Austin's chest as the carriage clipped along the bumpy road. She remembered his warmth, softly spoken words, kisses on her forehead, his arms around her waist and shoulders.

Cheval could dream of Austin forever, but she also recalled a kind-looking woman's face. She remembered that the woman had warm, gentle hands, a sweet smile, and a soft voice that inspired trust.

"Oh, you're awake and almost sitting up, too."

Cheval's eyes popped open. The woman she'd been thinking about walked into her room. Cheval knew immediately she was Austin's mother, although she didn't remember that anyone had actually told her that.

"How wonderful! My goodness you look so much better than when Austin brought you here. I believe you have more color to your cheeks and lips this morning, too. And your eyes have lost that glazed expression that frightened all of us." She stopped beside the bed.

The older woman looked frail with her light-green eyes, pale complexion, and dark-brown hair, but her vivacious smile and tone of voice belied that notion. She was a woman of strength.

"You're Austin's mother."

"Yes, dear." She smiled cheerfully. "We met, but you were more or less asleep, I think. You looked dreadful when Austin brought you up the stairs in the middle of the night. I worried you wouldn't make it until morning."

"I've been sick."

"That's making light of your condition. You were seriously ill, young lady. Seriously."

"What—how long have I been here?"

Mrs. Radcliffe clasped her hands together in front of her. "Oh, not long, dear. Less than a week. Once we got you settled in a warm bed and started giving you proper medication and my own secret-recipe chicken broth, you started getting better." She patted Cheval's arm. "Your fever went away. Those horrible coughing fits subsided, and you started resting through the night."

"Yes, I can tell that I'm not coughing very much this morning."

"You'll feel more like your old self as each day comes along."

Cheval moistened her lips and raked her hair away from her face with the palm of her hand. "How's Austin?"

Mrs. Radcliffe folded her arms across her chest and huffed. "Back at work, I'm afraid." A worried wrinkle appeared between her eyebrows. "As soon as your fever broke, he made arrangements to return to Baltimore. I begged him not to go back to town for the rest of the week, but he said he'd been away from his business too long as it was.

"He took that long trip to Europe, you know, and he says he's behind in everything. He's been handling the business since his father died five years ago. He was so worried about you, dear. He's already sent Jubal back once just to get word of your progress."

Disappointment settled over Cheval. She'd so hoped Austin was here so she could tell him how sorry she was about that man hitting him and how she was overwhelmed with gratitude for Betsy's generosity. But, maybe he was right in leaving before she fully recovered. Seeing him would only make it harder to leave him. She loved Austin with all her heart, but she couldn't forget what he'd done.

"Yes, I know about the trip to Europe." Cheval took a deep-sighing breath. "It was nice of Austin to bring me here and so very kind of you to offer your home to me."

"Austin told me to tell you he'd be back to check on you in a few days. He asked me how long I thought it would take for you to recuperate, and I told him at least two weeks. I'm pleased to say you're making wonderful progress. Do you feel like eating?"

"Yes," she said, wanting to get her strength back as soon as possible. She had to find a way to live without Austin in her life. "I'm sorry to have intruded on your home. I'll always be grateful to you for allowing Austin to disrupt your life like this."

"Don't be ridiculous," she said, brushing aside Cheval's comment. "Austin wanted you here, and so do I. You're presence not only gives me company, it gives me something to do other than to look after myself. It can get quite lonely out here sometimes with only the servants to talk to."

"Thank you," Cheval whispered, realizing she was getting tired.

"Well, now, I'm going to let you rest while I have the cook prepare a tasty dinner for us. I told Austin when he returned we'd roast a goose and glaze it with apple butter. It's divine and one of his favorites. I'm sure you'll love it, too."

The Maryland countryside was beautiful, enchanting, bewitching, Cheval thought as she lounged on a chair in the back garden of the Radcliffe estate. She didn't want to go back to the hustling crowds and noise of downtown Baltimore, but she couldn't accept Beatrice's hospitality much longer. She grew stronger each day.

Cheval had walked through the flower garden three times that day, gaining more strength each time she made the trip. Another day of rest and she'd be ready to declare herself well enough to start applying for employment as a governess. It had been more than six months since she'd left the Duncans. She hoped any gossip surrounding that had been forgotten.

Cheval lay back in the lounge chair and shielded her eyes with her hand as she looked beyond the trees on the outskirts of the property and to the flaming blue-and-red sky of late afternoon. The day was so perfect and peaceful she didn't want it to end.

Austin's face appeared before her as it had so many times since she'd recovered. In one way she hoped he'd return before she left his house, but in another she worried about what they would say to each other. She didn't want their last words to be in anger. She was sure he'd have things to say to her about running away from his town house.

She closed her eyes and thought back to how he'd seemed so worried about her in that office at police headquarters, but she also remembered he felt guilty that he was the reason she was there. She couldn't help but wonder how he really felt about her.

That night in his arms, she'd known that he cared for her, but what did he feel now that she'd succeeded in returning Bo to his mother? Was he angry with her for all she'd done to accomplish that? And exactly how did she feel about him? She loved him with all her heart. Of that there was no doubt. But after hearing Betsy's story of how she didn't want to live when she discovered her son gone made her know she'd done the right thing.

"Beautiful, isn't it?"

Cheval looked around and saw Beatrice Radcliffe standing on the slate patio in the middle of the garden. She wore a sunbonnet, and a thin shawl draped her slender shoulders.

"Yes, summer is my favorite time of year. I hate those cold, gray days of winter. I like sunshine and warmth even though Baltimore is more noted for its drab, rainy weather than for its sunshine."

Mrs. Radcliffe walked over and took the chair beside Cheval. She chuckled lightly. "Where's your bonnet? Your skin is going to get red and splotchy. You'll end up with as many freckles as my son-in-law, Bradley Thornhill."

Cheval's wide smile turned into a laugh as she thought about the red-faced lawyer and how he'd insisted on putting her in her place. She had to admit that she now felt kinder toward Bradley than she had at first. She'd always be grateful he'd given her his coat.

"Do you know him?"

Cheval nodded. "We've met. Right now I don't care about my skin. I'm so happy to feel the sunshine on my face that I can't worry about a pink nose and red cheeks."

"Well, I have orders to take care of you, and burning your skin is not in your best interest."

"I guess not." She looked up at the magnificent expanse of sky and smiled. "I don't know any way to explain it except to say I'm so happy to be alive. I'm feeling so much better, and I want to enjoy every minute of this day and all its beauty. I don't want it to end."

Beatrice sat so quietly for a few minutes that Cheval glanced over at her. A faraway expression clouded her eyes. She fondled a gold broach that rested at the base of her throat.

"Are you all right?" Cheval asked.

"I remember a day much like this one," Beatrice said softly. "Maybe it wasn't as warm, but there was a beautiful stillness as there is today."

The tone of Austin's mother's voice caused Cheval to sit up straighter. There was a thoughtful quality to the expression on her face that piqued Cheval's interest.

Beatrice looked out over the garden as with sightless eyes. "It was only a little over five years ago, but it seems much longer than that to me now. I was in the same position you are, only I'd been sick much longer. I'd been bed-ridden all winter and most of the spring, too. I don't know why, but the beauty and the stillness of this afternoon reminds me of that day. It's odd really. I haven't thought about it in a long time."

"What made the day so special?" Cheval asked, not wanting to be forward but sensing the woman wanted to talk about that particular afternoon.

Her hand remained at her throat, her fingers slowly caressing the brooch. "I'm not sure special is the right word. In one way it was the worst day of my life, and in another it was the best day of my life."

Cheval heard emotion in her voice. She prompted, "I'll listen, if you want to talk about it."

"Yes, I think I do." She untied the satin ribbon underneath her chin and pulled off her bonnet, exposing herself to the fading sunlight she'd just reprimanded Cheval about. "I've only talked with Austin about it and not with him for a long time now. It was the most frightening day of my life."

"What happened?"

The faraway quality didn't leave her eyes. "As I said, I'd been sick most of the spring. The coughing and fevers had lingered. On a day like this one, I was feeling so much better that Austin decided to take me for a ride in the carriage. We rode all over the countryside. Heaven couldn't have sent us a more beautiful day. I didn't want it to end, so Austin was reluctant to head home even when the day grew late.

"Austin and I were attacked by three robbers. The war hadn't been over all that long, and there were a lot of men looking for some kind of work. It was a bad time for a lot of people. Austin freely gave them his money and my reticule. I hated to give it up—it was one of my favorites and it didn't have anything in it but an extra handkerchief. But then they wanted this."

Her hand went back to her brooch. Cheval saw a tremble in her movements. "I didn't want to give it up. My husband had given it to me as a wedding gift. No, I thought it was far too precious to me."

Keenly interested in the story, Cheval asked, "What happened?"

Beatrice fiddled with the neckline of her dress as she recalled the story. Cheval watched the woman's eyes change from a light shade of green to a deeper color. She sensed the woman was actually reliving that day in her mind.

"Austin took on all three of the men."

"My goodness, how? Did they have swords or guns?"

"Oh, my yes. Both guns and swords. Austin rose in the carriage and cut the neck of one of the robbers' horses. That took care of one of the men for a few moments. Austin jumped from the carriage and whacked the horse on the rump, hoping it would take off running and get me out of the way, but the old horse just bucked and snorted. I was so frightened I didn't know what to do. I saw one of the men go down. He was covered in blood and didn't get up, so I knew he was dead.

"But then both the other two men challenged Austin at the same time. Swords were clashing; there were shouts and grunts. I was beside myself with worry. Austin's an excellent swordsman, but so were the other two men. I screamed when I saw one of the men's swords slice across Austin's stomach. I remember frantically looking around for some way to help. I'd never used a sword, so I knew I couldn't help that way."

"Austin was fighting two men at the same time?" Cheval asked, worried even though the incident had happened years before.

"Oh, yes. It was frightful. Austin started yelling for me to run. I realized then his goal was to see me safe. I jumped from the carriage, intending to run for help, but one of the robbers caught me around the waist, almost lifting me off the ground.

I saw Austin charging toward us. I saw the blade of the robber's sword coming toward my chest. Austin couldn't reach me in time. I closed my eyes, knowing I was going to die. But then a gunshot rang out. The sword fell from the man's hand and he crumbled to the ground."

"Who shot the robber?" Cheval asked, completely caught up in the story.

Beatrice smiled. "The most dashing man I have ever seen. He was splendid. He wore a coat of purple satin, trimmed with white and silver embroidery. His gold epaulets were thick and his buttons shiny. The scabbard at his side was the fanciest I've ever seen. His hair was lightly powdered beneath his tricorn hat with its red plume."

Cheval couldn't imagine who would make Austin's mother carry on so about his appearance. She'd obviously been impressed by the man. "Who was he?" she asked again.

"Oh, my dear, it was Jerome Bonaparte, Napoleon's youngest brother."

Cheval gasped so loud Beatrice looked her way. Cheval's mind immediately filled with questions, with answers, with hope.

"Yes, dear, strange as it seems. At the time, Jerome lived here in Baltimore with his wife Betsy Patterson. I'm sure you know their story. Everyone has heard it."

"Yes, I know it." Cheval's voice was husky. She suddenly felt weak again. In a rush of understanding, Cheval started fitting together all the pieces of Austin's behavior.

"Jerome saved my life and Austin's, too. After shooting the man who held me, Jerome helped Austin take care of the last robber. Exhausted, Austin fell to his knees. Blood poured from his side and arm, dripped through his fingers, and he fell to the ground in front of him."

"He was grateful," Cheval murmured.

"Oh, it was much more than that," she said with conviction. "Austin couldn't have saved me. There was no time. And he couldn't have held out against the last robber much longer either because he'd lost so much blood. And he had been weakened by the fight. Grateful? Oh yes, he was grateful, but he's also indebted to him. He told the flamboyant young man that he owed him his mother's life and vowed to act upon any favor Jerome might ask. All Jerome need ever do was to call on him. He'd be forever in his debt."

"I understand now," she whispered. Now she knew why Austin had agreed to take the kidnapped little boy to France. He was fulfilling a vow. Why hadn't he told her? Why hadn't she forced him to give her his reasons?

But she knew why. She'd told him *no* reason would be good enough. No reason. Could she have been wrong about that? Suddenly she was too confused to think properly. Had she been too hard on Austin?

"Of course what could Jerome Bonaparte ever need from Austin?" Beatrice continued. "Napoleon controls most of Europe, and he's made Jerome a king. What else could Jerome want?"

His son. Jerome didn't have his son; and Austin, with his ships, was the perfect choice to handle that job for him. She was the one who'd been wrong. Circumstances were such that it had been the right thing for Austin to do, just the wrong thing for Betsy Patterson.

"Of course, no one in Maryland could be happy about the shabby way Jerome treated Miss Patterson or what Napoleon did to her. But I—I will always be grateful to Jerome Bonaparte for saving me and my son that day."

"And you should be." Her voice was husky with emotion. "I only wish I'd known about this sooner. Austin never told me."

"And he probably never would. A man's pride is different from ours. They don't like to be considered weak or in need of help. They like to think they can take care of us with no one's intervention. I'm sure to this day Austin wishes he could have handled all three of those robbers without Jerome Bonaparte's help."

"Yes, I believe that to be true, too." Cheval bowed her head and whispered, "I need to talk to Austin."

Twenty-two

"Miss Worthington, what are you doing here?" Thollie asked when she opened the door and saw Cheval standing on the stoop. "How are you feeling? I thought you were sick?"

"I have been. I'm much better now."

"Well, you're still a might pale. Mr. Radcliffe didn't tell me he was expecting you." Thollie paused and looked down at Cheval with her big brown eyes shining. "Is he expecting you?" the housekeeper asked, gripping her hips with her hands, making her skirt hem hike on both sides.

Cheval smiled. "He's not expecting me. But, may I come in and wait for him?"

"Of course." She stepped aside and allowed Cheval entrance. "Mr. Radcliffe is working late hours these days. I usually have dinner ready for him about eight. He eats and goes right to bed. Then he's up by daylight and on his way back to his office."

After stepping into the parlor, Cheval took off her hat and her cape and handed them to Thollie. "Is Jubal here? I'd like to speak to him if he is."

"Um-hum." She nodded. "He's here. Right now

he's in the kitchen having his supper with me before he goes to pick up Mr. Radcliffe at the office."

Cheval swallowed hard. This wasn't going to be easy. "May I see him?"

"Won't bother me none. Come on in here. I'll get you a cup of tea."

Cheval took a deep breath to settle her nerves as she followed Thollie into the small kitchen. Jubal stood up and backed away from her as she entered. It hurt to know that he didn't want to be near her, but she couldn't blame him for feeling that way.

"Jubal, how are you?" she asked, wanting to smile at him, but not sure she should or that he'd welcome it.

"Fine," he answered.

That wasn't much to build a conversation on. "I—the only thing I know to do is say I'm sorry for hitting you that night. I hope it didn't hurt you too badly and that you're fully recovered.

"I'm fine," he repeated, not taking his gaze off her face.

"I've never been happy that I did it, but at the time, I felt I had no other choice. I knew you would have stopped me and I couldn't allow that. I hope you'll accept my apology and maybe one day forgive me."

I know why you did it," he said, wiping his mouth with the back of his hand. "But that don't make it right."

"No, it doesn't. I committed a wrong trying to

right a wrong. How could that be the right thing to do?"

He nodded and looked down at his dinner plate.

She was keeping him. She clasped her hands together in front of her and held them tight. "I'm in no position to ask anything of you, I realize, but when you go to pick up Austin tonight would you allow me to ride with you and not tell Austin I'm in the carriage until he gets there?" She didn't add that she was afraid he might decide not to come out of his office if he knew she was waiting for him.

She was so unsure of everything concerning her relationship with Austin. She'd made it clear they had no future because she couldn't forgive him or trust him. How could she make Austin understand that while she still didn't agree with what he'd done, that now she understood.

Jubal hesitated.

Her heartbeat increased. Would he deny her?

"You can go. I won't tell him you're there—unless he asks me."

That was fair enough.

"Thank you." She turned to Thollie. "Please finish your meal. If you don't mind, I'll wait in the parlor until Jubal is ready to pick up Austin."

"Damn, what a hell of a night," Austin said to Jubal as they walked out of his office and into the drizzling summer rain.

"Yes, sir."

Austin pulled his hat low and his coat collar up to keep the rain from running down the back of his neck as he and Jubal hurried over to the carriage parked just past the front of the building. It might be the middle of June, but a nighttime rainfall could chill a person to the bone.

Jubal reached the covered carriage first and jumped up on the driver's seat while Austin jerked the coach door open and stepped a foot up on the passenger step. He froze. Light from the street lamp spilled into the carriage and lit Cheval's face. For a moment he thought he was seeing an apparition.

What was she doing out of bed, out of his mother's house, out on a rainy night like this when she'd recently been so sick?

"You're getting wet," she said. "Come inside."

"I can't believe you're out of bed, let alone out on a night like this," he said angrily.

Austin pulled himself inside and shut the door with a bang behind him. He took the seat opposite Cheval, then gave the ceiling two hard raps with his hand to let Jubal know it was all right to take off. He removed his wet hat and threw it on the seat beside him. With his fingertips he wiped dripping water from his face and neck.

Light came through the windows into the cab from the lanterns attached to the side panels of the carriage. Austin glanced at Cheval again. She held out a handkerchief for him. A stirring started in his manhood. Damn, how he'd missed her!

She'd always been able to move him with just a look. For a moment he had to simply look at her. Her eyes glistened in the dim light. He wanted to grab her and hold her so close to his chest nothing could pry them apart. But no, she'd made her feelings for him clear. He knew how she felt about him. He even understood. He'd done what was required of him in getting her out of jail and taking care of her until she recuperated. Nothing else was needed or expected.

"Do you care nothing for your health?" he asked, taking the handkerchief from her.

"Thanks to you and your mother's good care, I'm well."

"You won't be for long. Not two weeks ago you were delirious with fever and coughing every other breath. Now you're out on a night like this. You're still much too pale. I can't believe Mama agreed to let you do this."

He wiped his face and neck with her handkerchief. Even though he used the small hankie quickly he smelled her sweet scent on it and it made him want to bury his nose in the softness at the base of her throat and breathe in deeply.

"Don't blame your mother. She didn't want me to leave. I convinced her I had to see you and I couldn't wait. She agreed her driver could bring me into town tonight."

He wanted to touch her, to hold her, to love her. But his pride said no. She had rejected him and denied his love. He wouldn't open himself to that kind of hurt again.

"There was no need for you to come here, Cheval. I was just waiting for you to get better before I went back and settled payment with you for your services. Naturally I'll see you'll well provided for."

Her eyes rounded. "Payment? What payment?"

"What payment, indeed! I haven't forgotten the money I promised you for taking care of Bo. Surely you remember?"

Affronted she exclaimed, "That has nothing to do with why I'm here!"

"What's the matter? Have you decided that to take the payment would soil your hands for life and you don't want dirty money?"

"No! How dare you suggest such a thing. Money has nothing to do with why I'm here. Besides, you don't owe me any payment. It's I who owe you. I stole money from you when we were aboard *Aloof*."

"Pennies."

This wasn't turning out the way she'd hoped. She wanted to ask his forgiveness for being so rigid, for not understanding, for not trusting that he had good reason for what he did. She wanted to love him, not argue with him.

"Your mother told me you were expected back to the country in a few days, but I didn't want to wait that long to talk to you." She paused then asked what was uppermost on her mind. "Why didn't you tell me about Jerome?"

"Jerome? What was there to tell other than that I was taking his son to him? You knew that."

"Why didn't you tell me he saved your mother's life and that you were indebted to him?"

"Dammit!" he whispered earnestly as he wadded the handkerchief she'd given him into a small ball.

"Why didn't you tell me?"

"It was none of your damn business for starters." He pointed a finger at her. "Nothing to do with you."

Her chest tightened, and she tried to swallow past a dry throat. She hadn't expected such a forceful argument from him. "How can you say that when you know that what has been keeping me from giving myself, my love, to you completely is the feeling that you were not the kind of man I should love? I've been driving myself crazy with wanting you, but thinking of you as a heartless man."

"In the beginning I didn't think I had to justify my actions or my reasons to you. Then when I wanted to tell you, you told me *no* reason would be good enough."

"That's because I thought you were doing it for some gain to yourself or your business." Cheval leaned forward. "Of course there's a difference."

"Why? Why should there be? Does it change the outcome of what I did?"

She struggled with her answer before saying, "No."

"Is the deed any less offensive to you because you now believe I had a good enough reason to do it?"

Cheval searched his eyes in the dim light. She couldn't lie. He'd see it in a heartbeat. But the truth might lose him to her forever.

"Is it?" he asked again.

"No," she whispered softly. "The outcome is the same, but I understand now that sometimes we don't have choices if we're to face ourselves each morning," she answered, remembering how much it had hurt her to hit Jubal and to leave Austin on the sidewalk when she knew he'd been injured. What she'd done hadn't been right for them, but it had been right for Betsy and Bo.

Austin sighed. "This conversation isn't even necessary, Cheval. I understand why you don't trust me or respect me and I accept that. There's no need to go over this. I can't change what happened."

She closed her eyes for a few seconds, unable to bear the pain she saw in his eyes. How could she have hurt him so much? She loved him. "I know it can't be changed, but now that I understand why you did it, I can accept it."

"You didn't trust me enough to have faith that I was doing the right thing for me so I could live with myself."

"No, I didn't. I have a mind, too. I have feelings and values that tell me what is right and what's wrong. I couldn't love you unconditionally."

Austin remained quiet, looking at her. The carriage clipped along at a leisurely pace, jostling them gently. She didn't know how to make him see that she loved him and needed him other than to simply come out and tell him so.

She tried to calm her racing heartbeat. "I left your mother's house to come tell you that I should have known you had reasons other than personal gain or you wouldn't have helped Jerome. I realize that now. I didn't understand how I could love you yet not be able to come to terms with what you had done. I can't explain it, except to say I believe my sister's loss clouded my reasoning. I know what losing her child did to Loraine. I know the anguish she went through that eventually drove her to kill herself. I've always wished I could have helped my sister overcome the loss of her son. I wanted to bring her son back to life and return him to her. I know that sounds strange, but I would have done anything to help Loraine.

"Austin, I didn't know how to handle your being party to something I considered so despicable."

"I know." His voice was soft. "And because of it, you have no respect for me."

Her own words coming back to her hurt. She moved over to the seat beside him. "I said it, but I don't think it was true even then. I would not have given myself to you and stayed in your bed if I didn't respect you, if I didn't love you."

He looked into her eyes. "You're rationalizing."

"No. I wasn't ready to admit that I saw past what you were doing and found a man I loved, respected, and wanted to spend the rest of my life with."

"I don't believe you."

Her heart filled with anguish. Was there no way to make him understand? "I've done a lot of things that were wrong, too, you know. I stole your gun and your money. I left you to the mercy of soldiers in France. I hit Jubal on the head. I left you—"

Suddenly Austin grabbed her upper arms and pulled her up close to his chest. His expression was intense. "What are you saying, Cheval?"

"That I love you. I want to be with you forever. When this carriage stops, you can leave me in the street; but it won't make me sorry I came here tonight to tell you these things."

"Don't tempt me with your sweet lips and words I've longed to hear, Cheval."

"Why not? All I've said is true. Jerome Bonaparte saved your mother's life and you felt obligated to him. Austin, I respect the honor that compelled you to keep the vow you made. That honorable man is the one I love."

"Don't make me more noble than I am, Cheval. I know my actions hurt people."

She looked into his beautiful eyes. Was he softening? Was he willing to forgive her rejection? "Sometimes we all have to do things that hurt other people."

A slight smile appeared on his face. He cupped the side of her face with his hand. It was warm. She turned into it and kissed his palm. The taste of him was tangy. With his free hand Austin picked up hers and kissed her palm.

She smiled at him. "I've loved you for a long time. Not without reservations at first, but they're all gone now. I'm bringing nothing with me to-night but unconditional love."

"I accept it and give you my love and my life."

Austin slid his hand to the back of Cheval's neck and pulled her too him and kissed her. Cheval savored the kiss. It was soft, sweet, romantic. She slid her arms around his neck and pulled him closer. She closed her eyes and surrendered to his touch, to her dreams of being his forever.

"I love you. I thought I'd lost you," Austin whispered. "And I didn't know any way to get you back. I couldn't change what I'd done."

She trembled with need for him. "And I thought you'd never forgive me for doubting you."

"The only thing you did to me was deny me your love, and now, if I have that, I have all I want or need for the rest of my life."

"You have my love, Austin. Forever."

"And you have mine. Say you'll marry me, Cheval."

"Yes, yes, my love. Nothing would make me happier."

"Hold me tighter," he pleaded as his lips sought hers for a long passionate kiss.

"The carriage has stopped," she murmured a few moments later.

"I don't care," he answered, kissing her lips, her cheeks, her neck. "I don't want to let you go."

"I'm sure Jubal wants to get out of the rain."

He looked down into her eyes and said, "Your kisses make me so crazy with need that I forget about everything and everyone else."

Cheval hesitated before saying, "Austin, we've come full circle to the place where we were the first time we met. I have no place to stay the night."

Happiness lit in Austin's eyes and he laughed. "Then allow me to offer my house and my bed to you for tonight and always."

"I accept," Cheval said and kissed him again.

Author's Notes

The love story between the beautiful Betsy Patterson and the immature Jerome Bonaparte is tragic but fascinating. While researching this book, I developed great admiration for Betsy's courage, wit, and determination. I felt pity for Jerome, who allowed Napoleon to rob him of such a strong-minded, intelligent, and appealing woman as Betsy Patterson.

All the information in this book about Betsy and Jerome is true except for the kidnapping. History tells no account of Jerome trying to kidnap his son. Jerome wrote Betsy several letters, first asking her to send his son to him, then later asking that she bring him. At one time, he offered to make her a queen and give her 200,000 francs a year if she would bring his son to Europe. During this time, Betsy refused all his overtures, but in later years Bo was allowed to visit his father in Europe.

In France, Napoleon had Jerome and Betsy's marriage annulled in 1806, but Betsy waited until 1812 to apply for a legal divorce in America. It was

...mored that Betsy and Jero...em spoke...met at the
...pera in France, but neithe...ome was the only
History books tell us t... only lover. After Na-
man Betsy ever loved a...nued to live in splendor
poleon's fall, Jerome...arriage Napoleon had made
because of the go...s known throughout Europe for
for him. Jerom...
his lavish s...ding, countless lovers, and reckless
behavior...e died at the age of seventy-five in 1860,
leaving no mention of his American son Bo in his
will.

Crushed once again by Jerome's hand, Betsy
spent the rest of her life trying to gain recognition
in France for Bo as a legal heir to the throne of
France. She never succeeded. She died in 1879 at
the age of ninety-four, outliving Bo by nine years.

Betsy asked to have carved on her tombstone
the words, *After life's fitful fever, she sleeps well.* Having read many accounts of her life, this author
believes she lied. She died as she lived, trying to
overcome, rise above, and rectify the humiliating
misdeed Jerome allowed when Napoleon had their
marriage annulled.

A woman who fought so hard against overwhelming odds and never achieved her goal couldn't possibly sleep well.

About the Author

The middle child in a family of seven, Gloria Dale Skinner grew up in a small town in the panhandle of Florida. Married for twenty-five years, she is the mother of two grown children. With her accountant husband, she has lived in Alabama, Connecticut, and New Hampshire, and now lives in Panama City Beach, Florida.

Gloria loves to read historical romances; those set in the South are her favorite. She considers doing research for her books to be fun rather than work because she enjoys it so much.

She was a Golden Heart Finalist, and she is also a winner of the coveted Maggie Award which is given by Georgia Romance Writers.

Gloria and her husband recently purchased and restored a house that was built in 1891.

WHAT'S LOVE GOT TO DO WITH IT?

Everything . . . Just ask Kathleen Drymon . . . and Zebra Books

CASTAWAY ANGEL	*(3569-1, $4.50/$5.50)*
GENTLE SAVAGE	*(3888-7, $4.50/$5.50)*
MIDNIGHT BRIDE	*(3265-X, $4.50/$5.50)*
VELVET SAVAGE	*(3886-0, $4.50/$5.50)*
TEXAS BLOSSOM	*(3887-9, $4.50/$5.50)*
WARRIOR OF THE SUN	*(3924-7, $4.99/$5.99)*